P9-BYM-150

Valparaiso Public Library
103 Jefferson Street
Valparaiso, IN 46383

Porter County Public Library

The Evil Wizard Smallbone

DELIA SHERMAN

Valparaiso Public Library
103 Jefferson Street
Valparaiso, IN 46383

vjbfi   VAL
SHERM

Sherman, Delia
Evil wizard smallbone
33410014113163   09/15/16

This is a work of fiction. Names, characters, places, and incidents are either products of the author's imagination or, if real, are used fictitiously.

Copyright © 2016 by Delia Sherman

All rights reserved. No part of this book may be reproduced, transmitted, or stored in an information retrieval system in any form or by any means, graphic, electronic, or mechanical, including photocopying, taping, and recording, without prior written permission from the publisher.

First edition 2016

Library of Congress Catalog Card Number pending
ISBN 978-0-7636-8805-9

16 17 18 19 20 21 BVG 10 9 8 7 6 5 4 3 2 1

Printed in Berryville, VA, U.S.A.
This book was typeset in Columbus MT.

Candlewick Press
99 Dover Street
Somerville, Massachusetts 02144

visit us at www.candlewick.com

For my goddaughter, Gigi, and her brother, Nick

✦ ✦ ✦ Prologue ✦ ✦ ✦

The great white wolf ran through the woods. Snow weighed on his back and shoulders, cold and heavy and wet, but he did not notice. He was on the hunt and he was hungry, though not as hungry as the pack that ran behind him, panting clouds of hot breath into the cold, damp air.

The pack was a coyote pack, and it smelled of rotten meat and motor oil. These are not natural smells for a coyote pack, and a wolf is not a natural leader for coyotes. There was, in fact, very little natural about this pack, except its hunger. It was a hard winter and game of all kinds was scarce.

A sea wind whipped the snow into the white wolf's eyes and brought a new and curious scent to his super-sensitive nose. He stopped and sniffed thought-fully. A boy. Young, human, full of rage and terror, and, yes, raw magic as well. Making for the enemy's territory. As was he. Curious.

With a furious howl, the wolf wizard Fidelou leaped forward, outpacing even the wind with his long strides. The scent grew stronger — the quarry was near. Ahead lay the Stream that marked the boundary of his enemy's land, the Stream that no magic could cross. The wolf wizard howled again, with triumph this time. He would give the boy a choice — to join the pack or feed it. He didn't care which.

But when Fidelou reached the Stream, all he saw was a clumsy trail in the snow leading to the pine tree he had felled last autumn in an attempt to bridge the enchanted water.

The wolf stood on the frozen bank and raised his nose to search the air again. He smelled salt and goats, chickens and cows and sheep and fish. And — wonder of wonders — the boy, moving straight for the enemy's lair. While his pack muttered and whined around him, Fidelou shook the snow from his shoulders and thought. If this was so, his enemy's last defenses must be weakening. Fire and Air had faded long ago, prey to Fidelou's attacks and their own inherent instability. Water and Earth, however, had stood firm. Until now.

And if they fell, he, Fidelou, would confront his enemy at last, and their battle would be spoken of as long as stories were told.

But first, the boundary must be tested. Fidelou turned away from the Stream, lowered his great head, and bared his long teeth, growling. The pack instantly groveled at his feet, bellies sunk in the clinging snow. Fidelou looked them over. A mangy bunch of curs, each more useless than the last — except perhaps his lieutenant, Hiram, and the she-coyote, Audrey. He would not risk them. That one cowering at the back, though — Doc, the so-called mechanic — was a fumble-fingered fool, unable to repair anything more complicated than a motorized bicycle. He would do.

Fidelou fixed the lean coyote's amber eyes with his own fiery gaze and growled. Whining pitifully, his head drooping almost to the ground, the unhappy coyote slunk forward and onto the ice. The wolf wizard watched as he padded cautiously to the middle of the Stream, taking care not to step on any of the rocks breaking the frozen surface. Except for the panting of the coyotes and the occasional eager whine, the woods were still. And then, *CRACK!* The ice broke open under the coyote's feet, plunging his hindquarters into the black water beneath.

The pack howled as their packmate scrabbled at the broken ice, searching desperately for something to hold on to. The current pulled him down, and with a final yelp, he disappeared under the ice.

Then the earth trembled beneath the coyotes' feet, and stones flew from the far side of the stream and rained down on them. Yipping and yammering, the pack turned and fled inland.

But the white wolf remained on the bank, balanced on the heaving earth, the stones bouncing off his thick pelt. He lifted his nose to the invisible moon and howled, a long shivering note of rage and defiance, then turned and followed his pack.

Chapter One

✦ ✦ ✦ ✦ ✦ ✦ ✦

Nick Reynaud didn't know where he was. He'd left the last town a while back, and now all he knew was that he was somewhere near the coast. No lights or houses or gas stations, only trees, black against the cloudy sky, with the road glimmering faintly between them. Night was falling, along with the temperature. He was cold and hungry, and not far from being scared.

As far as he could tell, it had been two days since he'd stood on the highway with his thumb out, waiting for a truck to pick him up and take him as far away from Beaton, Maine, as the road would go. It had taken a while, and the driver who eventually stopped was pretty suspicious. But it had worked out all right in the end.

Nick smiled. He'd fooled that guy but good. Getting him to believe Nick was going home instead of running away had been easy. Persuading him to drop Nick outside Bath had taken some fast talking, but Nick was good at fast talking. Sometimes he'd even been able to talk Uncle Gabe into beating up on his cousin Jerry instead of him. But not nearly often enough. Which was why Nick was running away. Again.

The first time had been three years ago, right after his mom died. He was only nine at the time, it was winter, and he didn't have a plan or food or anything, so it was probably just as well that the police had picked him up before he got too far. The second time, he'd been almost eleven and much better prepared. He took off after school with a bag of chips and a hot dog and twenty bucks he'd earned doing odd jobs for Mrs. Perkins next door. When his cousin Jerry caught up with him at the bus station, Nick had been buying a ticket to Bangor. After that, Uncle Gabe made Jerry walk Nick to and from school every day.

Jerry was sixteen, and as far as Nick could tell, his greatest ambition in life was to beat up every man in

Beaton by the time he turned twenty. He liked to practice on Nick.

Nick had put a lot of time and thought into planning his next escape, and he thought he'd done a pretty good job. He'd boosted a map and a flashlight, extra batteries, some trail mix, and a bottle of Coke from a gas station. He'd stuffed his emergency kit and some clean clothes into Jerry's old backpack and hid it under his bed, ready to grab when he saw a chance to make a clean getaway.

Things hadn't worked out according to plan.

The week before Christmas, Nick had gotten into another fight at school, and the principal had called Uncle Gabe to come pick him up. After getting yelled at by his boss for leaving work early and lectured by the principal about Nick's bad attitude, Uncle Gabe was ready for a few beers. When they got home, he gave Nick a couple of licks on account and locked him down cellar, promising him the rest of his larruping later.

Nick decided he wouldn't be around later.

He crept up the cellar stairs and listened at the door. A deafening hubbub of revving, screeching, and crashing told him Uncle Gabe was watching the stock-car races, turned up high. Nick figured he could probably blow the house up right now, and the old so-and-so wouldn't notice until he was halfway to the moon. With a last wistful thought for the backpack upstairs under his bed, he smashed a crowbar through the nearest window, scrambled out into the scrubby backyard, and made tracks.

As he trudged through the snow, Nick couldn't help thinking about the flashlight and the trail mix he'd had to leave behind. It could have been worse. He had his jacket and boots, and the suspicious truck driver had stood him a hot dog and a Coke. But his boots were old and his jacket was thin and the hot dog had been a long time ago. He felt like he'd been walking forever. His belly was as empty as a hole in the ground, his feet were like concrete blocks, and he was shivering like a wet dog. He wanted to rest, but everybody knew sitting down in the snow was dangerous, and he hadn't run away from Uncle Gabe's belt so he could freeze to death. He put his head down and pressed on.

After a while, he saw a double-wide trailer set up on cinder blocks a little ways back from the road. There was a light shining through the curtains. He was saved.

He banged on the metal door. It opened a crack, releasing a puff of warm, cigarette-scented air.

"Sorry to bother you," Nick said. "I'm lost. If you'll give me a hot meal and a warm place to sleep, I'll do anything you need done. I can fix things . . ."

The door slammed shut.

Nick yelled one of Uncle Gabe's favorite words and gave the trailer door a farewell kick. His feet were so cold, he couldn't even feel it.

He hit the road again.

It began to snow. Fat, heavy, wet flakes clung to Nick's hair, clogged his boots, and slid icy fingers down between his neck and his jacket collar. The wind picked up, needling his already stinging cheeks. He balled his fists in his pockets, bent his head, and forced his legs to keep going.

White swirled around him until he was walking blind, surrounded by snow and cold and the insistent whine of the wind. Time passed, unmeasurable, and still he walked, his nose dripping and his eyes streaming with frosty tears. He couldn't feel his fingers or his toes. For a while, he thought he felt a heaving under his feet, as if the ground were bearing him forward on a snowy wave. Must have been his imagination.

Some time later, the snow let up. Behind the clouds, the moon was high. He could just see a snowy road stretched out in front of him, with trees growing thick on each side. He was so tired, he could hardly stagger. There was some reason he shouldn't stop and rest, but he couldn't quite remember what it was.

Then the howling started.

It was far off at first, spooky, like the sound track of a horror movie, sliding up the scale and holding, long and hollow, before breaking off and starting again. Nick picked up his pace a little.

A rabbit galloped past him and dove into the underbrush. A deer leaped across the road, wheeled, wide-eyed, and took off in another direction.

The howling sounded again, louder and much closer.

Nick broke into a stumbling run. The road narrowed,

curved, morphed into a path through the woods. The howling was still behind him and the going increasingly rough and clogged with undergrowth. Doggedly, he floundered on.

The path ended at a frozen stream.

It wasn't a friendly-looking stream. Rocks stuck out of it like gravestones, and the snowy ice between them looked jagged and sharp. He couldn't cross here. He clambered along the bank until he saw a pine tree lying across the stream. It wasn't exactly easy to walk on, but he managed it, clinging to the brittle snowy branches with numb hands. At the far end, his foot caught in a tangle of roots and he fell facedown in the snow. He was too tired to move.

But when the howling swelled, closer than ever, Nick was on his feet and running through the woods. It took him a minute to realize that he was running on a path, and another to see that the path was straight and dry and padded with pine needles. There was a light ahead of him, glowing through the branches like a yellow moon. It promised shelter and food and warmth, and Nick followed.

The path ended. Nick leaned against a pine, panting cloudily and staring across a good-sized clearing at the house the light came from. It was almost too big to be real, with roofs that blocked out half the sky. It had dozens of windows and a forest of chimneys. A deep wraparound porch ended in an octagonal tower with a pointy roof and round windows from which light poured like honey over the mounded snow. He'd never seen anything remotely like it, not even on TV. A house like that could only belong to rich people. And while he didn't know any rich people personally, they probably would hate some random stray banging on their door even more than the trailer person had. They'd take one look at his uncombed black hair and his broken tooth and his ratacious jacket and call the police, who'd probably send him back to Uncle Gabe, who might not actually kill him but would absolutely make him wish he was dead.

Which was exactly what he would be if he stayed out here in the cold with the wolves.

The howling behind him rose to a furious crescendo, and Nick launched himself into a shambling run that carried him across the clearing and up onto the front porch. Half sobbing, he pounded on the big oak door. It flew open with a tooth-wrenching shriek of hinges. A narrow beam of yellow light blinded him, and a bony hand grabbed his arm.

"Let go!" Nick gasped.

The light pulled back, and a pair of rimless round glasses floated into view. Nick blinked. A beard like an extra-large dust bunny came into focus under the glasses.

The beard opened. "What do you think you're doing," said a gruff, creaky voice, "banging on the door this time of night?"

"I'm lost," Nick said. "And there are wolves after me!"

"A likely story." The old man gave Nick a shake. "Can you read?"

"*Read?* Are you nuts? Why?"

"Answer the question."

As a general rule, Nick was against answering questions truthfully. In his experience, any truth you gave away was likely to be used against you. "No," he said sullenly. "I got a condition or something—the letters don't make sense. Can I come in before I freeze to death?"

The old man set the light on a nearby surface and rummaged one handed in the pockets of his long coat, muttering "Durn house," and "Jeezly mess," and "This better be good." Finally, he pulled out a small white rectangle and thrust it under Nick's nose. "What does this say?"

Nick squinted at it. "It's a white card with black writing."

The card disappeared. "Can't be too careful. Don't need some jeezly boy reading things that don't concern him."

As he pulled Nick inside, the door swung shut with a solid *thunk*. Two large black dogs stalked out of the gloom and snuffled busily at Nick's knees. Nick stiffened. He wasn't used to dogs.

The old man released his arm. "That's Mutt and Jeff," he said. "They don't bite." He chuckled. "Not hard, anyways."

Nick didn't believe a word the old man said.

Because Nick could read perfectly well, and this is what he'd read on the card the old man had shown him:

EVIL WIZARD BOOKS
ZACHARIAH SMALLBONE, PROP.
Used Books, Maps, Local History, Speculative Fiction, Arcana
Open by Chance and by Appointment,
Fridays–Sundays from May to September

❧   ❧   ❧

A little while later, Nick was sitting in a kitchen. His feet were in a bowl of warm water, his shoulders were draped in a striped Hudson's Bay blanket, and his hands were wrapped around a mug of hot milk. The kitchen was tidy and oddly cozy, with red-checked curtains over the windows, an old-fashioned iron stove in one corner, and a stone fireplace with a rocking chair beside it. There was an orange cat in the rocker and a second cat, black, curled up on a braided rug. A picture calendar with the days crossed off in blue pencil hung over the sink.

The old man whose card said he was an evil wizard was hunched over the stove, frying sausages in a cast-iron pan with his long black coat skirt flapping around his boot tops. He was also wearing a hat like a bashed-in stovepipe. He hadn't taken either of them off, though the kitchen was perfectly warm.

Nick didn't believe in wizards, evil or otherwise. Not in the real world, and certainly not in Maine. Even when he was a little kid, Nick had known that fairies and wishes and heroes who overcame dragons and evil wizards were all just make-believe and daydreaming. However, if there *was* such a thing as an evil wizard, Nick thought he'd have a coat just like Zachariah Smallbone's. He might even have two black dogs, although they probably wouldn't sit with their tongues hanging out, begging for bites of sausage. They probably wouldn't be called Mutt and Jeff, either.

Nick wasn't sure about the cats.

Smallbone plunked a plate of sausages and baked beans on the table, and Nick attacked them with the eagerness of a boy who hadn't seen food for a while. As he scraped up the last bite, the dogs heaved twin sighs of disappointment and curled up on the rug. The black cat leaped onto the rocker, hustled the orange tiger out of its nest, tucked its paws under its chest, and closed its pale-blue eyes.

Smallbone forked another sausage onto Nick's plate. "What's your name, boy?"

Despite the sausages and the cozy kitchen, Nick didn't even consider telling him the truth. Wizards might be made-up, but evil was real. "Jerry Reynaud."

Smallbone's beard bobbed thoughtfully. "Hmph. You don't look like a Jerry. You don't feel like a Jerry. You don't smell like a Jerry or act like a Jerry or sound like a Jerry. I'll call you Foxkin. Where you from, Foxkin?"

Nick took a deep pull of milk, then launched into the story he'd invented to explain what he was doing wandering through the woods on a snowy evening.

He was proud of that story. It was artistic and, he thought, convincing. It involved a bike and an errand to an imaginary cousin living down the road and the snow and the front wheel frame breaking and Nick's taking a wrong turn and getting lost. While Nick talked, Smallbone tipped the black cat out of the rocking chair, sat down, and lit a long white pipe.

"Very good," he said when Nick was done. "Very

good indeed. You're an inspired liar, Foxkin. You don't embroider unnecessarily, you give just the right details, and you know when to stop."

Nick put on his best innocent look. "I don't know what you're talking about."

"Fox by name, fox by nature." Smallbone stared at him through curls of foul-smelling smoke. "You can't fool me, you know. So you'd better not try. Now," he went on, "it just so happens that I could use an apprentice. You're scrawny as a plucked chicken and numb as a haddock, but you're here, so you'll have to do. It'll be the usual arrangement: room and board and whatever I feel like teaching you in return for seeing to the animals, cooking, keeping the place clean, and generally doing as you're told."

The sausages and beans curdled in Nick's stomach. "Apprentice? I don't want a job. I mean, I'll work to pay off dinner and all, but I need to go home soon as the snow stops. My uncle — I mean, my father — is — will be worried."

Smallbone gave a low, dry, evil-sounding chuckle. "You ain't going nowhere. From the look of you, I doubt this uncle of yours — I mean father — cares whether you live or die. If he even exists. You're a waif and a stray, my Foxkin. You knocked on the door and you asked for shelter. Well, you got it. And now Evil Wizard Books has got you."

He rose to his feet, and the dogs jumped up like they'd been stung and ran into the front room, their tails tucked between their legs. The cats hissed and streaked after them. The old man lifted his arms, and his round glasses shone like silver coins and his white hair and bony fingers crackled with energy.

"I am the Evil Wizard Smallbone." His voice swelled and clanged like iron bells. "I know spells of binding and release, transformation and stasis, finding and losing. I learned them by experiment and example and luck. But most of all, I learned them from books. And you'll never learn a single thing I don't choose to teach you, because *you can't read*!"

Nick stared, openmouthed. The evil wizard lowered his arms and straightened his hat. "Well," he said mildly, "now we're all clear where we stand, you can take a bath."

"What?"

Smallbone's beard bobbed impatiently. "How old are you, boy?"

Nick was too disoriented to lie. "Twelve."

"Plenty old enough to know what a bath is. You're rank, Foxkin. In plain English, you stink. And you look like you been drug through a knothole backwards. Bathroom's through that door over there. Don't spare the soap."

Chapter Two

✦ ✦ ✦ ✦ ✦ ✦

Something was tickling Nick's nose. He groaned and buried his face in his pillow. He knew he was dreaming because it smelled of lavender instead of motor oil.

The tickling moved to his ear, along with the sound of breathing and something wet and . . .

"Yow!" Nick rolled out of bed with a bone-shaking thump, whacking his elbow so hard he saw stars.

Since his mattress at Uncle Gabe's was on the floor, he knew he must be somewhere else. Which meant he'd succeeded in running away from Beaton. And now he was — oh, yes — in a big house in the middle of nowhere owned by a crazy old dude who claimed to be an evil wizard.

Nick sat up, rubbing his elbow. The room was just exactly the kind of bedroom his mom would have loved, from its blue-checked curtains to the desk by the window to the painted wooden bed, where a small orange cat was peering at him out of the folds of a bright quilt. It mewed, jumped down, and butted against his leg. Nick scratched its ears and tried to remember what had happened last night.

He remembered taking a bath in a bathtub perched up on lion's paws, hot enough to soak the last of the cold right out of him. The towels were warm, too, and the long flannel shirt Smallbone gave him to sleep in. Nick thought it looked uncomfortably like a nightgown, but it was either that or the filthy clothes he'd come in. He didn't like sleeping in his clothes, but sometimes he had to—when the heat was off at Uncle Gabe's, for instance. Times were tough, Uncle Gabe said. Oil was expensive. And a man couldn't live without cable and beer.

Did Smallbone have cable? Nick wondered. Did Smallbone even have a TV? It didn't seem likely.

After the bath, the old man had picked up a lantern

that smelled strongly of kerosene and seemed to create more shadows than it chased away. He led Nick through the gloomy front room and up a steep stair to an even gloomier hall where rows of brass doorknobs glowed in the flickering light. Smallbone turned one of them and pushed open a door onto absolute blackness.

"Here you are," he said. "Sweet dreams." And he'd taken the lantern back downstairs, leaving Nick to find his way to bed in the dark.

Now it was morning, and the room filled with mouthwatering smells of frying bacon and coffee. The orange cat mewed and trotted out the door. Nick's stomach rumbled hopefully. There was a chair by the bed with a pile of clothes folded across the cane seat. Nick got up and shook out, in turn, a set of embarrassing long underwear with a drop seat, a plaid shirt, a pair of bib overalls, and lumpy knitted socks. A quick, desperate search in a chest of drawers turned up a pair of corduroy knickers, a tiny frilled shirt, two pairs of linen sheets, and another nightshirt. Nick put on the clothes from the chair and went in search of breakfast.

The hall was long and shadowy. When Nick turned toward where he thought the stairs were, he saw a kid glaring at him suspiciously.

Nick scowled and swaggered. The kid did the same.

Oh.

Nick laughed. It was the patched overalls and faded flannel shirt, that's all, making him look like a hick from Hicksville on the planet Hickooine. Before he left, he'd have to get his own clothes back. He was leaving, no doubt about that. But not until he'd rested a couple of days, found out where the nearest town was, made some plans. It wasn't like the old man had done anything particularly threatening, after all—just waved his arms around and talked like a nut job. If things got weird, Nick could always run away. He was good at running away.

He clattered down the steps to the front room. He'd been too sleepy to notice much the night before, but now he saw that it was filled with tall, dark shelves stuffed solid with books. It was also dim and chilly and stank of mold. The back of his neck prickled, like somebody was watching him, wary and a little hostile.

The dogs, maybe. Or the spiders that had spun all those webs. He passed through as quickly as possible, following the smell of bacon.

The kitchen was bright and warm. Smallbone was busy at the stove, his black hat tipped crazily to one side. "Breakfast's ready," he said. "Eggs are cooked solid and the bacon's burnt, but that's all you deserve, sleeping half the day."

Nick slid into a chair, and Smallbone slapped a plate of bacon and eggs, sunny side up and perfect, onto the red-checked tablecloth. The black cat jumped up and sniffed delicately at the bacon. Nick flapped his hand at it. "Scat!"

Unfazed, the cat sat down beside the plate, cocked its hind leg, and got down to some serious grooming. Nick gave it a shove. It hissed like a boiling kettle and leaped from the table to a narrow shelf over the stove, where it crouched between a salt box and a pottery jar and glared out resentfully.

"You want to watch out for Hell Cat," Smallbone remarked. "She bites."

"So do I," said Nick, and dug into his eggs. The

dogs from last night stationed themselves on each side of his chair, and the little orange cat jumped into his lap and patted his hand with a soft paw. Nick broke off a bit of bacon.

The old man settled himself in the rocking chair and got out his pipe. "Tom can always tell an easy mark," he said.

Nick gave Tom the bacon anyway. He crunched it neatly, then jumped down and sauntered off. The dogs yawned and kept on hoping.

Having filled his pipe and lit it, Smallbone fixed Nick with his glittering spectacles. "I suppose you ain't a farm boy, Foxkin?"

Nick swallowed his egg. "Nope."

Smallbone said, "It ain't rocket science. You'll feed and water the livestock, spread fresh bedding and suchlike. Collect eggs. Milk the goats."

Nick's fork paused halfway to his mouth. "Milk the goats?"

"You'll pick it up." The old man sounded horribly cheerful. "It's easy as splitting wood, once you know the trick. You do know how to split wood, don't you?"

Nick shook his head. There might not have been much heat in Uncle Gabe's house, but what there was came from an oil furnace. "If you're an evil wizard, how come you don't just do it all by magic?"

Smallbone grinned, displaying a dentist's nightmare of crooked yellow teeth. "Because that's what an apprentice is for."

This conversation was going nowhere good. "I said I'd do one job, to pay you back," Nick said. "But then I got to move on."

"One job." Smallbone's dark eyes narrowed behind his glasses. "I see. Well, you can clean the shop, then. But wash the dishes first. I hate a dirty kitchen." He emptied his pipe into the fire, wrapped a muddy-gray scarf around his neck, and went outside.

The shop. That must be the book-filled front room. He remembered the card Smallbone had shown him. Evil Wizard Books, huh? Stink City Books would be a better name. Muttering, Nick left the dishes on the floor for the animals to lick and went to look for a vacuum cleaner. He wasn't particularly surprised when he didn't find one. There was, however, an ancient straw broom and a tin bucket in the mudroom, and a basket of clean rags under the sink. Nick stuffed his pocket with rags, filled the bucket, and carried it and the broom into the shop. He might not be able to keep out of trouble, but he could clean, no problem. His mom had worked for a cleaning company and used to take Nick on jobs when he wasn't in school. He'd grown up helping her sprinkle water on floors to keep the dust down and polish windows with vinegar and newspaper. He even knew how to wind up cobwebs on a broom handle like dirty cotton candy.

This was a good thing, because Evil Wizard Books was well supplied with cobwebs. They drooped from the corners and hung in heavy swags between the rows of tall bookcases. They veiled the big bay window behind the shop counter like ragged curtains and completely covered a mysterious box-like shape that Nick thought might be an old-fashioned cash register. Besides the cobwebs, there was plenty of grime — on the windows, mostly, but also on the floor, which looked like it hadn't been swept or scrubbed in maybe a hundred years. Nick saw tracks in the dust where

Smallbone and the dogs had walked to the door and back, and the smears of his own wet boots.

The air smelled sour and musty.

If it hadn't been for the snow and the wind and the cold and the memory of wolves howling, Nick might have stolen a heavier jacket and some food and taken his chances in the woods. But Smallbone's sausages had been delicious, also his eggs, and it was nice to feel, if not exactly safe, at least warm. Besides, Nick might be a liar, but his mom had always said it was important to keep promises.

Reversing the broom, he took a swipe at the nearest web. It danced away like a curtain in a light breeze. He swiped at it a couple more times with the same result, almost as though it knew he was trying to get rid of it.

Nick pulled a rag from his pocket, wrung it out in the bucket like his mom used to do, and swiped it over the grimy counter.

The dirt didn't even smear.

He rubbed harder. Tom jumped up by his elbow, curled himself next to the shrouded cash register, and watched through slitted eyes. The rag turned black, but the counter stayed as grimy as ever. It felt like trying to blow out one of those trick birthday candles. It wasn't magic, of course. Magic — except for the card trick, nothing-up-my-sleeve kind — didn't exist. Nick was very clear on that. Still, there was obviously something going on.

Nick threw the rag on the floor and swore. Tom jumped down off the counter and padded away.

A voice behind him made a *tsk, tsk* noise, and Nick spun around.

Smallbone was standing on the stairs with his coat fluttering like something out of a late-night horror movie. "Best watch your tongue, Foxkin," he said. "The books in this shop don't take to bad language."

Nick swore again, using one of Uncle Gabe's best swears, then said, "You want this stupid shop cleaned, do it yourself. I'm out of here."

"You ain't going nowhere," said Smallbone.

Nick had heard that before, from Uncle Gabe. "How you going to stop me, old man?"

"I'll turn you into a spider."

Smallbone's voice was perfectly calm and matter-of-fact. He obviously believed he could turn Nick into a spider, and for a second, looking up into the flat silver of his little round glasses, Nick half believed it, too. Then Smallbone worked his jaw in a munching way, and Nick remembered he was just a crazy old dude who thought he was a wizard.

He laughed.

Smallbone's beard bunched up threateningly. "You think you're clever, don't you, Foxkin, can see right through the old crackpot like he's a jeezly clean window?"

Nick shrugged. "You said it — I didn't."

Smallbone raised his bony fist high. "Just remember, you brought this on yourself." He began to speak words in no language Nick had ever heard before, his voice clanging and swelling. Nick wanted to run, but he couldn't move. All he could do was watch Smallbone swelling up and up like a giant balloon as the bookshop faded into a shadowy mist.

Chapter Three

✦ ✦ ✦ ✦ ✦ ✦ ✦

Smallbone Cove was one of the prettiest towns on the Maine coast. It was tucked at the end of a deep, rocky inlet with a view down the Reach of little forested islands and distant blue hills. The weather was always practically perfect. In summer, it rained often enough to keep the small farmers happy and no more, and a brisk offshore breeze cleared the fog before anybody was ready to go to the beach. Its shore was free from blackflies, and its woods were free from mosquitoes. The winters were mild (for Maine), with a minimum of nor'easters and a maximum of days above zero. Violets and white trilliums bloomed early in Smallbone Cove, and the bright leaves of fall lingered late.

Whatever the weather was like in the rest of Maine,

in Smallbone Cove, the Fourth of July was always clear and sunny.

In summer, tourists flocked to Smallbone Cove like bears to honey. They loved it because it was quaint and relaxing, a little slice of the good old days, when life was slower and less complicated. Kids jumped rope in the parking lot to rhymes about building walls and blowing winds, and the only snacks available were all homemade.

There were no computers in Smallbone Cove and no electronics. At Smallbone Cove Mercantile, Lily and Zery Smallbone rang up homemade jams and sunscreen on a big brass cash register like the ones in every other shop in town. Telephones had cords and dials and lots of static on the line. There was no Smallbone Cove police force because there was no crime, not even any sketchy-looking characters hanging around at night. Of course, you had to go to Blue Hill if you wanted to eat anything but seafood and veggies. There was no cell-phone reception and forget about wi-fi, but most people thought it was kind of nice to be away from the Internet — for a few days, anyway.

In winter, when the tourists were gone, the adult Smallbone Covers fished, raised animals, and made things to sell in summer. Their kids went to the smallest school in Maine. It was too small to exist, really—its twenty-five students should have ridden the bus to Blue Hill. But somehow they didn't—just like the library didn't have wi-fi like every other library in Maine and the citizens didn't pay any state or local taxes. It was as if the State of Maine didn't know that Smallbone Cove existed.

The other thing the Covers didn't do was leave Smallbone Cove. They didn't go on vacations; they didn't go away to college; they didn't even go shopping in Blue Hill. The adults didn't seem to mind, and if they did, they didn't complain. They ordered their souvenir T-shirts and groceries and professional supplies over the phone or even by mail. They understood that staying inside the Town Limits was part of the price they paid for living in a practically perfect place.

The other part was looking after Zachariah Smallbone, the proprietor of Evil Wizard Books.

Nobody talked about him much, but everybody

knew that he was the founder of Smallbone Cove, that he was over three hundred years old, and that he was the reason that Smallbone Cove was the way it was.

When Dinah Smallbone was five, she'd asked her mother if Smallbone was really an evil wizard like in the fairy tales.

Lily had given her one of those looks mothers give kids when they ask an awkward question. Dinah, who was all about asking awkward questions, saw it often.

"I've never seen him do magic — not anything I'd call magic, anyway," Lily said carefully. "And he's never done anything I'd call evil, unless you count tearing strips off anybody who talks to him when he's not in the mood for talking. But my grammy used to tell stories that'd curl your hair, about him turning folks into frogs and calling up demons and hurricanes and such."

Dinah thought about this. "Maybe your grammy was making them up."

"No," said her mom, "she couldn't. Grammy couldn't make up a story to save her life. If she said Smallbone turned folks into frogs, then that's what he did."

"Is that why he doesn't have to pay for anything, even the special orders?"

"Well, he keeps Smallbone Cove safe, too." Lily took Dinah's shoulders and gave them a squeeze. "Listen, honey. You know I told you how people aren't comfortable talking about certain things? Smallbone's one of those things. I'm glad we had this talk, but you better not try and have it with anybody else."

Dinah nodded. She didn't really understand why certain subjects made adults uncomfortable, but she did understand that nobody would discuss them with her. It was a disappointment that Smallbone fell into that category. She was curious about how anybody could live three hundred years and not just wither up and blow away.

Dinah was curious about many things. When she was six, she'd decided she was going to be a scientist and learn how and why things worked. By seven, she'd discovered that books will tell you things that adults will not, and she started to spend all her spare time in the library. When she was eleven, the Smallbone Cove librarian gave her an after-school job as her assistant.

The librarian's name was Miss Rachel Smallbone, and in Dinah's opinion, she was the most interesting person in Smallbone Cove. She wore thick glasses that magnified her eyes into huge pools of darkness. Her lips were thin, her nose small and flat, and she wore her mottled gray-and-white hair tucked into a bun at the nape of her neck. She spent her days by the library's front window in a wheeled chair with a desk fastened across the arms, writing a book on the history of Smallbone Cove and keeping an eye on things.

As Miss Rachel's assistant, Dinah helped her go through the Smallbone Cove archives, which consisted of old books and papers that had accumulated over the years. Since she couldn't help reading what she was sorting and discussing it with Miss Rachel, the job went very slowly. But Miss Rachel didn't seem to mind and always answered Dinah's questions, however awkward — including the one about what had happened to her legs.

"Oh, Smallbone did that."

She sounded so cheerful about it that Dinah was surprised and just a little suspicious. "Mom says she never heard of him doing anything really evil," she said.

"That's because it happened before she was born, dear. And it wasn't long after that the wolf wizard and his were-coyotes started prowling the Town Limits again, so it didn't get talked about much."

Miss Rachel fell silent, but Dinah knew there had to be more to the story than that. "So," she said carefully, "he just walked into town and blasted you? That's pretty evil."

Miss Rachel laughed. She had a deep, hoarse laugh like a bark that only came out when she was really amused. "As if he'd take the trouble! No. It was all because Silas's grandfather John—he was little Johnny Smallbone then—said I wouldn't dare steal a pumpkin out of the evil wizard's pumpkin patch. We were fourteen, you see, and that's what passes for courting at that age. Anyway, I took the dare and Smallbone caught me. He threatened to turn me into all kinds of horrible things, but in the end, he just withered my legs." She shook her head. "It was a long way home, dragging myself and the pumpkin through the woods in the dark, but I made it. Johnny felt terrible."

"You brought the pumpkin?" Dinah exclaimed.

"Smallbone said he thought I'd earned it."

❧   ❧   ❧

Recently, Smallbone Cove had become a slightly less perfect place to live. All summer, the tourists had complained of being kept awake by mosquitoes and howling coyotes. By Labor Day, they'd all gone home and nobody came back for autumn leaf-peeping. In November, the winter storms had hit heavy and hard, making deliveries difficult. The Christmas food order turned up so late, Lily had begun to worry that it wasn't going to arrive at all, which would have been fine if it hadn't included Smallbone's monthly order of meat. It showed up at last on the morning of Christmas Eve, along with a box of decorations and all the presents the Covers had ordered to give to one another.

After a busy morning unpacking and distributing orders, all that was left to do was put up the decorations. Zery Smallbone helped his wife tack a bright-red banner with MERRY CHRISTMAS spelled out in gold foil above the counter, climbed off the ladder, and stretched.

"I'm in the mood for a game of checkers," he said. "Dinah, set up the board."

Dinah unfolded the checkerboard on top of a pickle barrel, pulled up a couple of stools, and laid out the pieces. Her father sat down and pushed a red checker forward. Dinah expected he'd beat her. He usually did.

The Mercantile was quiet except for the sounds of her mom folding sweaters on the counter and a faint buzzing, like a distant hive of hornets.

Her dad pushed a red checker into the last row. "King me," he said.

Dinah crowned his checker. The buzzing grew louder.

"Bikers," her dad remarked. "Funny time of year for them." He jumped his king across the board, capturing all Dinah's checkers.

"Aw, Dad!"

The buzzing swelled to a coughing roar, then cut

off. As her father reset the checkers, the Mercantile's glass door flew open, letting in a blast of frigid air and two men in brown leather jackets.

Dinah shivered, and it wasn't just the chill. She'd always thought of herself as brave, and she was, about things like skinned knees and worms and climbing trees and swimming out over her head. But there was something about those bikers that made her skin crawl. They were dirty and skinny and they smelled terrible — not just BO terrible, but like they'd been rolling in something old and rotting. It was all she could do not to retch.

"Afternoon," Lily said in a bright shopkeeper's voice. "Can I get you folks anything?"

The bigger of the two bikers went up to the counter and leaned on it. There was a picture of a howling coyote on the back of his jacket, under the words HOWLING COYOTES painted in spiky yellow letters, outlined in red. "A pack of smokes and some beef jerky."

"I'm sorry." Lily sounded anything but. "We don't sell cigarettes and we don't sell meat. You'll have to go to Blue Hill, I'm afraid."

The second biker's eyes narrowed, mean as a junk-yard dog's. "That's funny. I smell meat."

"Special order," Lily said.

He bared his teeth. "Sure it is. For us."

"Hand it over, honey," the first biker said, "and nobody'll get hurt."

Dinah's dad jumped to his feet, sending the checkerboard flying and the checkers rolling across the floor. His face was flushed and he was snarling. Dinah had never seen him so mad.

"Back off!" he barked.

The big biker laughed. "Who's going to make me? Sit down, fatty, or Sid here will take a bite out of you."

The second biker growled and lunged, teeth bared. Zery Smallbone plopped back into his chair, panting. Dinah released her breath in a frightened little puff.

"Meat's in the freezer in the storeroom," said her mom, her voice even colder than the freezer.

The big biker turned to his companion. "You heard the lady."

Helplessly, Dinah and her parents watched as the

Howling Coyotes took every bit of Smallbone's special order, threw it all into plastic bags, and screeched away in a cloud of black exhaust, leaving a tense silence behind them.

"*Dang* it," Lily said shakily. "That kind of thing isn't supposed to happen. It's in the Contract. No mosquitoes, no snakes, no drugs, no shoplifters, no tax collectors, and no scruffy, no-good, vagabond thieves, with or without motorcycles!"

Zery got up and hugged her and Dinah. "There's something bad wrong."

"Will Smallbone fix it?" Dinah asked.

"It's not that simple, honey," her mom said. "For Smallbone to fix it, somebody has to tell him it's broken. Which means somebody has to go to Evil Wizard Books and knock on his door and stand in that horrible dark old bookshop with the spiders and the rotting books and tell him something's gone wrong with his magical Sentries. And that his Christmas ham is gone. If all he does is turn us into frogs, we'll be getting off easy. No, I think I'd rather deal with the Howling Coyotes."

Zery said, "You'll have to tell him sooner or later, when he comes for the meat."

"Even he's not going to be running to town in this weather. With any luck, I'll get it replaced before he shows up. In any case, I'd rather tell him on my turf than his."

"It's all his turf," Zery reminded her.

"I know, but at least this part of it is clean." Lily sighed. "If those bikers come around again, I'll reconsider. In the meantime, let's just call the meat their Christmas present and go down to Eb's for dinner. I hear he's making gravlax."

Chapter Four

+ + + + + + +

Nick was on his back, his arms and legs curled into his chest. Wet snuffly noses tickled his face, and anxious doggy whines echoed in his ears.

He opened his eyes and saw Smallbone's rimless spectacles glittering like tiny moons against a backdrop of books.

"You feeling human yet, Foxkin?" Smallbone asked.

Nick stretched experimentally. Nothing hurt, exactly, but he felt achy, like he'd had a fever, and his mouth tasted like dust and copper. His arms and legs felt weak and wrongly jointed, and there seemed to be too few of them. Which made no sense, because he still had two of each, fingers and toes intact.

"I'm asking," Smallbone went on in a conversational

tone, "because you've been a spider for the best part of a week."

Nick sat up so fast, the books swam around him. "You're kidding."

"I was you, Foxkin, I'd think twice before I called me a liar."

Nick was not in the habit of thinking twice. It felt too good to say what was on his mind, even when it got him in trouble. "Because you can turn me into a spider? Maybe. If I believed you. I bet you just drugged me or something."

Smallbone shook his head. "Stubborn, ain't you, Foxkin? Maybe I should have called you Jackass. Keep an eye on him, boys," he said to the dogs. "I got things to do." And he stumped off.

Slowly, Nick got to his feet. They seemed smaller and farther away than they should. He swayed uncertainly. Mutt and Jeff steadied him with their warm, solid bodies, and he petted their sleek heads. Wagging muscular tails, they herded him gently toward the kitchen, where he got himself a glass of water. As he drank it, his eye fell on the kitchen calendar. There was a blue-penciled cross through every date up to December 26. Last he remembered, it had read December 21.

He'd missed Christmas.

Nick told himself he didn't care. At Uncle Gabe's, the only difference between Christmas and any other winter day was reruns of *A Charlie Brown Christmas* and *Miracle on 34th Street* on TV. Uncle Gabe might have brought home a mangy tree he cadged from his friend at the tree lot and pitched a fit because he couldn't remember where he'd put the decorations. Last year, he'd given Nick a sweater from the church charity box. It was way too big. Jerry had laughed, Nick had kicked him, and it all ended up with Nick spending Christmas Day in the ER. That's when he got the broken tooth.

No, Nick didn't mind missing Christmas.

He did mind missing five days out of his life, though. He set the water glass on the draining board. Maybe he hadn't missed them at all. Maybe the old man was just messing with his head. Without a TV or even a radio, Nick couldn't know for sure what day it really was. But something had happened—that was for certain. Now he was thinking about it, he could remember a thread twitching under his feet and a fly buzzing and struggling against his sticky silk trap. He remembered sinking his teeth into its body, wrapping it in silk, and feasting on its liquid insides when it was ripe.

Nick sat down hard in Smallbone's old rocker, feeling slightly sick. It was true. He had really been a spider. Magic was real, and Smallbone was just what he claimed to be: a genuine, card-carrying evil wizard.

A cold nose nudged his hand. Nick looked down. Mutt—or maybe Jeff—was gazing up at him with eyes the color of pumpkin pie, his forehead wrinkled and worried. Nick stroked the black velvet ears. He wished that Mutt—he was sure it was Mutt—really was his dog. And while he was wishing, he wished his life in Beaton was a bad dream and Smallbone was a character in a horror film and his mom was alive and life was the way it used to be before they moved in with Uncle Gabe. But that would be another kind of fairy tale than the one he seemed to be stuck in, the kind that had fairy godmothers instead of evil wizards, the happily-ever-after kind that really wasn't true even if the scarier ones might be.

"Well, if that don't beat the Dutch!" The old man—
the evil wizard, Nick reminded himself—glared at him
from the door. "It's past noon!"

Nick looked at him blankly.

"I want my lunch!" Smallbone said. "You can cook,
can't you?"

Nick almost laughed. There hadn't been a lot of
cooking in Uncle Gabe's house since Nick's mom died,
just lots of cold cuts and frozen dinners, Dinty Moore
stew, and SpaghettiOs out of a can. "I can't do anything." He gave the old man a sly look. "Maybe you
should let me go home."

"Not a chance." Smallbone sat in the rocker and
got out his pipe. "Behind that door is a larder. Pull out
some potatoes, some onions and carrots, and a head of
cabbage, and I'll tell you how to make a New England
boiled dinner."

Nick wanted to tell Smallbone what he could do
with his New England boiled dinner, but the spider
episode was fresh in his mind, and he was hungry.
Under Smallbone's direction, he peeled and chopped,
filled a big pot with water, and put it on the stove to

heat. Then he opened the refrigerator to get out the corned beef and saw a large glass jar full of round white things floating in a cloudy liquid.

His stomach lurched. "What's *that*? Eyeballs?"

"Pickled eggs," Smallbone said. "The eyeballs're in the freezer. I wouldn't eat what's in the striped bowl, either, unless you got a taste for beetles. And don't touch that package there. That's powdered frog."

Nick found the corned beef and put it in the pot, then made sandwiches with the pickled eggs and mayo while Smallbone smoked and commented on his progress.

When the sandwiches were made, Smallbone shook the plug out of his pipe and stood. "I like my supper at six." He took a sandwich and headed for the door, pausing to say, "I expect you'll have the shop clean by then," before he disappeared.

Nick didn't intend to clean the shop. He was done with Evil Wizard Books, and he was done with Smallbone. Warmth and sausages didn't make up for knowing he might get turned into a bug if he messed up. He looked at the clock—two thirty, plenty of time to put some miles between him and Evil Wizard Books before dark. He didn't know exactly where he was, but there was bound to be a town nearby, or a gas station, or an antiques shop—somewhere with a telephone and a TV and no wizards, evil or otherwise.

There was a slightly moldy ham and half a loaf of bread in the larder. Mutt and Jeff watched with drooling interest as Nick made sandwiches and found a large checked napkin to wrap them in.

He'd miss Mutt and Jeff—Tom, too. He'd never had a pet before. His mom had brought home a kitten once, a fluffy tortoiseshell scrap of fur with big yellow eyes. Uncle Gabe had grumbled, but he'd given in. The kitten had lasted about a week, sleeping on Nick's pillow, lapping milk, playing with pieces of string. And then it was gone. Mom said it must have run away, but Nick was pretty sure Uncle Gabe had gotten rid of it.

The dogs followed Nick into the mudroom and watched, eyebrows twitching, as he dug out boots, peacoat, woolly muffler, and mittens and put them on. It seemed wrong to leave without saying good-bye, so, feeling kind of foolish, he knelt down and rubbed their velvety ears while they whined and licked his face. Then the cats arrived, clearly wondering what the fuss was about. Tom joined the lovefest, but when Nick tried to pet Hell Cat, she hissed and swiped at him with open claws. She missed.

It was time to go.

Anxious to avoid walking all around the house, Nick tiptoed through the shop to the front door, his skin twitching with the sense that he was being watched by unseen, angry eyes. Nothing stopped him, though, not even the animals. The door was unlocked and failed to creak when he opened it.

Outside, the sky was gray as a dirty sheet. A freezing wind tossed dry snow from the drifts against the house and bit at Nick's throat and nose. He pulled his scarf up over his mouth. On the other side of the clearing, he saw a road, not very big, but paved and plowed. Next to it was a wooden sign, capped with snow. From where he was standing, Nick could just make out that it had EVIL WIZARD BOOKS painted on it in big black letters, like any tourists in their right mind would stop there.

Maybe it looked better in the summer.

Nick tromped across the porch and down the snowy steps into the long shadow of the corner tower. Unlike the rest of the house, the tower was built of stone, with a round window set high in each side. He cast a measuring glance at the nearest blank eye and, feeling horribly conspicuous, headed out across the windblown snow —

And found himself going up the porch steps.

Nick gritted his teeth and tried again. This time, he got almost halfway to the road before he bounced back to where he'd started. On the next try, he barely made it down the porch steps.

Nick tried taking different routes; he walked backward; he took little tiny steps; he took leaping strides. He went out the back door and walked down the long, neatly shoveled path that led to the woodshed and the big red barn where the goats that Smallbone wanted Nick to milk must live.

That time, he ended up actually walking through the back door into the kitchen.

By now, the hard gray light had faded and the

snow had started up again. Grimly, Nick fetched a hatchet out of the woodshed, tied a rope to the handle, and pitched it into the snowy ground. He checked that it had caught and pulled himself forward to meet it. And then he did it again, hauling himself toward the road bit by bit, farther than he'd ever come before, all the way to the EVIL WIZARD BOOKS sign. He heaved his improvised grappling hook to his shoulder for a last throw . . .

And found himself on the front porch, with the hatchet stuck quivering in the door frame.

Smallbone opened the door and turned his spectacles from the hatchet to Nick. "Running off, are you?"

Nick swallowed a shameful lump in his throat. "Nope. Just wanted some air."

Smallbone let the lie hang between them. "Dust got to you, eh? Well, tomorrow's another day."

⚜ ⚜ ⚜

They ate the New England boiled dinner. Smallbone grumbled at the overcooked cabbage and made lavish use of the mustard, but he didn't turn Nick into anything. In fact, he didn't speak to Nick at all, except to direct him in feeding the animals and washing the dishes and the floor. When everything was shipshape, he picked up his lantern.

"Come along, Foxkin," he said. "Chore time."

The night was cold as a deep freeze and black as Smallbone's hat. Nick crunched down the path after the lantern, shivering. It was warmer in the barn, if smelly, and even darker than it was outside. Nick stood just inside the door, listening to an excited chorus of clucks and *maa*s, as Smallbone lit another lantern and hung it on a hook.

A raucous bray made Nick jump and spin, fists raised, to see a donkey's fuzzy gray face by his elbow, long ears twitching curiously.

"Noisy cuss, ain't he?" Smallbone said, pseudo-sympathetically. "Name of Groucho. Groucho, this is Foxkin."

Cautiously, Nick held out his hand and Groucho lipped it. His nose was very soft.

Nearby, a buff-colored hen perched on a straw bale like a feathery toilet-roll cover. Smallbone said her name was Daphne. He had seven hens, plus a rooster called Apollo.

Among the lies Nick had told Smallbone was the one about not knowing anything about animals. When he was in fourth grade, his mom had enrolled him in 4-H. He'd had four chickens, which he'd kept in the backyard until his mother died, when Uncle Gabe had sold them. Nick hadn't minded leaving 4-H—he couldn't stand listening to the other kids talking about their parents and their projects. He'd missed the chickens, though.

Unlike Nick's chickens, who had laid their eggs in the coop he'd built for them, Smallbone's chickens nested everywhere, even in Groucho's manger. They were a lot feistier than Nick's chickens, too, and pecked at his fingers when he reached under them, looking for eggs. The goats, on the other hand, crowded to the front of their pen and bleated at him in a friendly way. One put its front hooves on the rail and nosed at Nick's shirt. Nick thought it was saying hello until he felt a tug and saw his scarf disappearing into the goat's busy mouth.

"Harpo will eat anything," Smallbone said. "Just give him a good shove. You got to be firm with goats or they'll be up to shenanigans." He scratched a slot-eyed doe between her ears. "This here's Thalia. The other two are Aglaea and Euphrosyne."

Nick groaned. "I can't remember that! I can't even say it. Why don't you call them something normal, like—I don't know—Betty? Or Nanny? Nanny's a good name for a goat."

"Because Nanny's not her name, of course. Names are important, Foxkin. You know something's right name, you know what it *is*. Knowing what something *is* gives you power over it."

"You don't care about my right name!" Nick snapped.

"Oh, I think I do, Foxkin mine. The question is, do you?"

When the goats had been fed and watered, Smallbone took Nick to the back of the barn, where a large pinkish-white lump snored gently in the straw. "This is Ollie," Smallbone said, hanging his lantern above the stall. "Finest Yorkshire hog on the coast."

He took an apple-size blue rubber ball out of a small bucket and shook it so a bell inside jingled invitingly. Ollie heaved himself to his trotters and squinted up at Smallbone, his saucer nose twitching eagerly.

Smallbone pitched the ball into the straw, and Ollie plunged after it with excited grunts, his little corkscrew tail awhirl. He rooted until he found the ball, then nosed it around the floor, pushing up a wave of straw with his nose and head to the accompaniment of much jingling and grunting.

Nick broke out laughing and glanced at Smallbone. What with the beard and the hat and the glasses, it was almost impossible to see the evil wizard's face, but Nick thought he might be smiling.

"Keeps him healthy," Smallbone said cheerfully. "He'll be good eating, come spring." He said some words Nick didn't understand, and the ball—streaked now with what Nick hoped was mud—sailed out from under Ollie's nose and into the bucket with a splash.

"Take that and rinse it off. Then you can fill the water troughs, and I'll show you how to milk a goat."

Chapter Five

✦ ✦ ✦ ✦ ✦ ✦ ✦

It was barely light out when Smallbone banged on Nick's door the next morning. "You want eggs for breakfast, you'll have to gather them."

Groaning, Nick slid into the hick clothes and staggered down the stairs.

Out in the barn, the chickens had hidden their eggs so well, Nick only found eight. He ate three for breakfast, black and crispy around the edges because he had the fire up too high, and a piece of charred toast. Smallbone disposed of two more, without comment, and went out to the barn to milk the goats. He didn't remind Nick about the shop. He didn't need to. The smell of mold and rotting leather was creeping down the passage into the kitchen. There was even a new spiderweb across the top of the connecting door.

Nick put the eggy plates on the floor and watched Mutt and Jeff rinse them with their long pink tongues. It didn't take a genius to figure out that cleaning the bookshop was some kind of test. Nick hated tests. In his experience, they were designed to separate the good kids, who knew the answers, from the bad kids, who didn't. He already knew he was a bad kid. Good kids knew how to stay out of trouble. Good kids didn't get turned into spiders and spend almost a week spinning webs and eating flies.

Or at least that's what tests were for in Beaton. It was anybody's guess what an evil wizard would be testing for.

Nick gathered up the plates and put them in the sink. Then he lugged a ladder out of the mudroom, trying not to trip over Mutt and Jeff, who were bouncing around him in the mistaken belief that this was some sort of new game. He propped the ladder against the wall next to the new cobweb, then climbed up and examined it.

Spiderwebs, as Nick now had good reason to know, are designed to trap things. A network of smooth threads allows the spider to navigate his web without sticking, but most of the threads are gluey, clingy trap threads. Sticky as they looked, the threads of this web felt like smooth cotton thread, and smelled sharp, like a thunderstorm. Also, a just-built web would have a spider lurking on it somewhere. This one didn't. In fact, it wasn't a real web at all. And neither, he suspected, were the others. But the fake ones just might stick to a real one.

All Nick had to do was find the one he'd spun.

He peered out over the rows of grimy bookshelves marching into the darkness. For all he knew, they just extended back forever into another dimension, in which case he might as well give up. Or maybe that web in the next aisle back, the one that wasn't all dusty and drapey and movie-like, was the one he was looking for, his web that he'd spun himself.

Nick descended the ladder and dragged it into the gloom, wishing Smallbone had left him a lantern. Back among the shelves, he heard something rustle. It was like a bad horror movie, he thought — the old house, the old man, the eyeballs in the freezer, the shadows, the mysterious noises. The prickly, uncomfortable feeling that someone was always watching him, someone with crazy eyes and possibly a knife, watching and waiting until just the right moment . . .

No. He wasn't going there. Sure, Smallbone was nuts, but it wasn't an ordinary, knife-in-the-dark kind of nuts. The noises were probably just the cats, hunting mice in the dark. And the airless feeling was just from breathing all that dust.

It was the right web. Once he climbed up and looked at it, he recognized it at once. A little lopsided, and the stay threads were kind of clunky, but for a spider new to the work, he thought he'd done a pretty good job. He pulled it down, wrapped it around his broom handle, and swirled it through the fake webs. They stuck to it like, well, magic. Before long, the broom handle was surrounded by a big silky cocoon of magic fake cobwebs. Nick gave it a tug and slid it off, leaving his web clinging to the broom handle. Encouraged, he swirled his way row by row right to the back of the shop—which was not so far after all, though very dark and stuffy—until all the cobwebs lay on the shop counter in fluffy gray rolls.

Tom, who'd been asleep by the cash register, woke up and patted a roll with a curious paw. It skidded a few inches, leaving a dust-free streak behind it, just like a miracle cleaning cloth in a TV ad.

Soon, Nick had not only cleaned the counter but polished it to a golden glow. He gave it a final, triumphant rub and grinned. One job done. That left only six extremely grimy windows and about a million dusty, rotting books to go.

Nick reviewed his options. He'd already tried running away. Hiding probably wouldn't accomplish much beyond making Smallbone mad enough to turn him into something even worse than a spider.

That left him with getting to work.

Nick slid a relatively clean roll of magic cobweb onto the broom handle and started dusting the first row of books. Close up, they weren't as smelly as he expected, and a lot more interesting. Random titles caught his eye: *Lunatics and Lycanthropes*, *Hexes Through the Ages*, *Haruspicy! Or: The Future Through Sheep Guts*, *100 Uses for a Dead Man's Hand*. He took the last title down and had just opened it when the dogs jumped up, barking happily.

"It's a sorry world," Smallbone said from the stairs, "where an evil wizard has to wait on his apprentice's convenience for his meals. It's past noon."

With the nonchalance of a practiced shoplifter, Nick ran his cobweb duster over *Dead Man's Hand,* closed it, and put it back on the shelf. "How am I supposed to know what time it is? I can't see. Aren't there any lights in here?"

"Don't want no flames around all this paper," Smallbone said. "And I don't hold with electricity. Chancy, newfangled stuff. You've got half an hour to get lunch on the table, or I'll turn your nose blue." And he went back up the stairs, the dogs at his heels.

Nick went to the kitchen, looked thoughtfully at the ordinary-looking lights and appliances, and spent a few minutes searching for switches and electrical outlets. He didn't find any. The fridge didn't even have a cord.

There probably wasn't a hot-water heater in the cellar or a furnace or anything normal, Nick thought as he put the leftover corned beef on a plate. The whole dang house probably ran on magic. Which brought up the question of why the old loon needed an apprentice at all, especially one who couldn't boil water, milk a goat, cast a spell, or — as far as he knew — read.

It didn't bear thinking about, but Nick thought about it anyway until Smallbone showed up in the kitchen at twelve thirty sharp, carrying a big leather-covered book. He read while he ate — which Nick's mother had always said was rude. When the last bite of corned beef was gone, he shut the book with a snap. "You can fetch a lamp from the mudroom, boy. If you're going to get that shop really clean, you'll need to see the dirt."

⚜ ⚜ ⚜

The lamp was tin with a glass chimney, and it burned kerosene. Nick set it on the counter, where it smoked and stank and cast dancing shadows everywhere. Then he got to work.

The magic cobwebs cleaned everything — windows, furniture, floor, books. They even took the tarnish off the big old cash register. Nick rubbed and dusted until his arms ached and his shoulders burned. When a roll got too grimy to work anymore, he put it back on the counter and picked up another. The dogs got tired of being tripped over and disappeared

✦ 61 ✦

upstairs. When Nick cleaned the big bay window, he could see the field of snow between the house and the road, crisscrossed with holes and scuffs and skid marks and tracks like a snake's.

The clock on the landing struck five, extra loudly. Time to make dinner, if he could find anything he knew how to cook. He wondered if Smallbone had ever heard of SpaghettiOs. He gathered up the dirty rolls of magic cobweb, carried them into the kitchen, and threw them on the fire, just like his mom had taught him.

A flash of multicolored light half blinded him, and a roiling billow of black and stinking smoke seized him by the eyes and throat, coated his skin, and invaded his nose with sticky, burning foulness. He rolled on the floor, choking.

A few very long minutes passed before Smallbone arrived on the scene. He took in the oily smoke, the gasping apprentice, and the seriously put-out cats yowling under the stove, fished in his pocket for a handful of white powder, and threw it onto the fire. The flames went out with a pop, and he raked what was left of the cobwebs onto the hearth, opened a window to air the place out, and got Nick some cold water.

"What made you think burning magic would be a good idea, eh? Danger aside, it's a jeezly waste. And it ain't good for the animals. Ah, what's the use? I've a good mind turn you into toast and butter you."

Nick glared over the rim of the glass. His chest hurt, and his face and hands prickled. "You could have warned me."

"You could have asked." Smallbone poked at the scorched cobwebs with a scuffed boot. "Go clean yourself up."

Nick marched into the bathroom and locked the door. Totally unsurprised to find that the tub was already full of gently steaming water, he shucked off his clothes, got in, and rubbed thin black curls of burned ork off his skin like peeling sunburn.

Electricity was dangerous, huh? What about getting turned into a bug? What about getting blown up by flaming magic spiderwebs? If Nick was Smallbone's apprentice, why hadn't the old coot told him what to do? So he could call Nick names? So he could watch him suffer? Was turning people into things any different from laying into them with a strap? And if it was different, was it better or worse?

Who cared? Not Nick. He was getting out of here, one way or another.

Maybe, he thought, adding more hot to the water, he could pretend to be all scared and docile, learn how to cook, take care of the animals, do what he was told, make Smallbone think he'd gotten Nick where he wanted him. Then, when the weather broke, maybe Nick could make his escape. At least it would keep Smallbone off his case.

Nick cleaned the grayish magic kludge out of the tub, put on his magic-spattered clothes, and returned to the kitchen. It was long past suppertime. A pan of congealing eggs and hash told him that Smallbone had fixed his own supper and left the dirty dishes for Nick to deal with. He'd also left a bucket, a shovel, and an iron rake beside the fireplace. Hell Cat was still under the stove, but Tom had moved to the draining board. Mutt and Jeff crouched in the corner farthest from the fireplace. The air smelled acrid and greasy.

So did the hash, but Nick ate it anyway, figuring he'd breathed in enough burned magic that eating some wouldn't make a difference. Then he heated up a bucket of water on the stove and dumped it on the floor.

The burned magic clumped into a thick gray glop, speckled with black.

Hell Cat slunk out from under the stove and poked at it with her paw. The glop shuddered. She pounced, claws out, and the clump popped out a foul-smelling, burned-magic fart, which sent her scuttling back to her hiding place. Nick shoveled the glop into the bucket. There was more glop underneath. He filled an iron stew pot with more water and put it on the stove.

An hour later, the floor was shining clean and Nick had made a start on the hearth, when the back door opened. "You don't want that magic crawling out again, you best put a board over the bucket," a gruff voice said. "You planning on staying up all night?"

Nick scraped up more glop. "Nope. Sleep well," he added sarcastically.

"Oh, I will."

Chapter Six

* * ✦ ✦ ✦ ✦ *

Inland of Smallbone Cove as the coyote runs is a part of Maine tourists don't often see. The land is rocky, scrubby, and flat. There aren't many paved roads, and those are more frost heave than pavement. The unpaved ones are muddy in spring and autumn, dusty in summer, slippery in winter, and bumpy all year long. Both kinds of road are dotted with little clumps of houses. Each clump has a name and a general store and a gas station and maybe a small post office or a library or a church. Some are well kept and pretty, with white houses and neat lawns and gardens.

The clump called Fidelou was the exact opposite of pretty.

It was, however, highly unusual. There aren't a lot of small towns in Maine—or any other state—that feature a medieval-type castle. Not the fantasy medieval-type castle, with pointy towers and lots of balconies for pretty ladies to wave from, either, but the low, solid, practical kind owned by someone who is prepared to be attacked at any moment.

Its windows were slits in the granite walls, and its doors were narrow and reinforced with iron. A black flag blazoned with a white wolf fluttered from each squat tower. More wolves were carved above the heavy doors and on the columns of the Great Hall. Against the wall stood battle trophies: a chariot shaped like a giant frog, a bison's head, a bright feathered cape, a pointy hat, a glowing sword. At the far end of the hall, a low platform supported a high wooden throne, a red velvet footstool, and a large and ancient wooden trunk decorated with a band of running wolves.

In the time the castle had stood there nobody had attacked it, but the wizard who sat on the throne had lived in a castle just like it four hundred years ago in his native France and was not about to change his habits just because he had moved to the United States of America.

The wizard's name was Fidelou, which means "Son of the Wolf" in French. He was a loup-garou, whose magic pelt changed him from wolf to man and back without need of spells or a full moon. He was evil and proud of it. His magic was all blood and destruction and greed. Back in France, he and his pack of wolf-soldiers had been feared throughout the land.

When he moved to Maine, he had added coyotes to the pack. They were better at surviving in the modern world than wolves were.

Fidelou did not like the modern world. It was too crowded and too hard to prey upon. His pack fell to traps and poison and men in airplanes with guns. In human form, they got put in jail. As a matter of pride, Fidelou did not go out and find new pack members; he waited for them to come to him, which didn't happen as often as it had in the old days.

So when a lantern-jawed teenager wearing a red Portland Sea Dogs baseball cap came into town on a rebuilt Yamaha, the were-coyote guard Hiram brought him straight to Fidelou, who was sitting in the Great Hall with his feet up.

The wolf wizard looked down his beaky nose at the newcomer, who was clutching his cap in both hands and pretending he wasn't scared. He smelled promising—desperate and aggressive, with a strong whiff of meanness. Fidelou liked bullies. They were so easy to intimidate.

"So, youngling," he growled. "You wish to join Fidelou's pack?"

The boy's hands tightened on his cap. "I might," he said, trying to sound tough. "Depends."

"For me, too, it depends." Fidelou bared his pointed teeth. The boy's eyes widened like a frightened deer's. "What are your talents, eh? What is it you have to offer Fidelou in return for his protection?"

"I can fight. And I can fix motorcycles."

The wolf wizard pricked up his ears. "Really?" Fidelou loved motorcycles. They were powerful and noisy and traveled faster than a wolf could run. They made the modern world bearable.

"Yeah," the boy said sullenly. "I'm the best. I can take a broke-down piece of junk and make it roar like a tiger."

"You do not lack in confidence, *mon brave.*" Fidelou leaned forward, elbow on one leather-covered knee. "What about a noble machine? What about a Vincent? Can you fix that?"

It was an important question. The Vincent Black Lightning was a shiny monster famous for going faster than any other bike in the world. When it went at all. For though Fidelou loved his Vincent, he did not understand it, and he rode it as if it were as indestructible as he was. As a result, it was always breaking down, and when it did, only a truly expert mechanic could fix it. Fidelou had drowned his last mechanic in the latest attempt upon Smallbone Cove, and the Vincent was now up on blocks in the courtyard, its engine silent and dead.

The boy's eyes shifted. "No problem," he said.

Fidelou smelled the lie, decided he didn't care. Any mechanic was better than no mechanic. If the boy didn't work out, Fidelou could always kill him. "*Bon.* What is your name?"

"Jerry," the young man said. "Jerry Reynaud."

"Well, then, Jerry. As we lack a mechanic just now,

you will take over the direction of Fidelou Gas and Motorcycle Repair."

Jerry grinned. "Sounds good." He hesitated. "The guys at the bar, they said something about coyotes. It sounded like a load of hooey to me, but I thought I'd ask, just in case it wasn't."

Fidelou sat back against the snowy fur of his pelt. "It is truth they have told you, Jerry. When you have earned it, I will give you a pelt and you will run with your pack-brothers and -sisters. Until then, you will do as you are told. I expect fidelity and obedience—to me and to all the full coyotes of the pack. Do you understand?"

Jerry nodded. "Yessir."

"You may call me Boss," said Fidelou. "Hiram, take him to the garage. And bring me a rabbit. I am hungry."

Chapter Seven

Uncle Gabe was looking for Nick with a flashlight. He must have been drunk, because the light flashed across Nick's eyes as he swung it every which way. In his hiding place, Nick breathed as softly as someone whose heart is thudding like a piston can breathe.

It wasn't softly enough. The light swung into his eyes and held. Uncle Gabe's hand, big as a giant's, spread over his head and . . .

Nick struggled upright, panting. Sunlight streamed through the blue-checked curtains onto the pillow. He wasn't in Beaton at all. That was a good thing. Except that he'd missed morning chores and breakfast wasn't ready and Smallbone was very particular about breakfast being ready when he came downstairs. The last time he'd overslept, the old man had made Nick's teeth grow until he couldn't eat anything at all.

Stupid dreams. It wasn't like Uncle Gabe was going to come after him. Uncle Gabe considered him a waste of time, space, and Dinty Moore stew. The only reason he put up with him was because he'd promised his sister he'd take care of her little boy. No, Nick thought as he scrambled into his clothes, he was free from Uncle Gabe. He had Smallbone instead, who was probably downstairs planning something special.

When Nick got to the kitchen, a pot of porridge was plopping gently to itself on the black stove. Smallbone had added a long mud-colored muffler to his black coat and top hat and was packing a small basket. He closed the lid and gave Nick a long-toothed and, under the circumstances, sinister grin.

"Land o' Goshen, Foxkin, you look like somebody left a dead mouse in your bed. That's no way to look on New Year's Day! I'm going fishing. Seeing as I already seen to the animals and you worked near half the night, you can take the day off."

Nick looked at the calendar. It had a new picture—of a covered bridge this time—and January 1 was circled in red pencil.

Smallbone slung the basket over his shoulder and collected a long rod from the corner. "Stay clear of my tower," he said. "If I find out you've been near it, I'll turn you into a slug and salt you." Then he whistled to Mutt and Jeff and followed them out into the bright coldness. Through the back window, Nick watched him trudge toward the wood, the dogs bounding ahead of him, black as licorice against the drifts. As the old man walked, the snow fountained out of his way as if he were using a snowblower.

I want to do that, Nick thought. Maybe he could learn from one of those books he'd seen in the bookshop when he was cleaning it. In any case, he'd like to get a look at *100 Uses for a Dead Man's Hand.*

He ran into the bookshop and looked at the MYSTERY section, where he thought he'd seen it. It wasn't there. Nor was *Recipes Every Witch Should Know* in COOKING or *How to Catch a Leprechaun* in FOLKLORE. Even ARCANA was stocked with nothing but books on the kind of magic that includes card tricks, disappearing handkerchiefs, and pulling rabbits out of hats.

Disgusted, Nick pulled *The Hobbit* out of SPECULATIVE FICTION and looked around for somewhere to read it. There wasn't one. And the bookshop, though clean, was cold, bare, and gloomy. He could just hear his mom saying it needed some cozying up. A rug, curtains, a chair or two, some lamps and tables to put them on would make it into a place you'd actually want to hang out in.

Evil Wizard Books had lots of rooms. There had to be stuff in them he could use.

Nick was not a kid to let grass grow under his feet. He ran upstairs and started opening doors. Most of the rooms were furnished like his, with a bed and a chest of drawers and not much else. Pushing his explorations farther, he found a little sitting room with a flowery rug, which he rolled up, dragged down to the shop, and spread in front of the counter.

He ran back up for an armchair.

A fancy bedroom with a four-poster bed yielded more chairs, a table, and a brass inkwell shaped like a raven. The next door he tried led to a kid's room with a crib and a life-size stuffed seal on wooden rockers. It was dusty and dim, and Nick closed the door without going in. There was nothing there he could use anyway.

Finally he turned a corner and found himself in a hall with gray stone walls. There was one door at the far end, made of heavy oak banded with iron, with an arched top.

It had to be the door to Smallbone's tower.

Blood racing, Nick went up to it and slowly reached one finger toward the latch. A spark leaped out and gave him the kind of electric shock you get after shuffling your feet across a carpet in winter, accompanied by a smell like overheated metal.

Nick shook his stinging hand and kicked the door, hard. A bolt of miniature lightning caught him on the leg, sharp as a needle.

So the tower was guarded. He wasn't surprised. He was, however, hungry.

He retraced his steps to the kitchen, made himself a ham sandwich, and went back to work.

Gradually, the bookshop began to look more welcoming. There were chintz curtains on the windows, chairs in the aisles for reading, a table on the rug, and three milk-glass lamps casting a warm glow over the rows of books. The air smelled pleasantly of lavender soap and lamp oil. Tom, who had been watching the process with interest, curled up on a comfy chair, and Hell Cat humped herself into a furry loaf on the end of the counter.

Then Nick heard a rattling back in the bookshelves. The nape of his neck began to prickle.

He picked up a lamp and followed the sound to the section labeled CHILDREN — USEFUL, and listened. Whatever was making the noise was definitely behind the books on that shelf — there. He raised the lamp, illuminating the nearest titles: *Goats Are Fun!, How to Sew an Apron, E-Z Spelz for Little Wizardz.*

E-Z Spelz for Little Wizardz?

Nick reached for the book. The spine felt warm and buzzed under his fingers slightly, like a tiny motor. He pulled it down.

The cover was bright blue, with a neon-yellow

wand and a sparkly red star under the title. A little-kid book, but a magic little-kid book. He opened it.

CHAPTER ONE: So You Want to Be a Wizard.

Warning!! A young magic worker should never try a spell without an experienced witch or wizard present to explain things and prevent accidents.

Nick had himself a good laugh over that.

Don't laugh. Magic is dangerous stuff, you know. There's still time to change your mind.

"I won't," he said, then felt like a ding-a-ling for talking to a book. But wasn't the book talking to him? He read on.

Magic isn't anything very special. Almost anybody can learn to do magic, just like almost anybody can learn to throw a ball. But to be really good, you need something extra. It's the same with

magic. If you want to be a witch or a wizard, the
first thing you need is TALENT.

Reading this book proves you have more
magical talent than most. Congratulations.

HOWEVER. Being a wizard takes more than
talent.

You have to really WANT to be a wizard. You
can't think maybe you'd rather be an engineer or a
superstar. You have to believe a cat can be a king and
pigs can fly, and a million other things most people
think are impossible. You have to know those things
can happen, then make them so. You need WILL.

Nick grinned to himself. Uncle Gabe always called
him pigheaded, and even his mom used to say he was
willful, so he guessed he was all set there.

Once you know it's possible to turn straw into
gold, you have to believe that YOU can do it. You
can't think maybe, probably you can—if you
don't screw it up, if you're in the mood. You have
to know that straw's going to turn to pure, solid

gold every time you tell it to. Truly great wizards know that magic is real because they make it real. They have CONFIDENCE.

There were lots of things Nick knew he was good at, but none of them seemed very magical. Lying. Stealing. Fighting. Screwing up. Pretending he knew what he was doing. Maybe if he pretended he was confident?

Bending reality takes a lot of work. When you're doing magic, you can't be thinking about lunch or a TV show or what might go wrong. You have to put your whole self—body, mind, and spirit—into doing it right. Spells focus your attention on what you're doing so that the energy you raise will go where you want it. You need CONCENTRATION.

Nick flipped ahead. The book was called *E-Z Spelz*. There had to be some actual spells in here somewhere. Turning straw into gold might be useful.

The next few pages were blank. Nick kept flipping.

Lines appeared.

Magic isn't like cooking, you know. You can't just start throwing stuff together and hope it all comes out okay.

Nick slammed the book shut. The last thing he wanted right now was another one of those lectures on focus and keeping on task and paying attention his teachers were always giving him. The air thickened, and a faint sharp smell, like an electrical short, tickled his nose. He sneezed and peered uneasily into the shadows. There was something there—he knew it, something watching and waiting and judging him.

Carefully, he opened *E-Z Spelz for Little Wizardz* with trembling hands. If the book wanted him to read a bunch of preachy rules before he could get to the good stuff, well, he'd read them.

He didn't have to follow them all.

Now, where were we? Oh, yes. CONTROL. As you'll soon find out, magic is energy, and the

energy comes from you. Use too little, nothing happens. Use too much, you'll use it up quicker. Use it wrong, you can do a lot of damage. Here are a few examples of what can happen if you miscast a spell. I hope you have a strong stomach. You'll need it.

There followed pages and pages of what could go wrong if a Little Wizard was weak on Concentration and Control. With sick fascination, Nick read about explosions, fires, tempests, and floods. "Inversion" seemed to mean people's skin turning inside out. There were pictures.

The list ended with "Death" and "Dismemberment."

Just when he thought things couldn't get any weirder, the next page contained an Aptitude Test. It wasn't like any test he'd had at Beaton Middle School.

1. Place your thumbs on your two favorite letters on this page.
2. Think of your worst enemy.
   Wow. He's bad, all right.

3. Think about what you would do if he was
   hanging off a cliff by his thumbs.
4. Pull a hair out of your head.
5. Tie a knot in it and put it in this circle: O
6. Say "Shelley Sells Sheep to Silly Sharks" six
   times fast.

And so on, for five pages.
When he got to the end, a neat paragraph appeared.

Your Will is off the charts, but you already
knew that. Your Confidence is a sometimes thing,
and your Control and your Concentration both
stink. As does your sense of self-preservation. It's
getting dark. Do you want the old man to catch
you? Oh, and you might want to cut up some
potatoes for dinner. Boiled potatoes go well
with fish.

Chapter Eight

✦ ✦ ✦ ✦ ✦ ✦ ✦

Dinah Smallbone was getting impatient.

More than two weeks had passed since the Howling Coyotes had hit Smallbone Cove Mercantile. Somehow everybody in town knew all about it, and they were considerably exercised. This sort of thing wasn't supposed to happen in Smallbone Cove. Wasn't it the evil wizard's job to protect them? What about the magical Sentries that were supposed to keep them safe? Lily called a Town Meeting in the white church to talk it over.

Miss Rachel Smallbone suggested that the towns-folk walk the Town Limits and sing to the Sentries, the way her parents used to do. Ham Smallbone said no full-grown man would be caught dead tromping around the woods in the middle of winter, singing to stone walls and streams. Jezebel Smallbone pointed out that nobody knew what the songs were, anyway, unless Miss Rachel happened to remember. Miss Rachel said, rather huffily, that she'd been a child when the custom fell into disuse, but she was looking into it.

Bildad Smallbone, who owned the Three Bags Full knitting shop, said the Sentries were wizard business and it was up to the Wizard Smallbone to see that they worked right.

"It's in the Contract, ain't it? That he gotta take care of us?"

Miss Rachel gave Bildad a look over the tops of her spectacles. "You ever read the Contract? Keeping the Sentries strong is our responsibility."

"It says we got to farm his land and work in his house and give him a portion of our daily catch, too." Saul Smallbone thought the evil wizard was a thief and a tyrant and didn't care who knew it. "But we don't, and he hasn't done nothing about it. What do you say to that?"

Then Ham asked if anybody had noticed that they

were in the middle of the worst winter in living memory. "I'm not going out in that," he said, pointing at the sleet whipping sideways past the windows. "And neither is old Smallbone—or the bikers or anything else. At least let's wait until the weather lets up."

Miss Rachel threw her hands in the air and wheeled herself out of the church.

They discussed it a while longer, but in the end, they decided to do what Ham had suggested. Nothing.

On the first day it wasn't actually snowing, Dinah put on long johns and a parka and boots and set out on the path that led to the Stream to investigate.

The Stream wasn't flowing. It was covered with snow.

That never happened. In Smallbone Cove, "As long as the Stream flows" was the same thing as saying "Forever." Dinah knew she should run back and tell everyone. But Dinah was a scientist down to her bones, and no scientist worth her microscope would theorize in the absence of hard data. She wasn't going anywhere until she knew whether the ice was just on the surface or went all the way down, in case that made a difference to whether the Stream was completely broken or only kind of broken, like a car that wouldn't start when it was raining.

Poking at the ice with a stick told her nothing, dropping a stone on it very little more. Dinah stepped onto the snowy ice, her heart racing. The Stream wasn't all that wide. Ten good steps, and she'd be outside the Town Limits.

There were all kinds of schoolyard theories about what happened to Smallbone Covers who tried to cross the Town Limits. You'd explode or go up in flames. You'd turn into a frog or a fish or a snapping turtle or a tree or a rock. Older kids dared one another to wade to the middle of the Stream or climb the Wall or cross the Stone Bridge that connected Smallbone Cove to the county road. Some of the bolder ones even took the dare. But nobody ever came anywhere near succeeding. First they'd get dizzy, and then their skin would start to twitch and prickle. If they kept going, they'd fall over like they were having a fit, and somebody would have to pull them back.

It was the sort of thing nobody tried twice.

Dinah had never tried at all. She was curious, not stupid.

But now, in the interest of science, she shuffled slowly over the frozen Stream, testing each step for creaking or cracking. She was almost halfway across when her foot hit something that felt horribly like a dead animal. She squeaked and jumped back — because she was all wound up, not because she was grossed out by dead animals. Scientists did not get grossed out. Last summer, she'd recorded the gradual decomposition of a dead skunk from flies through maggots to bones.

Dinah brushed the snow away, revealing an untidy bundle of fur, stiff with ice but not completely frozen. Poking it with a stick told her there wasn't an actual animal inside it.

This was even better than the skunk. Carefully, she spread out the crackly pelt. It was perfectly preserved, head and legs and tail still attached, no tears or holes or ragged edges. It was a pretty color, too, cream and sand and black all mixed, with a long fluffy black tail. She'd take it home, maybe put it in her bedroom for a rug. She'd have to get the smell out, though. Even in the cold, she was aware of it. Not bad, exactly, but pungent, like the smell of seaweed at low tide.

She threw it over her shoulders.

What happened next was not something Dinah was ever able to remember clearly. One minute, she was gagging and trying to throw off the horrible thing. The next, an icy agony was stabbing into her forefeet, forcing her to dance backward, yipping with pain, until she was back on the shore she'd just left.

Whimpering, the young coyote licked her paws until they stopped tingling, then got up and lifted her nose to the air.

The world was full of sounds and smells: water running under thick ice, the scratching of a small animal in the undergrowth, the distant scent of goats and chickens and smoke.

She licked her chops and yawned. She was hungry.

Following her nose, she trotted toward the goats until she ran into a barrier that set her fur on end. Ice stabbed through her veins, and she tumbled backward, then picked herself up and fled, yelping. After a while, she stopped, shook herself, and sniffed again. Fish, salt, smoke, prey. And stronger than all of these, warm and beckoning, the smell of her pack, of her mother and father, of safety, of home.

Shortly afterward, the coyote that was Dinah Smallbone bounded out of the woods onto a hard surface that smelled of oil. Her nose told her she'd found her pack, but all she could see was two-legged animals far bigger than she running around like prey and making loud noises that hurt her ears. Panicked, she tucked her tail between her legs and made a mad dash for her den.

She hit another barrier and sat down with a surprised yip. Caught between the terrifying noises behind her and the smell of home before her, she scratched desperately at the barrier, whining and howling until she was hoarse and spent. She curled up against the barrier and went to sleep.

She woke up in a dark place that smelled of stone and salt and meat and water. And there she stayed for what seemed to her like a long, long time.

Chapter Nine

+ + ✦ ✦ ✦ + +

Nick hated winter. Winter was chilblains and freezing feet, cold food and not enough of it. Winter was school and being bored out of his mind and fights at recess and having to go down to the principal's office and listen to lectures about the importance of anger management and impulse control.

Winter was when Nick's mother had died.

One day, she'd been laughing and cooking pot-au-feu and reading fantasy books to him at bedtime. The next, it seemed like, she'd been coughing and skinny and pale. Uncle Gabe said it was only a cold, but a lady who worked at the cleaning service said colds didn't last three months and talked her into going to the hospital.

She never came home.

That winter was when Uncle Gabe went from crabby to mean, from a guy who liked a couple of beers when he got home to a guy who got drunk at work. That winter was when he lost his job at Beaton Garage. He was a genius mechanic, so the Sunoco station took him on, and he got into a fight with a customer and had to move on to Joe's Motor and Body Shop.

Winter was the pits and lasted way too long. If Nick had a choice, he would have skipped it entirely.

This winter was a little different. Nick was warm and dry and had plenty to eat. He didn't have to go to school with dimwits who made fun of his clothes and called him names and jumped him at recess. He had Mutt and Jeff and Tom to keep him company, more science fiction than he could read in a year, and he was learning magic. All in all, this winter was better than most, or it would have been if it hadn't been for Smallbone.

Nick couldn't figure Smallbone out. Nothing about him made sense. He was a wizard who said he knew all kinds of spells, and yet he did barn chores by hand, like an ordinary person. Nick's dirty clothes disappeared and clean ones appeared to replace them, but all the meals had to be prepared and cooked. The stove ran by magic, but the kitchen fireplace had to be fed with wood that had to be chopped and hauled. All the evil wizards Nick had ever read about had minions — plural — to help them spread their evil empires. Nick was Smallbone's only minion, and as far as he knew, the evil empire consisted of some farm animals and a bookshop no customer in their right mind would ever stop at.

And there was the fact that, after forcing Nick to accept that he couldn't leave Evil Wizard Books no matter how hard he tried, Smallbone proceeded to ignore him. He spent all day up in his tower work-shop, coming down only for meals that he ate while reading a book propped against the sugar bowl. Sometimes he'd stick around afterward and tell Nick how to make some dish he liked, but mostly he didn't speak at all. It was as if he was trying to pretend he still lived alone.

As puzzling and bizarre as the old man's behavior was, it did leave Nick plenty of free time. Every morning, he got up to a world of swirling white and fought the wind as he followed Smallbone's magic path to the barn, fed and watered the animals, gathered the eggs and milked the goats, then came back to make breakfast. Every night, he fell asleep to the wind rattling the windows and Tom purring on the pillow by his ear. In between, he played with the dogs and—whenever he felt reasonably sure Smallbone was safely out of the way—read *E-Z Spelz for Little Wizardz* in the nest of cushions he'd made for himself in the back of the bookshop.

He'd started with a spell for lighting a candle without a match. It was kind of like learning to ride a bicycle. At first it was hard, and then it was like something switched on inside his head and he didn't even have to think about how he did it. Other spells were harder. They called for ingredients he couldn't find and rituals you needed time to complete. He was always aware that Smallbone might come in and turn him into something horrible.

He didn't want to go through anything like the spider episode again. It wasn't so much *being* a spider that bothered him — the spider had been perfectly fine with it. But that spider hadn't been Nick. It had just been a spider, and the Nick who remembered his mom and hated his uncle had been nowhere.

It was enough to give anybody nightmares. Nick had them anyway, mostly about Uncle Gabe, but sometimes about Smallbone, too, and they were horrible. He always woke in a rage, thrashing around and trying to yell.

One night, he lit the bedside candle, pulled *E-Z Spelz* from under his pillow, and opened it at random.

Spells of Protection are easy to cast. People have been casting them for thousands of years, and the paths of magic are worn smooth. Bow-Wowzer Meowzer is a beginner's spell. It depends almost entirely on Will—which makes it perfect for a stubborn cuss like you. It won't keep the old man from turning you into a frog if he feels like it, so you better keep working on that Control. But it

should keep him—and anybody else you don't invite in—out of your room.

Next morning, after Smallbone had stumped up to his tower, Nick went looking for a yardstick, a handful of salt, and some iron nails. He took them up to his room, locked the door, and propped *E-Z Spelz* against the pillow.

The spell itself was dumber than dumb, like something a little kid would make up to keep the monsters under the bed from coming to get him. Following the instructions, he dribbled unbroken lines of salt (not too thick, not too thin) along the threshold and the windowsills. He stood on a desk chair and laid a nail on the door frame and one above each window. He used the yardstick to find the exact center of the room so he could stand there and turn around three times, dribbling salt in a circle with his right hand and reciting.

E-Z Spelz didn't explain why or even how this worked. Nick had to make up his own mind about how reciting, "Bow-Wowzer Meowzer, Bow-Wowzer

Meowzer! Fly, bad spirits, fly!"—with or without throwing salt around—was going to protect him. But he had no doubt it had done something. The air felt thick and a little prickly, like just before a thunderstorm. There was that smell, too, like hot metal, that he was beginning to recognize as the smell of magic. For a moment, Nick thought he might pass out or throw up. Then there was a kind of *snap,* and everything went back to normal. Except Nick knew, absolutely and without doubt, that Smallbone couldn't come in to spy on him or turn him into something creepy while he was asleep. Smallbone couldn't come in at all.

Nick smiled. And then he laughed. And then he whooped out loud.

He opened the book again. Maybe he could find something that would help him get away. Maybe he could break the confusion spell on the yard or fly over it or—

You're a young wizard. Remember, you need to learn to walk before you can run, and patience is a virtue.

Patience is a virtue! Nick couldn't believe it. Why did everybody have to lecture him all the time and tell him what to do? He wanted to be a wizard, not a Sunday-school teacher! He slammed *E-Z Spelz* closed, threw it under the bed, and ran out of his room. Suddenly, it was too small and the house was too big and he had to get out and go somewhere or he'd burst.

He pulled on a jacket and headed for the barn, which was warm and shadowy and full of the small noises contented animals make. Nick petted Groucho, stamped at the chickens to watch them run, and threw Ollie's ball in his water trough. Ollie got it out, splashing water everywhere, and rootled it through the straw, his tail whirling happily. Somehow, it wasn't as funny as usual, especially since Nick didn't know the spell to float the ball back and Smallbone would be mad if he didn't find it in its bucket.

Nick climbed over the rails, and Ollie looked at him. His tail was still twirling, but without the fence between them, the pig looked very big—even bigger when he turned and took a step forward. Nick backpedaled, slipped on a pile of something squishy, and landed flat on his back in the muck. Panicked, he kicked out at Ollie, who was coming to investigate.

It was a solid kick, and it caught the pig on his sensitive snout. Ollie squealed like a whistle and scuttled to the back of the pen, where he stood with his hindquarters to Nick and panted anxiously.

Nick picked himself up and climbed out. He hated everybody and everything in the world, but mostly he hated the way he smelled. An unpleasant session with some straw and a quick scrub under the pump got rid of the worst of it, but he was left with a dripping jacket and a damp butt and the uncomfortable feeling that he'd been a complete jerk. He liked Ollie. Like the goats, Ollie played with Nick. Unlike the goats, he didn't make Nick feel like a birdbrain.

He hung the jacket from a peg to dry, then sat on a bale of hay next to the pigpen with his back to the rails.

He was wondering how you apologized to a pig when he felt a gentle touch on his shoulder and a rubbery snout snuffled at his neck.

❧　❧　❧

After supper, when Smallbone was at the barn, Nick fished *E-Z Spelz* out from under the bed and opened it, prepared for another lecture on patience and control and maybe kindness to animals.

Magic is dangerous. Which is why you need to learn to make a pentagram.

A pentagram is a Little Wizard's Best Friend. A pentagram helps you focus. Any spell you cast inside a pentagram will be stronger. If the spell is particularly dangerous, the pentagram will contain it. If you can't have a senior wizard to help you with your spelz, you'd better have a pentagram handy.

Ready?

Nick found himself nodding.

Good. You'll need a yardstick. Also a piece of
string with a thumbtack on one end to mark the
center and chalk on the other to make the arms
even. And when you've got a perfect one, you can
learn to cheat at marbles.

Chapter Ten

✦ ✦ ✦ ✦ ✦ ✦ ✦

One morning Nick woke to silence and a hard, pale sky. The snow had stopped, but the air was cold enough to freeze snot. By the time he'd finished the chores, the weather had cleared. In the sunlight, Evil Wizard Books looked like a crystal palace in a snow globe, chimneys and roofs all frosted and glittering.

When Nick returned with the milk and eggs, Smallbone had already made breakfast. "Eat up, Foxkin. We're going into town. I'm out of tobacco and I haven't picked up my Christmas ham."

Nick's heart gave a lurch. A town meant people, a telephone, maybe even a police station. A town meant a possibility of escape. Which was all he really wanted, right? The bookshop and the animals and magic were all fine, but they didn't make up for Smallbone and his acid tongue and the constant fear of bug-hood.

Smallbone gave Nick a look under his bushy brows. "Just in case you're thinking of making a break for it, remember that the townsfolk are Smallbones, every one of them. They know what's due their evil wizard, even if you don't."

Nick returned the look with interest. "I can't wait to meet them."

A little while later, Nick was trudging through the woods behind Smallbone. He was carrying an empty straw basket on his arm for purchases, and he'd tucked a bacon sandwich and *E-Z Spelz for Little Wizardz* in his jacket pockets, just in case.

Smallbone's path wound through the woods, climbed a steep rise covered with prickly blackberry, then plunged downhill to a rocky beach. Nick squinted up at the seagulls mewing and gliding down the sapphire sky, and wondered where he was.

"When you're done gawking," Smallbone said, "you can help me with the skiff."

A sturdy boat was turned upside down on the rocks

like a turtle, with its oars beneath it. Nick brushed the snow off and helped the old man drag it down to the water.

Smallbone's beard twitched. "Don't suppose it's any use asking if you can row."

"Nope."

"I'll teach you come spring. Hop in and don't fidget."

Nick threw the basket in the boat and stepped in gingerly, gripping the sides as he felt the boat lift and stir under him. Smallbone pushed the skiff off the sand, scrambled aboard, sat down facing Nick, and headed out into the Reach.

Nick had never been in a boat before. He gripped the sides while the wind cut through his jacket like a saw and the cold waves stung his hands. When he looked ahead, there was Smallbone, all bristly white hair and glittering glasses, scowling as he pulled on the oars. Nick turned his eyes to the little islands that were scattered along the Reach, ringed with rocks like massive loaves of brown bread sprinkled with floury snow. Some were big enough to walk around on, but most were too small to hold more than a few trees. The world smelled of pine and wood smoke and cold.

Nick felt like laughing.

Before long, they rounded a rocky point and headed into a deep, sheltered cove. Nick made out a weathered dock surrounded by a flock of boats like oversize geese. Behind them was a row of gray and white buildings and a white clapboard church with a sharply pointed steeple topped with a black weathervane shaped like a seal. The whole scene was dusted with glittering snow, like the most touristy kind of Christmas card.

Nick tucked his frozen hands into his armpits. He didn't care what Smallbone said: somebody was bound to help him. He'd find a nice woman — women usually felt sorry for Nick until they got to know him — and spin her a tale about family in Bath or Boothbay or whatever, and he'd be on his way in no time.

With an expert flick of his oars, Smallbone pulled up against the dock, threw a rope over a post, tied it fast, and took off, his black coat flapping, his black hat jammed down over his wild white hair like a stovepipe over a bird's nest. Nick scrambled after with the basket.

There weren't many people around. An old guy was coiling rope next to the gas pump on the wharf, and there were a couple of pickups parked in the lot, but Nick didn't see anybody he felt he could talk to. The stores were boarded up tight for the season. With nowhere to run, Nick followed Smallbone down the street. They passed a neat white clapboard house with an old-fashioned public phone booth to one side of the front walk and a sign to the other identifying it as the Smallbone Cove Public Library. A woman was looking out one of the windows. Maybe she'd lend him a quarter for the phone. Maybe she'd hide him in her cellar.

Nick caught her eye and smiled. She looked a little startled but smiled back.

Down the street, a woman in a red parka was heading toward them, waving a red-mittened hand. "Mr. Smallbone," she called, her voice ringing in the nippy air. "Thank heaven you're here! I was just coming to see you."

Smallbone ignored her.

She patted the basket hanging on her arm. "I've got your meat order right here. And there's something I want to talk to you about."

Smallbone didn't answer.

"Please listen, Mr. Smallbone," she said, tight and desperate. "I invoke the Contract."

Smallbone stopped so suddenly that Nick nearly crashed into him. "The Contract, eh? You making a formal petition, Lily Smallbone?"

The woman gripped the basket. "I am."

Smallbone scowled, his hat tipping forward. "Land o' Goshen, Lily, you know better than this. There's a time and a place for petitions and this ain't neither the one or the other."

Lily opened her mouth. Smallbone trained his spectacles on her. She closed it again, turned, and stomped back the way she had come.

Wondering what had just happened, Nick followed Smallbone and the woman to what looked to be the only open shop in town. It had "country store" written all over it, from the rustic wooden benches on its porch to its sparkling bay window filled with jars of candy and homemade jam. There was a wooden plaque over the door: SMALLBONE COVE MERCANTILE EST. 1780, LILY AND ZERUBABBLE SMALLBONE, PROPS. A red gingham sign on the door told passersby that it was OPEN.

Nick followed Smallbone into the warmth and took a deep breath flavored with vinegar, wood smoke, and fresh-baked bread. Two men in heavy sweaters playing checkers on a pickle barrel beside the shop window looked up and stared at him with eyes so dark they were almost black. Nick smiled, trying to look pathetic and trustworthy. They returned to their game.

The woman called Lily deposited her basket on the shop counter next to a glass case filled with fancy baked goods. She took off her parka, revealing a sweater decorated with seals and a round face that was probably pleasant when she wasn't in a temper. Her sleek brown hair was splotched and streaked with gray.

"So, Mr. Smallbone," she said briskly, "how can I help you?"

Smallbone produced a creased paper from his

pocket and unfolded it. "Here's my list. Cornmeal, salt, tobacco, ham, vanilla, washing powder, ammonia, bacon, corned beef—the usual. Oh, and you can give me some of them fresh cinnamon buns—a dozen will suffice. Some other odds and ends. You can see for yourself."

Lily took the list without looking at it. "With respect, Mr. Smallbone—"

Smallbone's beard bunched. Lily looked at the list. "Jeans. Wool jacket. Underwear, boy's size fourteen. Flannel shirts." She cocked her chin toward Nick. "This gear for him?"

"Ayuh," Smallbone said. "This here's my new apprentice. You'll be seeing him from time to time, running errands and suchlike." He leaned forward confidentially. "You'll want to keep a sharp eye on him. He's crooked as a hairpin."

Lily turned to Nick. Her eyes were like polished black stones. Nick called up his best smile. If he wanted these folks on his side, he had to pretend to be the kind of kid they'd like—a kid with manners, a kid they could trust. He whipped off his cap and stuck out his hand. "Pleased to meet you, ma'am," he said, making firm eye contact. "My name's N —, um, Jerry."

"Call him Foxkin," Smallbone said. "Better yet, don't call him anything at all. There's nothing you can say he needs to hear, barring 'Put that candy bar back where you got it.'"

"My name really is Jerry, ma'am," Nick said. "Jerry Reynaud. And I'm not a thief. My bicycle broke when I was on my way to my cousin's house, and then it started to snow and I got lost. Mr. Smallbone took me in, which was nice of him, I guess, except now he won't let me leave."

Lily quirked her eyebrow. Nick dropped his hand.

"Crackerjack liar, ain't he?" Smallbone asked cheerfully. "I might almost believe he had a cousin if I didn't know better." He gave Lily a graveyard smile. "Come around to Eb's in half an hour, and we'll see about that petition."

✤ ✤ ✤

Eb's turned out to be a clam shack, or rather, a Klam Shak. Its tiny-paned windows were draped with old fishing nets hung with glittery red and green glass balls for Christmas. A slate sidewalk board listed the specials: mackerel, fresh and fried; fish pie; salt cod. Nick, who didn't like fish, hoped they had hot dogs, too.

Inside, a dozen broad-faced men and women with dark eyes and streaky hair like Lily's sat at Formica-topped tables. They stopped talking when Nick and Smallbone came in. A couple with two kids—all of whom, strangely, had gray hair—slid hastily out of the last booth and moved to an empty table as a tall man in a stained apron bustled up, wiping his hands on a dishcloth. "'Morning, Mr. Smallbone, sir."

Smallbone bared his teeth. "If I could just get everybody's attention here, Ebenezer, I got something I want to say."

And then he launched right into his speech about what a big liar and thief Nick was. If anything, he laid it on thicker than he had at Smallbone Cove Mercantile. Nick's hope of making friends with the locals, already pretty weak, lay down and died.

"That about covers it." Smallbone turned to the man in the apron. "We'll have a couple of bowls of clam chowder, Eb, and a Coke for Foxkin here." And then he sat in the empty booth.

After the speech, Nick figured he couldn't ask for a hot dog instead. But the clam chowder turned out to be better than he expected. His bowl was just about empty when Lily appeared at Smallbone's elbow.

Smallbone put down his spoon. "Couldn't wait for me to finish, could you?"

"It's been thirty minutes," Lily said. "Zachariah Smallbone, I petition you to hear me in the name of the Contract between you and your people."

Smallbone munched his jaws irritably. "All right, all right, I'm coming." He drained his bowl and dried his beard with his napkin. "I'll be gone for a spell, Foxkin. You can wait for me here."

Alone in the booth, Nick scraped up the last drops of chowder and finished his Coke and wondered if there was any chance of pie. The bench wiggled as bodies slid into the booth behind him.

"Evil wizard's in town, I hear," a deep voice said.

A woman answered. "Ayuh, Saul, he is that."

"'Bout time," said a third voice — a man's, nasal

and whiny. "Things're going to hell in a handcart around here. What about that coyote we saw in the street? Never seen a coyote in town before."

"Of course you haven't, Ham," said the woman. "They can't cross the Town Limits."

"Well, this one did," Saul said glumly. "It'll be tax collectors next."

"Hush," the woman said. "That coyote's bad enough. Makes my skin crawl, hearing it howl all night. I don't know why Lily insists on keeping it in her house, especially with her Dinah so sick and all."

"It ain't in her house, Jezzy," said Saul. "It's out back in the storeroom, with the freezer for Smallbone's meat."

"It's strange they took it in," Ham said. "Lily said they wanted to save it to show to Smallbone, but they could of done that just fine if it was dead. What'll they do if it gets loose?"

"Get et, I expect," Saul said.

There was an uncomfortable silence, and then Jezzy said, in a let's-change-the-subject kind of way, "Did you know Smallbone's got a boy with him?"

Nick sat very still. The conversation sounded like it was about to get really interesting.

"Does he?" Saul's tone suggested he didn't care what Smallbone did.

"A real bad seed. According to Smallbone, anyway."

"Stands to reason, doesn't it?" Ham asked. "I mean, who else would go work for an evil wizard?"

"I heard he had apprentices," Jezzy went on, "but I never seen one before."

"My granddad said there used to be lots of 'em, one after another," said Saul. "None lasted long, though."

"What do you reckon happened to 'em?"

"Granddad said he thought the old man ate 'em to keep himself young. Or threw 'em to the wolves."

"That's nasty, Saul," said Jezzy.

"So's Smallbone," said Saul.

Jezzy said, "I can't help feeling sorry for them."

"That's because you're soft," Saul said. "It's not like they're from around here."

At that point, Eb came up to take their orders — two mackerels, one raw, one fried, and a fish pie for Jezzy.

Nick huddled into the corner with his Coke, his

mind racing. Obviously, nobody in Smallbone Cove was going to help him. He had to get away, and he had to do it fast. The hard part would be leaving Eb's without anybody noticing. And then he'd have to start walking again and hope that Smallbone didn't come after him. Or the townsfolk. And that he didn't get picked up by the police, who would certainly send him back to Uncle Gabe, who might not eat him but would probably beat the tar out of him and shut him down cellar on stale bread and water until he was eighteen.

He was getting ready to slip off to the men's room and see if it had a window he could crawl out of, when Smallbone showed up, looking like an evil Santa with a canvas duffel slung over his shoulder and his basket on his arm.

"Still here, Foxkin?" he asked cheerfully. "Good." He reached into the basket and pulled out a sweater and watch cap knitted in heavy blue wool. "Lily says Merry Christmas, a little late. Hurry up and get 'em on. I want to get home before dark."

Nick doubted Lily had said any such thing, but he

stood up and pulled the thick sweater over his head. It was too big, but it was warm.

In the next booth, Jezzy, Ham, and Saul were staring at their plates like half-eaten fish was the most interesting thing on earth.

A bad seed, was he? Who deserved to be eaten by wolves? Fury rose in Nick like an electrical surge, and he jostled their table. Startled, they looked up. Nick gave them a toothy grin. Their round black Smallbone eyes swiveled back to their plates, but not before he'd seen the fear in them.

Nick couldn't help swaggering a little as he followed Smallbone out into the snowy street. There might be an upside to this wizard's-apprentice thing. Too bad he wasn't likely to live long enough to enjoy it.

Chapter Eleven

+ + ✦ ✦ ✦ + +

In their natural state, coyotes are never confused. If something smells like prey, they hunt it; if it smells like another predator, they run away. If they're caught in a trap, they struggle to get out. If something threatens them and they can't run, they challenge, then attack.

There was nothing natural about the situation of the coyote in the storeroom. She was in a trap that was also somehow a den. Every so often, two humans brought food into the den (or trap). They smelled a little like prey but also like pack, like family. Whenever the door opened, she didn't know whether to growl and snap or rub against them and whine like a cub.

She slept a lot, as caged animals do, but sleep brought no relief. Sometimes she dreamed of running in the woods, hunting with a big white wolf. Sometimes she dreamed of having eggs and orange juice for breakfast and going to school. In either case, she woke up howling.

The whole thing felt like a thorn in her brain. Except it was an imaginary thorn, and she knew it was imaginary and that coyotes don't usually imagine things.

The door opened, and the coyote smelled something even more confusing than prey-that-was-family. It was neither prey nor predator nor human, but something horribly *other,* prickly and unpleasant. It stung her sensitive nose and tickled the soft lining of her mouth. Terrified, she retreated into a corner, ears back, teeth bared, hackles bristling, and snarled.

Her mother was beside her, rubbing her head with her cheek, surrounding her with her scent. The young coyote pressed herself to her mother's side, whining.

The evil-smelling stranger made noises. They were huge and heavy and stank of ozone. The world came apart and then, suddenly, the noises became words.

"Dinah! Dinah Smallbone!"

That's me, thought the coyote that wasn't a coyote anymore. *I'm Dinah Smallbone.*

She felt very sick. She was sweating and trembling and she ached all over, as if with fever.

She moaned.

"Dinah, honey! Can you hear me?"

It was her mom, sounding frantic with worry. Dinah wanted to tell her she could hear her just fine, but her mouth wasn't working right.

The voice that had first called her name said, "I'd get that pelt off her before it takes hold again."

Somebody—her dad—lifted a weight off Dinah she hadn't realized was there until it was gone. She moaned again and opened her eyes.

She was lying with her head on her mother's knees, looking up at an old man in a black coat and a tall black hat. *Smallbone,* Dinah thought. *That's the Evil Wizard Smallbone.* His glasses flashed as he stuffed a furry bundle into a canvas duffel.

He looked at her and his beard bobbed. "I got some questions for you, young lady."

"Not until she's had a bath and some food and some solid sleep." Her mom's voice was fierce as a wolf's growl. "I'm grateful you brought her back, and I want to know what happened as much as you do, but you can see she's not herself."

Dinah whimpered and closed her eyes. She didn't want to answer questions. She didn't want to sleep, either, in case she dreamed about being a coyote, or maybe woke up and found out she still was one.

There were whispers and shuffling, then the door creaked shut. Dinah took stock of herself. She was hungry. She was still achy, but she was no longer feverish. More important, she could wiggle her fingers, feel her arms and legs. They were human. She was human. She could remember what being a coyote had been like but wasn't ready to think about it yet. The experience was still too tender, like a skinned knee. But part of her—the part that liked to know things—was thinking, *Huh. I was a coyote. I wonder how that works.*

Chapter Twelve

+ + + ✦ + + +

The trip back to Evil Wizard Books was a lot faster than the trip out. Smallbone dug into the water with each stroke as if he wanted to hurt it, muttering under his breath. What with the wind and the seabirds, Nick couldn't make out what he was saying, but from the look on his face, he was willing to bet it involved cursing.

Nick would have been cursing himself if he'd dared.

He wasn't scared, of course. If there was one thing about himself Nick was proud of, it was that he wasn't scared of anything. Being scared made you weak, and the weak got broken. After his mother died, Nick had made up his mind that he was going to be one of the strong ones. Which meant that things that made weak people scared — spiders and evil wizards, for instance — just made him mad.

Right now, he was mad as a wet cat. He was mad at Saul and Ham, who didn't care what happened to any kid who didn't come from Smallbone Cove. He was mad at Jezzy, who knew he was evil because he was with Smallbone — as if he'd had a choice. Most of all, he was mad at Smallbone, who kept him tethered to the barnyard like a straying dog and threatened him with transformation every time he did something wrong.

Smallbone might call himself an evil wizard, but really he was just a bully, like Uncle Gabe. With magic, which made it worse.

It was a good, hot, roaring mad. Nick built it up as he helped haul the boat onto the shore and walked back through the woods as the sun moved down the sky. By the time he got to Evil Wizard Books, he was ready to explode.

Smallbone opened the kitchen door, and the dogs erupted into the mudroom, crazy with joy and a day spent indoors. Jeff reared up, put his paws on Nick's shoulders, and swiped his tongue across his face.

"Get down!" Nick yelled, and gave Jeff a kick that sent him tumbling among the boots. He yipped and cringed, his black velvet forehead pleated with confusion. Nick wanted to throw the basket at him, or maybe throw up.

Smallbone's glare could have scorched ice. "If I'd known you was the kind of no-good who went around kicking dumb animals, I'd have left you to freeze in the snow!"

Nick glared back. "And now you're going to turn me into something horrible, right? Go ahead, then!"

Now that the worst was about to happen, Nick wished, as he always did, that he'd kept his mouth shut. Still, it was oddly satisfying to make the inevitable happen instead of just waiting for it. It showed he was stronger than whoever was beating up on him. He could push their buttons until they cracked, then take what they dished out without caving in or begging for mercy.

The words of the spell fell around Nick like a rock

slide. His body grew cold and numb. He just had time to regret what he'd done to Jeff before the kitchen faded from sight and sound and his thoughts stopped.

❧   ❧   ❧

Nick woke up smelling bacon. At least, his head was full of the scent of something rich and meaty and smoky. A moment later, he remembered that it was bacon, and that the gnawing sensation in his middle meant he was hungry.

A hot, wet, soft thing slopped over his ear, accompanied by panting and high-pitched whines. He opened his eyes to see worried amber eyes peering at him a muzzle length away.

The surface he was lying on was hard — a floor, he thought. But what was that warm weight on his hip? He brushed at it. There was a thump and a resentful yowl, and a lean black cat stalked past his face, her tail quivering like an indignant exclamation point.

"Bacon's almost done, Foxkin," a gruff voice said.

Nick got up slowly and removed the bacon to a waiting plate, then cracked eggs into the frying pan until he ran out of room.

"Hungry, eh?"

Nick turned. There was a man sitting at the kitchen table. A name came into Nick's head: Smallbone, that was who the man was. The Evil Wizard Smallbone.

He looked like a badly made scarecrow.

Nick blinked. "You turned me into something, didn't you? I don't remember what it was."

"Rocks don't remember much of anything that takes less than a hundred years to happen. Watch it, boy! Them eggs is going to burn."

Nick dished up the eggs and sat down. The world was sparkly around the edges, as if he'd been in a dark room for a long time.

His thoughts caught up with Smallbone's words. "A rock?"

"Granite. Handy for drying the kitchen cloths, though I did have to step over you every time I wanted to mend the fire. Hell Cat staked you out as her favorite sleeping spot. Eat up."

Nick ate. After he'd absorbed three eggs, four pieces of bacon, and two slices of bread, he noticed Tom sitting beside his plate and gave him a bite of bacon. Mutt and Jeff whined at him in stereo. He fed them, too, and rubbed their heads. Their ears were dense and soft in his hands, their bacon-breath warm on his skin.

After a while, they went away.

Nick looked around. Smallbone had gone and Hell Cat was delicately licking the grease out of the frying pan. Nick wandered into the bookshop.

It was dark in the shop, apart from an island of light around the oil lamp on the book table. One of the books was propped against the others. Nick read its title: *Fairy Tales from Many Lands.* He went and picked it up. It was heavy and solid in his hands, the kind of book a rich kid's grandma would buy, with a thick padded cover. A gift from the bookshop, Nick wondered, or just a random book?

There are no random books, he thought, and took it up to his Bow-Wowzer-protected room.

Tom was curled up on his bed. He shoved him aside, settled against the pillows, and started to flip through the pages. A few stories in, he came to a picture of a flock of white birds flying above a sinister bearded guy in a fancy embroidered coat and a fur-trimmed hat. A title in curly letters read, "The Wizard Outwitted."

Nick turned the page and began to read.

"The Wizard Outwitted" was about a boy whose father apprenticed him to a sinister bearded guy for three years. As anybody who'd ever read a story would have known, the bearded guy was an evil wizard. Like Smallbone, he collected apprentices and made them cook and clean while teaching them zero magic. He also had a habit of turning them into rocks when he was mad. Of course, the boy learned magic anyway. The part of Evil Wizard Books was played by the wizard's beautiful daughter.

After a year or two divided between being a rock and studying magic, the boy sent an enchanted bird to his father to tell him where he was and how to rescue him. The old man went to the evil wizard's castle, where he had to pick his son out of a flock of twelve white pigeons, twelve roan stallions, and twelve handsome young men, all alike one another as peas in a pod. Coached by the magic bird, the old man chose right every time, freeing the boy from his evil master.

So the boy and his father went home, but the story wasn't over. There were eleven other apprentices to rescue, not to mention the beautiful daughter. Using the magic he'd learned, the boy tricked the wizard out of enough money to keep his parents comfortable for life and killed him in a wizard's duel. Then he married the wizard's beautiful daughter, who didn't seem to care that her husband had broken her father's neck.

Of course, her father had been trying to eat him at the time. But still.

By the time Nick finished the story, he'd recovered from his post-rock daze enough to wonder what the bookstore was trying to tell him. "The Wizard Outwitted" was a dumb story. Why did the boy trust his father to save him after the old man had traded him for a sack of coins? Why didn't the wizard know his daughter was sabotaging him? And where had he been keeping all those old apprentices?

True, the boy's situation and Nick's were similar, but Nick didn't have a father—not one he'd ever heard about, anyway—and though he wanted to get away, he certainly didn't want Uncle Gabe coming for him.

Finally, there were no suspicious flocks of pigeons or herds of horses or even piles of stones lying around that could be Smallbone's former apprentices.

It just didn't add up.

As Nick closed *Fairy Tales from Many Lands,* he noticed that the front cover was thicker than the back. He poked it, and it gave a little. There was something hidden inside it.

He tore back the endpaper, uncovering a crackly yellow packet. When he touched it, his fingers tingled. He pulled back his hand, then took out the packet and unfolded it. It was a chart of some kind, crossed and recrossed with fine lines and curves drawn with brown ink. There were numbers, too, some written on the lines and some between them. It was clearly magic and important enough to hide. But what did it mean?

The grandfather clock on the stairs chimed the half hour, impatiently, as though it had done it before. Nick jumped up and ran down to start lunch.

The chart filled Nick's head as he chopped cold corned beef and onions and peeled potatoes for hash. It was obvious that he was meant to have it. Maybe what the bookshop was trying to tell him, he thought as he put the potatoes on to boil, was that he was the hero of this story. Maybe *E-Z Spelz* was teaching him how to outwit Smallbone and rescue himself. Maybe tests were part of being a hero. Maybe the chart was the thing he needed to learn that would set him free.

In any case, it fascinated him. He wanted—no, he *needed*—to know what it meant.

That night, he stashed the chart in his bureau, under his shirts. And he cast Bow-Wowzer Meowzer on the drawer, just to make sure.

Chapter Thirteen

✦ ✦ ✦ ✦ ✦ ✦ ✦

Next morning, Nick bounced out of bed feeling ready to take on the world. He could protect himself and milk a goat, he could draw a perfect pentagram and light a candle, and under his clean shirts he had a cool secret chart he just knew would be his ticket out of Evil Wizard Books, once he learned how to use it.

He couldn't wait to get started.

At breakfast, Smallbone said, "You're looking mighty chipper."

Nick swallowed a mouthful of egg. "Must be left over from the rock spell," he said blandly. "It's mighty restful, being a rock."

"I didn't do it to give you a rest. I did it to calm you

down. You'll be taking the evening chores from now on and keeping the wood box filled. I got important work in hand." Smallbone cleaned out his pipe and put it on the mantel. "There's a chicken in the deep freeze. You remember what I told you about roast chicken?"

Nick didn't, but he could look it up in *The Joy of Cooking*. "Yep."

Smallbone gave him a narrow look, whistled for the dogs, and left.

As soon as he was gone, Nick had *E-Z Spelz* out of his pocket.

⚜ ⚜ ⚜

The next week passed in a blur of chores and magic.

E-Z Spelz was silent on the subject of charts with numbers, but it did start teaching him more actual spells. Some were more E-Z than others. Levitation gave him a lot of trouble, and he didn't seem to have the knack of conjuring visions at all. But the spells having to do with water or fire or wind or stone came natural as breathing. He made little whirlpools in the animals' water troughs and chased Hell Cat off the kitchen table with magically aimed water squirts. He learned a spell for finding lost objects and another for lifting and moving little ones, which must have been what Smallbone had used to retrieve Ollie's jingle ball. Nick tried to use it to gather eggs. It sent the chickens into cackling hysterics, but it worked — maybe a little too well. Eggs, new and not so new, zoomed at him from the hayloft, the rafters, behind the mangers — all the hidey-holes discovered by generations of wily hens. He ducked, but they smashed into him anyway. When it was all over, he was covered with egg slime and smelled like a sulfur pit. He managed to wash off most of the stink before Smallbone came down for breakfast and covered up the rest by burning the bacon on purpose.

Smallbone didn't notice. Smallbone was spending every waking hour in his tower workshop, appearing only for meals, looking more than ever like a badly made scarecrow and smelling odd. Sometimes it was paint and sawdust. Sometimes it was the hot metal and ozone that was the smell of magic.

After a few days, the chickens got used to the egg-gathering spell. It was funny to see them bobbing in the air like feathery balloons, peering underneath themselves and saying *werk*. Nick started using the same spell to clean the kitchen when Smallbone was out of the way. He lit the lamps with magic, too. It came so naturally that he slipped once and did it when Smallbone was in the room, but the old man was patting Mutt and didn't notice.

When he realized what he'd done, though, Nick went cold. If he didn't want to get turned into a slug and salted, he was going to have to be more careful.

❖　❖　❖

A few days later, Smallbone left Evil Wizard Books after lunch, saying he'd be back for supper. When suppertime came and went, Nick, who'd made spaghetti, found himself watching out the window for the gleam of lamplight on a curling wave of snow.

It was almost nine when Smallbone finally showed up, looking fierce and carrying a dinged-up old lantern in his hand. He eyed the set table, the simmering pot of sauce, and the spaghetti draining in the sink. "Heat up them noodles and I'll be down directly. Better make a fresh pot of coffee, too. It's some nippy out."

He disappeared with the dogs, who'd spent the

evening whining and pacing by the door, bouncing joyfully around him.

Nick set a kettle on the stove and fumed. He was just a convenience, like the stove and the hot water and the laundry that did itself. He couldn't go anywhere: he couldn't do anything. And the only person he had to talk to was an evil wizard.

It was almost enough to make him wish he hadn't run away from Beaton. But then he wouldn't have the bookstore or the animals. And he would have Uncle Gabe.

Still, he was getting sick of being stuck in one place all the time.

Next morning, Smallbone came down carrying a large leather satchel.

Nick looked up from the slightly lumpy pancakes he had sizzling on the griddle. "What's that?"

"Something I should have done a long time ago," Smallbone said unhelpfully. "Hurry up with them flap-jacks, Foxkin. We're going into town again."

This time, they walked, with Nick carrying the satchel over his shoulder. It was heavy.

Beyond the woodshed, a clear if somewhat icy path led eastward through the woods. Under the trees it was very quiet, except for the occasional whoosh and thud of wet snow sliding off a branch. A load landed on Nick's head, soaking his blue watch cap and sending icy trickles down the collar of his jacket.

Smallbone, of course, was untouched.

The path came out at a small pond, iced over and snow covered, plunged back into the trees, crossed a bridge over a frozen creek, and fed onto the main street of Smallbone Cove. Some kids heading for the hill behind the church with sleds stared as Smallbone and Nick stalked by behind a wave of snow.

When they reached the Mercantile, Smallbone banged on the door, right under the CLOSED sign.

A window went up on the second floor. "Go away," a male voice shouted.

Smallbone banged some more.

Zery's head appeared at the window. "It's Sunday morn—Oh. It's you."

Smallbone stepped back and glared upward. "Tell Lily the Evil Wizard Smallbone wants to talk to her."

Zery disappeared and the window slammed shut. Nick peered through the shop window and saw Lily hurrying out of the back with her shirt buttoned cock-eyed, a this-better-be-good look on her face. Behind her were Zery and a girl about Nick's age. Nick looked away quickly. Girls made him nervous.

Lily opened the door. "'Morning, Mr. Smallbone. What can I do for you?"

Smallbone met her glare with glittering intensity. "Town Meeting. Now."

"Town Meeting's not until June," Lily said.

"I'm calling a special one," Smallbone said. "Get hopping."

Lily sighed. "You heard the evil wizard, Zery. You and Dinah start knocking on doors. I'll take the car and hit the farms."

"Dinah can stay here," Smallbone said. "I got some questions for her."

Dinah's mother looked unhappy.

"I'll be fine," Dinah said. Her voice was firm, like she didn't mind being left alone with an evil wizard and his probably evil apprentice.

"You heard the girl," Smallbone said. "Now get going."

Lily and Zery got, but not before hugging Dinah and telling her they were proud of her — for what, they didn't say. It made Nick want to roll his eyes, or maybe punch something — he wasn't sure which.

The door closed behind them. Dinah wound her hands together. Like most of the other Smallbones Nick had seen, she had strangely colored hair — white, in her case, with black patches that might have been dyed, if a girl who wore fluffy sweaters with cats on them was the type to dye her hair. She was short and solid, and her eyes were Smallbone Cove black. Right now, white was showing all around her irises. Clearly, she wasn't as calm as she had sounded.

Smallbone fixed Dinah with his spectacles. "I want to hear how you found that coyote pelt, girl, and you better not leave nothing out."

Dinah took a slightly shaky breath and told Smallbone how she'd walked out on the icy Stream and found a coyote pelt that had turned her into a coyote when she put it on.

Nick listened open-mouthed, glad he wasn't the only person outside a fairy tale ever to get turned into something he wasn't.

"And what did the Stream do?" asked Smallbone when she stopped talking.

"The Stream? Nothing. It was all ice, like I said."

"All the way down?"

"I don't know. Like I said, I was testing it."

"Hmph," Smallbone said. "And what happened after you got turned?"

Dinah looked at her feet. "I can't say."

"What do you mean, you can't say?"

"I can't, that's all. I remember, kind of, but it's like a dream, all feelings and smells. It's hard to talk about." She lifted her dark eyes. "I'm sorry. I wish I could."

Nick wished she could, too.

"Well," Smallbone said, "no use in beating a dead horse. What a jeezly mess." He glanced at the clock over the counter. "I think I got time for a Moxie. Bring one for Foxkin, too."

With the expression of someone who is hoping she's doing the right thing, Dinah took two brown glass bottles out of the cooler and brought them to Smallbone. He opened them and handed one to Nick. "Drink up."

Nick took a cautious sip. An intensely bitter wash reminiscent of tar and pine needles flooded his mouth and nose. His tongue felt like it had been scoured with Brillo.

Smallbone laughed like water going down a drain. "If you could just see your face!"

"The bitter taste comes from gentian root," Dinah chimed in helpfully. "It's supposed to be good for the digestion, but it hasn't been scientifically proved."

Smallbone took a long swallow and smacked his lips. "*Children* don't like it. I guess that tells us where you stand, eh, Foxkin?"

Nick wiped his face on his sleeve, put the bottle to his lips, and chugged. The bubbles went up his nose and the bitterness caught at his throat, but he persisted. When the bottle was empty, he burped loudly. "Yeah," he said. "I guess we do."

Dinah giggled. Nick shot her a glare in case she

was laughing at him. She wasn't; she was smiling. His ears grew hot.

"I see folks heading for the church," Smallbone said. "Foxkin, if you're done showing off, it's time to go."

⚛ ⚛ ⚛

When Nick was little, his mother used to take him with her every Sunday to St. Mary Magdalene. The last time he'd gone was more than three years ago, for the funeral, but he remembered shadowy aisles and high-backed pews, an altar with a gold cross, windows like kaleidoscopes, and the nose-tingling perfume of incense and hot candle wax.

The Smallbone Cove church was not like that. It was a big open box. The walls were painted the cloudy green of sea glass, and the windows were made up of dozens of small panes, also faintly green, with a rippled texture that gave a wavy undersea look to the sunlight pouring through them. A dozen rows of backless benches faced a wooden stage that was set up with a piano, a beat-up lectern, and two chairs. There were no crosses anywhere, even on the steeple.

Smallbone stalked to the stage, climbed the steps, and lowered himself into the bigger chair. It was dark and heavy, with carving on the arms and back, like the rector's chair at St. Mary's. Only the arms of the rector's chair didn't look like reclining seals, and the legs and back weren't held up by carved seals balanced on their back flippers.

"Pass me that satchel, Foxkin," Smallbone snapped. "And see if you can manage to sit still."

The second chair was free of seals but very hard. Nick fidgeted uncomfortably as the townsfolk trickled in: Eb and the staff of the Klam Shak in stained aprons, fishermen in worn foul-weather gear, shopkeepers and farmers in oilskins and parkas. There were old folks with canes, babies in arms, toddlers in strollers, and kids of assorted ages. By the time Lily herded the last of the latecomers onto the benches, Nick had counted maybe three hundred Smallbones, all staring at the evil wizard and his apprentice.

What chiefly struck Nick, looking at them all together like that, was how alike they were. There was something about the shape of their faces, the size of their noses, and those wide-spaced, ink-black eyes. Except for a few of the teenagers who'd dyed theirs blue and pink, everybody's hair was brown or white or gray, blotched or streaked with black. They didn't look quite human, and Nick found himself wondering if Smallbone had called up a town of fairies to serve him, or even demons.

Lily walked to the front. "That's all of them," she told Smallbone.

"You'd best get started, then."

Lily faced the townsfolk. "I call this Town Meeting to order." Her voice was deep and resonant, a good voice for addressing a roomful of people. "All rise."

Benches creaked as they got to their feet.

"Smallbones, are you all assembled?"

"We are," answered the townsfolk in slightly creepy unison.

Smallbone stood, his old black coat flowing around him like a movie wizard's robes. "Who are you?" He used the voice he used to turn boys into rocks. The little hairs rose at the back of Nick's neck.

"We are swimmers and fishers," came the answer. "We are beasts and men."

"Where do you come from?"

"We come from the north, from the wide beaches and the raging waves of the sea that shows no mercy."

"What are your rights?"

"We have the right of freedom of the sea and the land for us and our heirs. We have the right of protection from any who would harm us or wish us harm. We have the right of long life beyond the use of our kind."

"What are your duties?"

"To honor and obey our Wizard. To give him the best of our catch and our harvest. To Walk the Bounds of the township at Midsummer and Midwinter, at the Equinox of Spring and the Equinox of Autumn, and to strengthen the Sentries. To come to Town Meeting and answer the Questions."

Silence fell. Smallbone glared down, beard bristling, wiry hair quivering with energy, spectacles winking like baleful diamonds. The townsfolk shuffled uncomfortably.

"Now we got that out of the way," Smallbone said in his ordinary voice, "I got some real questions. You might as well sit down."

This was obviously not part of a usual Town Meeting. The townsfolk resumed their benches, exchanging startled glances.

"Comfy?" Smallbone asked. "Now. When was the last time you clowns walked the Bounds?"

The townsfolk stared at him, then looked away — at their feet, out the wavy glass windows, at the ceiling, anywhere but at Smallbone. Nick knew how they felt. Smallbone's voice had been full of acid, as if he already knew the answer and was daring them to lie.

A wheelchair detached itself from the end of a row and rolled down the aisle. It was propelled by an elderly woman with a white bun screwed to the back of her head, wearing a puffy down jacket like a giant pink marshmallow and a grim expression.

"Ah, Miss Rachel," Smallbone said.

Miss Rachel engaged her brakes. Her glasses, Nick noted, were bigger than Smallbone's and turned her eyes into giant pools of black. "It's been quite some time since it was done properly. My granddaddy and his friends used to do it — at least that's what they said they were doing. My grandmother said it was an excuse to drink and bark at the moon four times a year."

A woman in a plaid barn coat stood up. "I heard the fishermen back then decided there wasn't any point traipsing around the Town Limits four times a year when the farmers could go out and check the Sentries any time. I do myself, when I think of it." She sounded defensive.

"And when was the last time you thought of it, Naomi?" Smallbone asked.

The woman called Naomi looked defensive. "I went to Lantern Glade just last year!"

"I see." Smallbone's voice was dry. "And was the Lantern burning bright?"

She shrugged. "It was in the middle of the day. Everybody knows you can't see a flame so good in the daylight."

Smallbone munched his beard. Naomi sat down.

A man in a sou'wester got up. "Weathervane don't turn," he said. "I'm surprised you ain't noticed it yourself."

Smallbone munched faster.

There was a commotion in the front row, where the Mercantile Smallbones were sitting. Nick looked down in time to see Dinah jerk her arm out of her father's grip and rise to her feet, looking mulish.

"The Stream's frozen," she said flatly. "It's not supposed to freeze, ever."

"The Stream flows free at midwinter," Smallbone chanted in his wizard voice. "The Lantern burns bright at midday, the Weathervane guides the Wind, and the Stone Wall stands against all harm. And if they don't," he added crabbily, "it's a sorry state of affairs."

"You mean the sorry state of affairs where we do all the work and give you food and anything else you want and you don't do nothing for us?" yelled a voice from the back.

Smallbone's beard bristled. "You listen here, Saul Smallbone. I drew the Town Limits and set the Sentries to guard them. I set the Wind to sweep away any who threatened the peace of Smallbone Cove, the Lantern to burn them, the Stream to rise and drown them, and the Stone Wall to bar their way. Even you must agree all that's worth a few provisions."

Saul got to his feet. The woman sitting beside him tugged at his jacket "No, Jezzy, I won't hush! I don't care what he did—or says he did—way back in the old days. Them Sentries are there to keep us in and keep us down, and you"—he pointed a stubby finger at Smallbone—"are a lazy old tyrant!"

There was a communal gasp as the townsfolk waited for the evil wizard to blast Saul into the middle of next week. Nick gripped the arms of his chair and held his breath, wondering what the old man would turn Saul into.

But Smallbone just laughed. "Lazy, am I? Well, maybe I'm tired out after all these years keeping you jeezly blubberheads safe from anything might hurt or worry you. You could at least thank me."

An older man popped to his feet. "You promised to take care of us! It's in the Contract! No predators, no danger except from the sea. And now there's bikers and mosquitoes and I don't know what-all rampaging up and down!"

"Bildad is right," said a woman. "And what about that coyote we saw last month, trotting down Commercial Street in the middle of the day!"

"Be fair, Zilpah," said Miss Rachel. "The coyote didn't actually hurt anybody."

Smallbone's beard bunched, and Nick thought he could hear his teeth grinding. "That wasn't no coyote. That was Lily's Dinah in a coyote suit she found by the Stream. Which"—his voice got louder—"wouldn't have happened if you numb-brained, no-good blubber-heads had kept up your end of the bargain the way you was supposed to!"

Nick looked at Dinah. Her head was bowed and her hands were clenched in her lap. Her father patted them gently.

Smallbone surveyed the crowd of round, anxious faces. "It goes against the grain, putting myself out for a pack of gormy cusses like yourselves. I've a mind to hole up in Evil Wizard Books and let Fidelou's pack do their worst."

"Fidelou?" Saul was still on his feet. "Fidelou ain't nothing but a boogeyman you made up to give you an excuse to keep us penned up here. Everybody knows there ain't no such thing as werewolves."

To Nick's astonishment, Smallbone seemed to find this funny. "I'll be hornswoggled if that ain't the most boneheaded thing I've heard in three hundred years! You got your own personal evil wizard and you don't believe in werewolves?"

"Wolves are wolves," Saul said. "People are people. You can't switch from one to the other like changing clothes. The world don't work that way."

Smallbone picked up the leather satchel. His spectacles glittered. "It don't? Well, I guess you Smallbones need some reminding about where you come from. Lily, come here."

Lily climbed up onto the stage, her lips thinned into a determined line.

Smallbone opened the satchel, pulled out a hairy bundle, and put it in her hands. The bundle unfolded like a furry flower into a sleek mass of pale gray spotted with brown that glistened in the underwater light as Lily shook it out.

It was a sealskin, with the head, tail, and flippers still attached.

Smallbone's voice was like a whip. "Put it on."

Lily tossed the skin around her shoulders. The head settled over her hair like a hood. For a breath, she was a woman draped in fur, so close that Nick could see her frightened eyes gleaming behind the dead, whiskered mask. And then she was a sleek harbor seal.

The Smallbones gave a collective gasp. Somebody screamed, and the babies started crying. Dinah was on her feet, her mouth ajar. Her father shouted, "Lily!"

The seal shuffled backward, barking unhappily.

"Shut up!" Smallbone roared in a voice that startled even the babies into silence. "That's what you are," he shouted. "Every last one of you. I pulled your ancestors out of the sea and gave 'em hands and feet and speech and thought so they could work for me. In return, I promised to keep 'em safe from anything that wanted to hurt them, wolves and coyotes included. That's what them Sentries're for. It's on account of your neglect that they ain't what they should be. So

I better hear a little less about how I ain't holding up my end and a little more about how you aim to hold up yours, unless you want to find out just how evil an evil wizard can be."

The silence that followed this speech was thick enough to cut with a saw. Nick wasn't surprised that Miss Rachel was the one who broke it.

"Fair enough," she said. "What do we do?"

"Stay away from the Town Limits," Smallbone said. "Do the Rituals. Even you clowns couldn't have clean forgotten them. The Equinox is next month. Oh, and give them bikers a wide berth. They're mean sons of guns."

Zery got up. "We'll do it—we promise. Now can you bring Lily back?"

Smallbone rose, marched over to the seal that was Lily, and laid his hand on her head, then stepped back as the sleek dappled body shuddered, flowed up to stand on two feet, and became Lily with a glossy sealskin draped around her shoulders.

Smallbone twitched it off and thrust it back into the satchel.

She tottered to Smallbone's chair and sat down heavily. "Well, that was a trip and a half," she said.

"Blubberheads," Smallbone muttered. "Nothing but blubberheads. Come on, Foxkin. We got work to do."

They strode past the rows of Smallbones, sitting stunned and silent on their benches. As Nick left the church, he heard a baby cry, and then a great swell of sound as the Smallbones of Smallbone Cove got over their shock and started to react.

Chapter Fourteen

✦ ✦ ✦ ✦ ✦ ✦

Jerry had left Beaton looking for somewhere he could hang around with guys like him, guys who liked motorcycles and didn't pay too much attention to things like speed limits and drinking age and the laws of property. What he'd found was a one-pump gas station off a two-lane road a mile away from a Podunk town. He couldn't hang out, and he couldn't make friends. He couldn't even hunt with the pack because he didn't have his pelt yet.

Fidelou Gas and Motorcycle Repair was the only point of contact between the Howling Coyotes and the outside world. Whoever ran it was responsible for taking delivery of the merchandise sold in the General Store and supplying gas to the pack when they hunted on two wheels instead of four legs. If he was a mechanic, he also ordered parts and patched up dents and straightened wheels. If he was good enough, he was allowed to touch the Boss's machine.

The town mechanic, the Boss told Jerry when he gave him the job, was the most important member of the pack.

That was not the way it felt to Jerry.

Back home, Jerry had considered himself a pretty good mechanic. Not in his dad's class, but still completely competent to fix anything, providing he had a manual and the right tools. But he couldn't fix the Boss's machine. He guessed that Fidelou Gas and Motorcycle Repair probably had the right tools, but without a manual, he didn't know what to do with them. Oh, he'd hammered out the dings in the fenders and waxed everything that could be waxed, but he couldn't get the motor to catch and he was afraid to take it apart completely in case he couldn't get it back together again.

It was a gray afternoon, nippy and windy and threatening snow. Jerry was out in the garage, staring helplessly at the Vincent. He was stumped. Not even the Boss was going to take a motorcycle on the road in this weather, but eventually there'd be a thaw. The Boss would want to ride his Vincent, and Jerry didn't think he'd listen to any excuses.

The frozen silence was broken by the rumble of an engine. Jerry adjusted his Portland Sea Dogs cap and went to the garage door.

A truck was turning off the county road, tilting and skidding as it crossed the icy asphalt to the rusty pump. Jerry swore. He knew that truck, from its rusty tailgate to its corroded front bumper. He ought to. He'd been tinkering with it since he could hold a screwdriver and driving it since his feet could reach the pedals. He'd taped the heavy plastic over the broken passenger-side window and installed the gun rack across the back. He'd hoped never to see it again.

The engine cut off, the door opened, and his father got out. "Hey, son!" he roared. "Aren't you glad to see me?"

Jerry glared at him. "How the hell'd you find me, Dad?"

His father hitched his jeans up under his belly. "Followed my nose, I guess. My fool boss decided he could do business without me. You and Nick were gone, so I thought I'd hit the road, see what turned up."

He strolled over to the repair bay. "My, my. Now that's what I call a fine machine." He stroked the round speedometer. "You know what it is?"

Jerry scowled. "It's a Vincent."

"It's a Vincent Black Lightning," Gabe said, as if Jerry hadn't spoken. "British built. Only made a handful before they went out of business. Most terrifying motorcycle ever made, before or since. Costs a fortune, if you can even find one. What's it doing here?"

Jerry shrugged. "It's the Boss's. I'm fixing it." Pride flared in his narrow chest. "I'm the town mechanic."

"Are you?" The old man bared brown teeth in an unpleasant smile.

Jerry clenched his fists and glared.

But Gabe wasn't paying any attention to him. Gabe was taking in the garage. "Mighty sweet setup you got here," he said, surveying the well-stocked tool bench.

"Roof over your head, nice work space. How about you share some of the sugar with your dear old dad?"

"It's not as sweet as you think," Jerry said. "The Boss expects you to work for nothing, and when he says 'Jump,' the only thing he wants to hear is 'How high?' And if he don't hear it, he'll tear your throat out and eat what's left."

His father laughed and gave him a whack on the shoulder that made him stagger. "You're a comedian now, huh? I bet your mean boss'll sweeten up real fast when I get this baby running." He ran his hand along the fuel tank, where the word VINCENT was painted in black on a chipped golden banner. "Let your old dad take a look-see." He knelt stiffly. "You know, as long as she has fuel and fire, she should run. Let's put in new spark plugs, clean the points, and adjust the carburetor. She's kind of dirty, too."

He looked up at Jerry. "Get me a spark-plug wrench, a small screwdriver, and a beer," he said. "I'm going to show you how an expert does it."

It was true. Whatever else Jerry's dad was, he was a genius with motorcycles. Jerry sighed. "Okay," he said.

"But first I got to take you to the Boss and introduce you."

Gabe shrugged and got up heavily. "Always happy to meet a guy can afford a machine like this. Where's he at?"

"Couple miles down the road," Jerry said. "I'll drive."

❅   ❅   ❅

Jerry generally didn't get into town unless Fidelou called for him or he had a delivery to make. There wasn't much action during the day anyway, what with coyotes being mostly nocturnal. Today, however, the open space in front of the castle was crowded with what looked like the whole pack of Howling Coyotes, on two feet and four, all of them intent on the castle gates.

As Jerry pulled up in front of the General Store, he heard the noise of a serious dogfight.

"I don't think this is a good time," Jerry said.

Gabe snorted. "It's a good time for me."

A chorus of snarls and hysterical barks and growls swelled, dropped away, and broke out again. "Really,

Dad, we better wait. The Boss's bite is worse than his bark, you know what I mean? You don't want him mad at you."

His father got out of the truck and started shoving his way through the crowd.

Jerry's sense of self-preservation fought his curiosity and lost. If there was a fight going on, he wanted to see it. Besides, as attractive as the thought of the Boss tearing his dad into pieces was, it would mean that he couldn't fix the Vincent. And if his dad didn't fix the Vincent, Jerry would be the next to suffer.

So Jerry got out of the truck and found a place where he could see what was going on without being too noticeable himself. Right out in front of the castle gate, a huge white wolf and a were-coyote stood in a churned-up mess of snow and mud, growling like a hive of wasps. Their heads were down, their legs stiff, their ruffs raised. They were both covered with mud and streaked with blood from a dozen bites and tears.

As Jerry watched, the were-coyote made a desperate leap. The wolf seized the coyote's foreleg in his great jaws and jerked his massive head. Jerry heard a crack followed by a scream that trailed into unhappy yipping. The wolf released the coyote's leg, shook himself from snout to tail, and flowed upward into Fidelou the loup-garou, his black hair wild, his eyes amber-bright, his wolf pelt dry and gleaming white.

He looked down at the were-coyote licking at his fractured leg between pitiful whines. "You are a fool," he said. "But you have given me a good fight. I will let you live." Fidelou gestured to his two guards. "Take him away and dress his wounds. It is over," he went on, raising his fierce yellow eyes to the watching pack. "You may sleep now. We hunt at moonrise."

Hiram and Audrey hauled the wounded coyote into the castle, and the pack began to drift away toward the trailers and the houses. Jerry wanted to drift with them, but his father was still there, standing in the muddy slush. His thumbs were hooked into his belt loops, his head was tipped to one side, and his eyes were narrowed like he was studying a troublesome engine.

Fidelou looked him up and down, transferred his yellow gaze to Jerry. "Who is this person?"

"He's my dad," Jerry said, his mouth dry. "He's a mechanic."

"A mechanic." The thin, dark lips twitched. "Like you?"

The cold sweat of terror ran down Jerry's back. "Much better. He knows all about Vincents."

The yellow eyes shifted toward Gabe. "This old mongrel? It is not possible."

"Neither's turning into a big old dog," Gabe said. "Yet I see you done it."

Fidelou leaned forward and sniffed, his narrow nostrils flaring wide. "Beer," he said. "Oil and axle grease. Sweat—old, not fresh. You do not fear me. You are a fool, then, or possibly mad."

Gabe's cheeks, already red from the wind, turned a mottled purple. "You bet I'm mad. It ain't right to treat a beautiful machine like you done. You don't deserve her, and that's a fact."

To Jerry's astonishment, Fidelou smiled. "It is beautiful, my Vincent, is it not?"

"No, she ain't," Gabe snapped. "She's pretty enough

on the outside, but her engine's banged up something pitiful. She could be beautiful, though."

"Ah." The smile grew wider. "You love my Vincent. *Bon.* I love it, too."

Gabe spat. "No, you don't. You love the power and the roar."

Fidelou's dark brows bristled, and a growl rumbled in his leather-covered chest. Gabe folded his arms, his face hard as a fist. Jerry stood open-mouthed, afraid to move, almost afraid to breathe.

Fidelou began to laugh. "You are right, *mon brave.* I love my Vincent because it is magnificent and it is mine. Now you are mine as well." He flung his arms wide. "Welcome to the Howling Coyotes, father of Jerry. Come into the castle and we will talk."

Chapter Fifteen

+ + + ✦ + + +

Nick trudged back from the Town Meeting, the satchel banging at his hip and the words of the ritual ringing in his ears. *We are swimmers and fishers. We are beasts and men.*

They were. They really were—even Lily, whom everybody treated like the unofficial mayor of Smallbone Cove. They were seals, or they had been until Smallbone hauled them out of the sea and turned them into people. It was wrong. Nobody should have the power to monkey with the nature of things like that, changing people into animals and animals into people just because they wanted to.

And what about this Fidelou? Nick remembered the howling that had chased him through the woods the night he'd come to Evil Wizard Books. Was that Fidelou? Was he the threat Smallbone had been talking about? What were the Sentries?

When they reached the pond, Smallbone turned and glared at him. "Out with it!"

"What?"

"You're already on the simmer," Smallbone said. "You'll boil over soon."

Nick scowled. "I don't know what you're talking about."

"Town Meeting. You're bursting with questions. By the Rules, you get three. Speak up, now. I ain't got all day."

Nick hesitated, looking for a question he thought Smallbone might actually answer. "Who's Fidelou?"

"He's a loup-garou. That's French for werewolf, but he can take any shape he's got a mind to. He sailed over from France three, four hundred years back, drifted down from Canada about the time I found the Cove. We got a history, Fidelou and me. He thinks he's the greatest wizard who ever howled, and I think he's a big sack of wild magic with the brains of a vole.

Powerful, though, and magic clear through. Not a drop of human blood in him. You know them islands all down the Reach? They're rocks we threw at each other, last time we fought."

"Did you really . . . ? Scratch that," Nick said hastily. "Um, how do the Sentries work?"

Smallbone started walking again. "They keep out whatever I don't want in my territory, mostly Fidelou. If they were working like they should, the Stream would have risen and swept them Howling Coyotes right off. Still would, if they tried to cross the bridge on four feet. Even as it is, Fidelou can't get in until they're all down." He picked up his pace. "Hurry up with that last question, Foxkin. I got work to do."

They passed out of the woods and into the meadow. Smoke curled from the chimneys of Evil Wizard Books, and its many windows twinkled in the thin sunlight.

"What'll happen if the Sentries fall?"

"Fidelou will blow in like a hurricane," Smallbone said shortly. "Then I'll fight him, and I'll win or he will. Either way, the Cove'll go to wrack and ruin. And now I'd like a little peace. You're a kid, ain't you? Go off somewheres and play."

Then Smallbone opened the back door, stalked inside, and closed it, leaving Nick outside in the snow.

Nick kicked the boot scraper. That hurt, so he levitated it as far as he could, which was almost to the woodshed. Then he trudged out through the snow to fetch it, because Smallbone would want to know how it landed all the way out there and Nick couldn't think of anything to tell him that wouldn't get him turned into something with too many legs, or maybe none at all.

When he finally came inside, the kitchen was empty except for a gently snoring heap of black and ginger fur on the rocker. Nick shucked off his jacket and marched into the bookshop.

It was quiet but not peaceful. The air quivered with tension, and even the clock seemed to be ticking faster than usual, like a panicky heartbeat. Or maybe that was him.

"Listen," he said. "*E-Z Spelz* is great, but if it comes down to a fight between Smallbone and this Fidelou guy, I'm going to need a weapon or more protection or *something*. Bow-Wowzer Meowzer just isn't going to cut it."

There was a brooding pause, followed by a storm of rustling and rattling back in the shelves, a heavy thud, then silence.

Nick lit the oil lamp and went to investigate. In the third aisle back, a fat leather-covered book lay on the floor in front of the NATURE section.

He picked it up. *101 Steps to the Animal You.* He appealed to the shadowy shelves. "How is this going to help?"

He didn't really expect an answer, so he wasn't disappointed when he didn't get one, unless you could count the strident bonging of the clock as it struck five.

Supper! he thought, and ran back to the kitchen, pausing only to slide *101 Steps* under the clock. He wondered if Smallbone would be willing to eat leftover chili.

But Smallbone didn't come down. He sent Mutt and Jeff, though, so Nick fed them, then retrieved the book and took it out to the barn to study after he'd done the evening chores.

The bookshop's latest gift was not full of illustrations and charts like *E-Z Spelz*. And although it was interactive, in the magical sense that it talked to him, it wasn't nearly as user-friendly.

I'm doing this under protest. You don't know enough about magic to read me. I'm not even the book you wanted.

"You got that right," Nick said. "Transformation is stupid. I want to learn how to call up storms and throw rocks and fire."

Of course you do: you're an elemental wizard. If you're any kind of wizard at all.

Nick flared up. "What do you mean? *E-Z Spelz* said I had lots of Talent and Will!"

***E-Z Spelz* also said you had roughly the**

Concentration of a hungry squirrel and the Control of a goat in a vegetable garden. You've got a nasty temper, too. Wizards have to keep a cool head.

"What about Smallbone?"

Print on paper shouldn't be able to look indignant, but this print managed.

Smallbone is one of the greatest human shape-shifters who has ever lived.

"I *know* that!" Nick yelled. "That's why I need to learn how to turn myself human again!"

AHA! You DO want to learn shape-shifting!

Nick snapped *101 Steps* shut, slapped it onto a hay bale, and fumed. After a while, he picked it up again and opened it. The pages were blank.

"I really hate getting turned into things. It wouldn't be so bad if I could turn myself back, but I don't know how. If that's what the bookshop wants you to teach me, I want to learn."

The page remained blank. Nick turned to the next. Blank. The next page featured the first of a series of woodcuts of spiders and rocks and crows. Nick kept turning. Words printed on five consecutive pages added up to a message:

Why.

Are.

You.

Still.

Reading?

Nick turned some more.

The last page read:

Congratulations. You're the Most Stubborn One of All. Maybe your totem animal is a donkey. Turn to the introduction. It's at the front.

Grimly, Nick flipped back to the first page, now filled with print.

Shape-shifting is hard—much harder if you're
not a natural shape-shifter, which we both
know you're not. This is because it's physically
impossible. For the most part, people are either
much bigger or much smaller than animals. Think
of the difference in mass between you and a frog,
for instance, or you and an elephant.

Am I going too fast for you here?

"No," Nick said. "I get it."

You better.

There are a lot of theories about excess mass
and so on, and maybe some of them are even true.
But for now, we'll just say it's magic and leave it at
that. You're not interested in theory anyway.

Because it's essentially against nature, shape-
shifting takes an unusual amount of skill and
concentration—even more than calling a storm,
and that's saying something. You can't stop or let
your mind wander or change it halfway through.
Because if you do, Bad Things will happen. You

can get stuck between shapes or explode or die. You can keep too much of your human mind and not know how to use your animal body, or you can keep too little and lose interest in turning yourself back. You have to know the spells dead cold and you have to keep your focus. Most important, you have to keep your animal and your human selves in perfect balance.

To do that, you have to know who you are.

Nick turned the page.

All righty, then. Let's get started.

Step 1: Finding Your Totem Animal

All human beings have a totem animal, whose spirit reflects and shapes their characters. If you want to learn Transformation, you have to find yours.

And then there was a list of questions, like the quiz at the end of a chapter in a schoolbook. Dopey-looking questions about what he'd do if this or that thing happened, like one of the psychological tests the school counselor gave him when he got in a fight.

He went to turn the page.

Oh, no you don't. Am I called *101 Steps to the Animal You, Except for the Steps You Don't Feel Like Taking*? I don't think so. This test is Step 1. If you don't complete it, you can't take Step 2. I *knew* you didn't really want to do this.

Nick fished the stub of a pencil out of his overalls and took the test. He threw in a bunch of wrong answers just to mess with it.

His totem animal was a fox.

☙ ☙ ☙

Next night, it began to snow again and kept on snowing as if it never intended to stop. And it didn't stop. Every trip outside was an Arctic adventure. If it hadn't been for Smallbone's paths, Nick would have spent all his free time shoveling his way to the barn and the woodshed.

After a day or two, Nick discovered that, big as

it was, Evil Wizard Books wasn't big enough to keep two crabby people from getting on each other's nerves. It felt like every time he wanted to go in the bookshop, there was Smallbone, scanning the shelves with his beard tipped up and his hat tipped back, or taking books down and poking at them as though he thought there might be something hidden in their covers.

Like, for instance, the chart Nick still had tucked away under his clean shirts.

That chart fascinated Nick. He'd take it out at night and stare at it, turning it this way and that, trying to make sense of it. He knew it made a pattern. He couldn't see it, but he could feel it, like the static on a car radio when you weren't near enough a town to get a clear signal. He wanted to beg the bookshop for something that would help him hear what the chart was trying to say, but even after Smallbone retreated into the tower, he never knew when the old wizard might show up. He'd even started doing all his reading in the hayloft. He didn't want to risk getting turned into anything before he knew how to turn himself back again.

101 Steps to the Animal You was giving him trouble.

Shape-shifting, apparently, didn't work the same way as the transformations Smallbone had used on Nick. *Animal You* had explained it in Step 2:

Think of it like this:

If you manage to keep hold of who you are while you're being transformed, then you're a shape-shifter, and can turn yourself back if you want to. If you shift yourself and get distracted and lose track of who you are, then you're transformed and will stay so forever, or until somebody else transforms you back.

Do you understand?

"Of course," Nick said. "It's simple."

No, it isn't. And you don't understand at all. But you will. You'll have to, if you want to get to Step 99.

"What's Step 99?"

The spell for turning yourself back into a boy.

And then there was a whole series of exercises on things like Lucid Dreaming and Balance and Meditation.

Nick hated these exercises, and he wasn't very good at them. If he hadn't been as stubborn as a goat, he would have given up at Step 10.

Apparently things weren't going well for Smallbone, either.

One morning, a hedge sprang up around the meadow, ten feet high at least, made of what looked like giant blackberry canes. It bristled with thorns as long as Nick's little finger and sharp as knives, as he discovered when he touched one. But when he returned to the barn that afternoon, the hedge had shrunk to a more realistic size, and when he came out again to make supper, it was gone.

The next day, a wave of water surged across the kitchen floor, drenching Mutt and Jeff, who were asleep on the hearth rug. Afraid for the books, Nick waded out to the bookshop. A cascade was pouring down the stairs, swirling around the grandfather clock, and drowning the bottom row of books. As Nick stood gaping, a carved wooden duck bobbed down the waterfall and bumped gently against his ankles.

He picked it up. It was beautifully carved and painted.

He put it on the table and sloshed his way to the front door and opened it.

He felt the water rush over his feet, freezing into a slick of ice on the porch and the front steps. *Flow,* he thought. *You don't want to be stuck in leather and wood and paper. You want to be outside. Hurry!*

One moment, he was alive with power; the next, he was swaying and shivering in the bitter cold. He slammed the door shut, leaned against it until his head stopped spinning, then turned and opened his eyes.

The floor was dry. So was the rug and the books and the stair and everything else that had been soaked a moment before.

The next day, the wind blew so hard, Nick could barely make it to the woodshed. When he got there, it was surrounded by a ring of fire that melted the snow for two feet around.

And although Nick had the bookshop to himself

now, the shelves were stocked with ordinary books with titles like *Fun with Armadillos* and *How to Be a Truly Effective Salesman*. There wasn't a magical title in the place.

Which brought him back to *Animal You*. He'd already reached Step 74. Twenty-five, no, twenty-seven more steps, and he'd be a shape-shifter — or at least he'd be able to turn himself back into a boy if he had to.

The next section was called "Knowing Yourself."

As far as Nick was concerned, he already knew as much about himself as he needed to. For years, everybody from Uncle Gabe and the principal to his classmates and their parents had been telling him that he was stubborn, untrustworthy, and moody, a compulsive troublemaker, liar, and thief. It was true, too. He didn't like anybody, he didn't trust anybody, and he wasn't scared of anything.

Animal You wasn't impressed.

If you think that's who you are, you might as well be a frog, because you'll never be a wizard. Come on, you've made it this far. It'll be worth

it. Animals are smart, in an animal way, but they can't do magic.

The fact that Nick knew this from firsthand experience just made him madder than he already was. "I'm a kid who wants to be an evil wizard," he said sullenly. "What else do I need to know?"

I get it. This is hard. You're scared. We should just forget it.

"I'm not scared!" Nick exclaimed.

Then do the danged exercise and quit bellyaching. Step 75: The Journey. You got a pencil?

Step 75 was a paragraph full of empty spaces. Nick had to fill them in to make a story, not thinking about it too much.

Walking through a (NOUN) , you come to a (PLACE) . It is (ADJECTIVE) . You go in. You see

a (NOUN) and a (NOUN). You (VERB) it. You go out into a (PLACE), where you meet a (NOUN). It (VERB) you. You (VERB) it with (NOUN). You find a (NOUN). You (VERB). You go back to the (PLACE). The (NOUN) is (ADJECTIVE). You leave. There is a (NOUN) in your pocket.

Nick picked up his pencil, grinning. He'd show that stupid book what he thought of its danged exercises. "Walking through a pile of dog . . ."

Okay, that rips it.

"What? I'm just doing what you said."

If you can't follow the Rules, then you aren't a wizard. And people who aren't wizards can't learn magic.

The page went blank.
Nick swore. The page was still blank.

Nick flipped through every page. Not a word in sight, not even a period or a comma. Nothing. Nada. Zilch.

A bubble of rage boiled up in Nick's belly, rose into his throat, and burst into a roar as he pitched *101 Steps to the Animal You* clear across the barn. It landed next to Groucho's pen.

Groucho stuck his nose through the slats and lipped at it curiously.

After a moment, Nick retrieved the book and smoothed its pages with trembling hands. None of them were torn, and the cover was only a little scratched. But inside it was still blank.

Nick climbed back into the hayloft, slid the offended book into the straw, and brushed Groucho's coat until he'd calmed himself down. The way he was feeling, the last thing he needed was to run into Smallbone. He'd be eating flies — or worse, scuttling around the kitchen floor with Hell Cat after him — in no time flat, with no way of coming back to himself again until Smallbone decided he was tired of doing his own cooking.

Or maybe Smallbone wouldn't turn him back at all.

The next day, he fished *101 Steps* out of the straw, just to check.

Step 75. Right after breakfast.

⚜   ⚜   ⚜

Walking through a FOREST , you come to a SPACESHIP . It is SHINY . You go in. You see a MACHINE and an ALIEN . You PET it. You go out into a DIFFERENT WORLD , where you meet a MONSTER . It TRIES TO EAT you. You KILL it with A BLAST OF FIRE . You find a WELL . You DRINK SOME WATER . You go back to the SPACESHIP . The ALIEN is GONE . You leave. There is a STONE in your pocket.

Nick studied the completed Step 75. It didn't say a thing to him, but at least he'd done it.

Finally we begin to get somewhere! Good.
Step 76: Facing Your Inner Alien.

Chapter Sixteen

✦ ✦ ✦ ✦ ✦ ✦

In Maine, February is the longest month of the year despite having the fewest days. For Jerry, this February was longer than most. It wasn't just the pretty much nonstop snow and wind that kept him stuck in a two-room house without a TV or even a radio to distract him. It was being stuck in that two-room house with his dad. Gabe had a way of making Jerry feel crowded and lonely at the same time that made him want to howl. The only thing that kept him from going crazy with boredom was the hope of earning his pelt in the spring. In the meantime, he didn't have much to do but play solitaire and hope the beer held out until the next delivery.

He was shoveling a path out to the gas pumps

to check if they were frozen one afternoon when a coyote appeared at the edge of the woods and turned into a girl wearing a buff-and-gray pelt with the head over her head like a mask. She pushed it back until the muzzle pointed at the sky as if it were howling. "Hey, Jer!" she said. "The Boss wants to see your dad. Better go get him fast. The Boss don't like waiting."

A special invitation from the Boss to the town mechanic turned out to include a snow-free path from the garage to the castle just wide enough to walk on. Still, by the time they got there, Jerry was freezing and wet, and his dad was red nosed and sullen. It didn't help that about the only thing they could see by the flickering torchlight in the Great Hall was the misty breath of the human Howling Coyotes, bunched together on the red carpet. A group of actual coyotes, with fur, sat and lay around the throne, where the Boss lounged comfortably on his white wolf pelt, his feet propped on the footstool, with Hiram and Audrey stationed behind him, scowling importantly.

Except for an occasional whine or sniff, the hall was completely still.

"I have summoned you," Fidelou said, "to witness my triumph. Smallbone's Sentries droop and wither like trees in a year of drought. When they fail—and they must fail—Smallbone Cove will be ours. It is only a question of a little push in the right place, at the right time, by the right hands. Those hands cannot be mine."

The Howling Coyotes shifted uncomfortably.

"I am a loup-garou," Fidelou went on. "I am magic, me, to the marrow of my bones. As long as there remains a spark of power in any of the Sentries, I may not pass. Yet many of you have crossed the Stone Bridge across the Stream and taken meat from under Smallbone's very nose. It follows then that human hands may complete the destruction my wolf magic has begun."

He grinned—an unsettling and inhuman grin. "Let those who have not yet earned their pelts come forth. Rejoice, pups! Your time has come!"

He hadn't even finished before Jerry was elbowing his way forward, grinning as ferociously as he knew how. This was his chance to prove that he was good coyote material, to earn his pelt and join the pack for real. His father might think he was a pain in the neck and a waste of space, but Fidelou needed him.

⚡ ⚡ ⚡

Night falls early in February. It had been dark for hours when the aspiring pack members hit the road to Smallbone Cove. Because of the hard winter and the slim pickings, there were only two: Jerry and a big guy with a bad attitude named Pete. Jerry didn't want to count his dad.

The light of a full moon filtered through the clouds, turning the sky a milky gray that matched the pelt of the great white wolf loping easily beside the road. Jerry rode on his old Yamaha, following the taillights of Pete's Harley, with his dad's pickup behind him. A light snowfall glittered in his headlights and stung his cheeks. For the moment, he was perfectly happy.

Fidelou led them to a field east of Smallbone Cove, where Gabe pulled a heavy duffel full of tools from the back of the pickup. It held, among other things, a big camping lantern that lit the way through the trees to what looked like a perfectly ordinary stone wall, covered with patches of lichen and moss and almost low enough to step over.

"Don't look like magic to me," said Pete.

Gabe snorted. "Really? Then how do you explain how come it ain't covered with snow?"

It was true. Not only was the Wall clear of snow, but so was the ground for a couple of feet in front of it. Jerry watched as big fluffy flakes fell through the camping lantern's beam and ran down the gleaming rocks to the soggy mess of leaves at the foot. He shivered, and not from the cold.

The Boss, on two legs now, pointed a long finger at the Wall. "Destroy it!"

There was a pause, and then Pete hefted a sledgehammer, stepped forward, and slammed it down with all his weight behind it. The sledgehammer hit the rocks with a resounding *CLANG!* Pete dropped the hammer, thrust his hands into his armpits, and swore. The Stone Wall was undisturbed. The sledgehammer, on the other hand, was cracked right up the middle of its iron head.

Gabe laughed. "I told you that wouldn't work. Step aside, boy, and let the old guy show you how it's done." He thrust the lantern into Jerry's hand and took a screwdriver out of the duffel. Then he knelt by the Wall and swore. "Can't see," he complained. "Bring that dang light closer."

If the Boss hadn't been there, Jerry might have told his dad what he could do with the lantern. But he wanted that pelt and he knew he wouldn't get it by acting out. He held the cone of light steady as Gabe scratched at the packed dirt and moss and rotten leaves that had built up between the top stones.

"This," he said as he worked, "is a dry stone wall. There's nothing holding it together but gravity and habit and some old moss." He gave one last dig and stood up. "That oughta do it. Pete, you want to give me a hand?"

It was obvious from the look on Pete's face that he didn't want to do anything but run home. The Boss growled. Pete got a crowbar and inserted the end under a capstone. Gabe positioned his own crowbar.

"On the count of three," he said. "Give it all you got."

Pete nodded. Jeff clutched the lantern.

"One. Two. Three."

The two big men leaned into their crowbars, straining. By rights, that stone should have popped off the wall like a rotten tooth. But all it did was shift and slide back a bit.

Cursing, Gabe put his hand on it and pushed.

With a wrenching grind, the rock slid toward him.

Pete jumped back. Gabe dragged in a hissing breath, then screamed once, hoarsely.

The flashlight beam wavered as Jerry leaned over his father's hand. The stone was back where it started, with Gabe's little finger caught in what had been a gap and wasn't anymore. It didn't look good. There was a lot of blood, and his father was bug-eyed and whimpering.

The Boss shoved Jerry aside, his black hair electric with fury. *"Imbecile!"* he snarled, and seizing Gabe's arm, murmured furiously under his breath. Gabe's arm grew long and thin and oddly jointed, then started sprouting black feathers.

The Boss gripped the wing by what looked like the elbow and pulled. Gabe screamed again and cradled the wing across his chest. The Wall was unchanged, except for a long black feather caught in a seam between two stones.

"The Wall holds," the Boss growled. He sounded more disgusted than angry. "Yet," he said, brightening, "it is weakened, I think. The feather may weaken it further. We will try again another night."

Chapter Seventeen

+ + + ✦ + + +

Nick spent the next week doggedly working his way through *101 Steps to the Animal You*. He discovered that, along with being stubborn and quick-tempered, he was passionate, bold, and active; that he was a good liar because he was smart; that he had an attitude because he hated being told what to do; that he liked animals better than people; that he liked spicy, salty flavors better than sweet, milky ones; that his favorite colors were red and dark brown. None of the steps seemed to have anything to do with magic. He stuck with it, though, until finally, finally, he turned the page and read:

Step 98: Turning Yourself into an Animal
    We have arrived at the moment you've been
waiting for. Below is the spell that will turn you

into your totem animal. Repeat it, think it, make
up a tune and sing it until you know it as well as
your own name. Don't be afraid to say it out loud.
It's like practicing layups. You can do them until
the cows come home, but it's not the same thing
as doing one in the middle of a real game.

The spell was short, but oddly slippery. It took a
whole day of practice before *101 Steps* was satisfied that
he knew it. Step 99 took even longer, mostly because
Nick really needed to be sure that he had it down cold.

Now he was sitting on a hay bale and leaning
against Groucho's pen, listening to the wind chase the
snow around the corners of the barn and the goats
chewing their cud. *Animal You* was open to Step 100.

It was very short:

Cast the Transformation.

"No," Nick said.

Text appeared under the spell, bolded and under-
lined. *Animal You* was annoyed.

What do you mean, No? That's what you want,
and you can't say you don't, because I *know* you.
You're scared.

"I'm not scared," Nick said. "I just don't want to. I wanted to learn how to turn myself back if Smallbone transformed me again, and I did. I'm good."

How do you know it'll work if you don't try
it out?

"Because I have Confidence," Nick said, and put the book back under the straw.

⚶   ⚶   ⚶

That night, he pulled the mysterious chart out from under his shirts and studied it. He still couldn't make sense of it, but there was something about it—the way it made his fingers tingle, the way the numbers almost spoke to him—that made his brain itch to understand it. He was sure it was elemental magic.

He was an elemental wizard. *101 Steps* had said so.

⚶   ⚶   ⚶

The next day, when Smallbone was safely shut in his tower, Nick went to the bookshop.

"I've finished the book you gave me," he said. "It was really useful, but I'm not really a shape-shifter. I want to learn to read that chart you gave me. I want a book on Elemental Magic. Please," he added, because he was learning that it never hurt to be polite to magical things.

He got his reward when a volume bound in red flapped heavily out of the darkness and landed next to the wooden duck on the table. Stamped in black on the cover were the words *The Elements of Elemental Magic.*

"Thank you!" Nick shouted, and took it out to the barn to read without even putting on his snow boots.

l am earth. My pages are made from trees, my ink from carbon. Though l am dry, l was born of water, and water clings to my fires. Fire and air were used in my making, and are bound into each word on my pages. One of these elements will speak more clearly to you than the others, but all must be kept in balance.

Do you understand?

Nick opened his mouth to say yes, remembered that wizards shouldn't lie, and said, "Not really."

Good. Not understanding must come before understanding. You will learn.

The Elements of Elemental Magic was different from *Animal You.* It never lectured him, and it never scolded. It gave him diagrams that it said were pictures of energy and told him stories about river gods and molten rocks and birds that rode the paths of the winds. And it gave him exercises, lots of exercises, that turned out to be spells.

The first one Nick tried sent a wind roaring through the barn, much to the consternation of the animals, who panicked as their bedding swirled and danced around them. It took Nick forever to calm them, particularly the goats. But they got used to it after a while. They'd stand in the corner and watch the soiled bedding sail out of their pen and the fresh straw sail in and scatter itself across the boards with weary patience.

He still had to do Ollie's pen with a manure fork. Pigs don't like change.

Next he built a snowman using only water magic. It took him a lot longer than it would have just to pile up the snow and shape it, and the final result looked less like a snowman than an icy cone with strange lumps sticking out of it, one of which was decorated with stones and looked sort of like a face if you squinted hard. He melted it down with a fire spell, after which he felt sick and a little weak at the knees.

The next snowman was a lot better.

After about a week of this, Nick woke one morning to the dazzle of sun on new snow. He'd stayed up late, as usual, puzzling over the chart, and he must have overslept. Smallbone would be furious.

Heart pounding, he ran downstairs. Smallbone was hunched over the stove like an angry raven, his white hair bristling and the skirts of his coat flapping in no wind Nick could feel. Hell Cat, perched above the stove on her favorite shelf, turned sapphire eyes on Nick and hissed.

"If it's staying up all night you like," Smallbone said nastily, "I can turn you into something nocturnal. An opossum, maybe. Put you over the Wall for Fidelou's coyotes to play with."

The familiar red rage coursed through Nick's veins. "I'd like to —" he began, and stopped. *Take a deep breath,* his *Animal You*–trained brain told him. *Do you want to test that shape-shifting spell right now?*

"What?" Smallbone snarled. "You'd like to what?"

"Say I'm sorry," Nick finished. "I won't do it again."

There was a tense pause, then Smallbone's coat settled like a hen's feathers. "You better not." He left the stove and sat down with his pipe. "Now you're here, you can make the coffee. I got work to do."

When Nick got out to the barn, the animals were watered and fed, with fresh hay in their stalls. He brushed the loose hair from Groucho's hide and played fetch with Ollie, then climbed up into the hayloft and got out *Elements of Elemental Magic*. He had a feeling it would have something to say, and it did.

> You really should know by now that magical
> energy is not endless. Your spirit is the battery
> that drives the magic. When it runs low, you
> become weak and tired. When you drain it, it may
> or may not return. You cannot become a master in
> a week, or even a month. You must be patient.

But Nick didn't want to be patient. The chart was beginning to make sense. It no longer looked to him like spilled spaghetti, sprinkled with numbers instead of meatballs. It looked like a complicated pattern. He couldn't tell what it meant, yet, but he felt like he was getting close.

> I plant the seeds of magic, send water to nourish
> them, bring the sun to warm them and the wind
> to cool their first leaves. The chart you speak of is
> the plant full grown. I cannot help you.

Warily, in case Smallbone was still around, Nick returned to the bookshop, hoping to beg for or find a more advanced book on Elemental Magic. The shop was willing. The books on the shelves were magic books. But the NATURE section, where the books on Elemental Magic were to be found, was bare of even dust and cobwebs. There wasn't a book to be found.

Smallbone had taken them all.

❖ ❖ ❖

Even in Maine, winter doesn't last forever, although in March it can feel that way. "The March Hill," they call it. Bitter windstorms are followed by thaws; snow squalls are followed by rain that turns everything into muddy, icy slush. People come down with colds and cabin fever. Anybody who can get through March without breaking a glass, a friendship, a secret, a promise, or somebody's nose is either a saint or on vacation in Florida.

Nick wasn't anybody's idea of a saint.

One morning, Smallbone put on his muffler. "Should be home by suppertime," he said. "Don't get up to no shenanigans."

Nick's heart rose, but he kept his eyes firmly on the sink, full of greasy dishes and soap bubbles. "No shenanigans," he said. "Check."

"Hmph," said Smallbone, and went out the door.

Nick counted to ten, then ran for the stairs, accompanied by the dogs, who leaped up ahead of him, almost as if they were leading him.

He'd given a lot of thought, in the past weeks, to what the inside of Smallbone's tower looked like. From watching old movies like *The Sword in the Stone* and *Harry Potter* and *The Time Bandits* with his mom, he imagined Smallbone's workshop as a dark room full of bones, mouse nests, and stuffed alligators, with maybe a caged demon in one corner. Long tables would hold glass alembics full of fluorescent green liquid bubbling over magic flames and iron crucibles for brewing potions. There would be a wand, black and knobby, with a claw at the end, several magic talismans, and at least one black-bladed knife for ritual purposes. The air would be thick and smoky and would smell of magic and, probably, blood.

He couldn't wait to see it.

It had been some time since Nick had been in the stone corridor that led to Smallbone's tower. He wasn't at all sure he could get in now. But he had found a lock-picking spell in *E-Z Spelz,* of all places, and he knew a way of turning lightning away that might get him past Smallbone's protection spell.

In any case, he intended to try.

The door to the workshop was just as intimidating as he remembered. He took a deep breath, concentrated, and muttered the lock-picking spell under his breath.

There was a small *click.*

His hand hovered over the latch. He could sense the lightning spell in it, waiting to sting him again. The latch was iron. Maybe if he called up magnetic energy out of the earth . . .

He concentrated. The thumb lever sank. He gave the door a kick, and it creaked open.

The dogs rushed past him and disappeared into the blackness. From the sound of it, they were climbing stairs, wooden ones. Nick squared his shoulders and went after them.

The steps were steep and high, almost ladder-like;

the walls nearly brushed his shoulders. Heart racing, Nick groped his way upward, half expecting the door to slam shut behind him or the steps to disappear. At the top, he stumbled on a step that wasn't there and fell into a choking, smothering mass of fabric. As he flailed at it, it parted on a blaze of sun and the smell of turpentine and dust. He stepped forward, blinking.

He'd been right about the books.

There were books stuffed into rickety brick-and-board shelves and books stacked within reaching distance of an old leather recliner. Books spilled across the floor and teetered in piles on the long trestle table under the far window, along with an old lantern, a pile of fur, a plate with half a sandwich on it, and a Bunsen burner. The books were bound in leather and metal, and they looked very old, but they were just books. The room, though admittedly cluttered, was just a room. There were no bones, no disgusting things in jars, not even a stuffed alligator hanging from a rafter. No rafters. The only real sign of magical activity was the silver pentagram inlaid in the floor, half obscured by Jeff's furry butt and tail.

Nick turned around. Under one of the four round windows, Mutt was stretched beside a low bench laid out with planes and chisels and a half-finished carving of a duck just like the one that had come floating down the steps in the bookshop flood. Behind it, more carvings crowded a long, curving shelf.

Nick moved closer. Smallbone's carvings were actually pretty good. They were all animals: cats, dogs, ravens, a bear, a family of gray harbor seals, an osprey, and, of course, ducks.

The cats looked like Smallbone's cats, down to Tom's fluffy tail and Hell Cat's suspicious expression.

Nick put down the little wooden Tom and turned back toward the books. "I'm Nick," he said. "You know, Smallbone's apprentice. I need some books on Elemental Magic."

Nothing moved except Jeff's tail, sweeping the silver pentagram free of dust.

"Please?" Nick added experimentally.

Nothing.

Nick swore softly, then picked up the nearest book. It was *Water and Earth: Elements of Growth*. Bingo!

Mutt trotted over to the curtain, whuffed softly, then barked.

Nick knew that bark. It was Mutt's happy-to-see-you-glad-you're-home bark. Smallbone must be back.

He looked around for somewhere to hide. Under the table was too open; behind the chair was too far away. And it was too late now anyway, because Smallbone was standing in the door, glasses blazing, beard bristling, coat skirts quivering with fury.

"What in Sam Hill do you think you're doing in my tower, boy?"

There was no good answer to this question. Nick clutched *Water and Earth* to his chest, feeling oddly calm. "Looking around," he said. "You left the door unlocked."

"Unlocked!" Smallbone growled. "I'll show you unlocked!" And he raised his hand in an all-too-familiar gesture.

Nick gritted his teeth. This was it. He couldn't stop Smallbone's spell, but he should be able to turn himself back — if he could just hold on to his human mind. Know who you are, *Animal You* had told him. All right. Who was he?

I'm Nick, he told himself. *I'm an elemental wizard, even though I don't know much about it yet. I like science fiction and I can milk goats and cook. I'm smart enough to make an evil wizard think I'm dumb. I'm Nick Reynaud of Beaton, Maine, and some old geezer in an ugly old coat can't make me be any different.*

The other times Smallbone had transformed Nick, everything had gone fuzzy or black, and next thing he knew, he was waking up with a set of strange new memories to sort out. This time, he felt the change as it happened. It was a little like having the measles and a little like riding a roller coaster and a lot like something he'd rather not go through again.

Then it was over, and Nick was still Nick, with all his human memories intact.

In a rat's body. With a rat's senses and instincts. It was like seeing double, only inside your head.

The smell of dog hit Nick like a sledgehammer, sending him scuttling to the safety of the wall. He scurried farther into the darkness, looking for a place to hide, his sensitive whiskers guiding him around and over piles of books, until he was stopped by something big and solid.

He sniffed carefully. Meat and wood and salt and age, and something dark and jumpy and sharp, like old blood and lightning.

Box full of magic, his boy-self said. *Danger,* his rat-self added. *Run away!*

He darted through a crack that led to the narrow space behind the wall.

As soon as he was safe, Nick peed and pooped on the floor. Then he sniffed what he'd done, because that's what rats do. One part of him confirmed that he was a healthy young male rat and that he was afraid. The human part thought, *Ew, gross,* and backed away.

I am Nick Reynaud, he thought. *My best friend is a bookshop. I know magic. I can turn myself back into my right shape any time I want.*

He could feel the words of the spell in his mind, ready to do their job, but his heart was beating too fast for him to concentrate. Which was probably a good thing, since the space between the walls would be a tight fit for a twelve-year-old boy, even a skinny one.

There was nobody to fight, nobody to yell at. He was alone and lost and, yes, he had to admit it, scared out of his mind. Half of him wanted to stay very still and hope it would all go away. The other half, the stubborn half, was telling him to get his furry butt in gear and search out a good place for his transformation.

He squeaked experimentally and listened to the echoes. The walls were there and there. All he had to do was go straight, and he'd be, well, somewhere else. The crack he'd escaped through couldn't be the only rat hole in the place. He scuttled into the darkness, squeaking at intervals, investigating with his whiskers anything that sounded promising. The first opening he came to was stuffed with steel wool. He tried to chew through it and only cut his mouth. The next crack was also blocked, and the next and the next. The next was stuffed with paper folded into a fat packet. When Nick gave it a hopeful shove with his nose, his whiskers tingled.

Magic, he thought, and left it alone.

Beyond that was a solid stone wall and a hole in the floor that smelled of dust and damp plaster, magic, and—was that bacon grease?

Rat-Nick was suddenly ravenous, but boy-Nick knew that getting lost in the walls was not going to help him. He retraced his route to Smallbone's workshop, stuck his nose cautiously through the crack, and sniffed. Smallbone and the dogs were gone, so he emerged.

The world was all blue shadows and green smudges; rats, apparently, are almost blind. Their noses, however, are super-sensitive. Besides dog and ancient wizard—and magic, of course—he could smell dust, paper, old fish, ashes, varnish, paint, stone, stale bread, fresh wood, chicken.

Mouth watering, Nick sniffed and scurried his way to the moldy remains of a chicken sandwich under the bench. Boy-Nick was revolted even as rat-Nick tore into it with sharp little teeth. When it was gone, both Nicks felt steadier. It was time to do some magic.

Nick noticed that his whiskers were all gummed

up with chicken. Nobody can do anything with gummed-up whiskers. He sat up and groomed them clean, then attended to his paws. He'd started on his haunches when he remembered that he was supposed to be turning himself back into a boy. His fur rose in panic. Suppressing the urge to lick it flat again, he began to recite the spell in his head.

It didn't work. He remembered the words, but they were just sounds. It was like when he meowed at Tom or baaed at the goats. It sounded kind of like animal-speak, but it didn't mean anything.

Will, Concentration, Control. It was so hard to keep his focus when everything smelled so interesting and his whiskers and fur kept sending him messages he couldn't quite understand. And he'd been doing spells all morning. What if he'd wasted his magic on gathering eggs and opening the door? What was he going to do?

Ratty panic overcame him, and he ran blindly for the darkness. He came to himself again under the worktable, crouching against a book that made his fur tingle. *Magic,* he thought. *I need more magic.*

Wasn't there a pentagram in the middle of the floor?

Nick scurried out into the light and stopped, his heart beating so hard he felt sick. All around him was emptiness, cold, hostile, unknowable. When he squeaked, only confused echoes answered him. Quivering from nose to tail, Nick slunk back to the safe, close dark under the table and groomed his fur thoughtfully.

Books. There were books all over the floor. If he stuck to the books, maybe he could get closer to the pentagram without having to go out into the open.

Whiskers twitching nervously, Nick ran through the uneven papery maze, squeezing between tall stacks, climbing over lower ones, making his way toward the electric smell of magic. Once he stepped on an open book and peered at the writing until his eyes would have watered if rats had tear ducts, but he couldn't read a word. Was it because his eyes were wrong for reading or because he'd forgotten how?

Why was he looking at this thing, anyway?

Some time later, Nick crouched at the edge of a terrifying open space. He'd forgotten exactly what he was looking for, but he knew it was out there and that he was going to go after it no matter how terrified he was.

With a defiant squeal, Nick launched himself into space and landed on something that stung his paws like ice. All at once, he remembered walking on two legs and seeing more than a few inches away. And he knew exactly how he could do those things again.

Nick closed his beady rat eyes and poured all his fear and all his trust into the words that would make him human.

The magic rushed through him, making his blood and his whiskers tingle painfully. Then the world tilted and turned itself inside out, taking Nick with it. Everything hurt, everything was falling apart, like Uncle Gabe's worst beatings, only ten times worse. Nick tried to squeal or scream but couldn't make a sound.

When it was over, he was lying on the floor. Boy or rat? He hurt too much to care.

There was a clatter, like metal rings sliding, and the clump of boots on the wooden floor, accompanied by the familiar stink of Smallbone's tobacco. Not the nose-busting blast it would have been for a rat, but a faint, human-size whiff.

Despite the trouble he was certainly in, Nick grinned.

"You got no call to be so cheerful, Foxkin," Smallbone said. "You've made an everlasting mess of my workshop and pooped all over my books." The boots thumped nearer. "You're white as a hake's belly. Here."

Something hard poked Nick in the ribs. Opening his eyes, he saw Smallbone bending over him, his hat squashed down over his wild hair. Bony fingers grasped Nick's shoulders, sat him up like a doll, and shoved a steaming cup into his shaking hands. It smelled of hot chocolate, with cinnamon and something slightly bitter he couldn't identify.

"Sage," Smallbone said. "It's good for dispersing magic. You called up enough just now to turn a goat into a senator. Next time, hold back a little; use just what you need and no more."

Nick swallowed the chocolate and glanced sideways at Smallbone. "Aren't you going to turn me into a slug and salt me or something?"

"Turn you into a slug?" Smallbone sounded amused. "Why should I do that? Just because you ain't as full-up numb as I thought?"

This conversation, Nick thought, was getting stranger by the second. "But I lied to you. I told you I couldn't read."

"So you did," Smallbone said. "But I didn't believe you. Better than a greased-pig race at the fair it was, watching you busily pulling the wool over my eyes."

Nick was getting annoyed. "Why didn't you tell me?"

"Because it wouldn't have been a real test if you knew you was being tested." The old wizard heaved himself to his feet. "And now, if you're done asking fool questions, it's past five, and I want my supper."

Chapter Eighteen

✦ ✦ ✦ ✦ ✦ ✦ ✦

After his day as a rat, Nick slept straight through two nights and the day between. When he woke, he sat up, feeling better than he'd felt in weeks. Tom, who had been asleep on his chest, picked himself out of the covers and meowed resentfully.

"I'm a wizard," Nick told the little cat. "I passed Smallbone's test. I'm going to be the best elemental wizard in the world. You just watch."

Unimpressed, Tom yawned, stretched, curled up on the pillow, and went back to sleep.

It was snowing, one of those heavy, wet snows that Maine can deliver in March. Nick ran downstairs, grabbed an apple from the barrel in the larder, threw open the back door, and called up a wind to blow the snow out of his way.

The wind wouldn't come. When he tried to reach for his power, there was nothing to reach for, just a damp blankness. Nick was clean out of magic. Furious, he marched, head down, into a wind he couldn't control and forked the soiled straw out of the pens and washed the buckets and worked the pump and even gathered eggs without a lick of magic to help him. It took him twice as long as it usually did, and the longer it took, the madder he got.

It had all been a trap. He imagined Smallbone up in his tower, carving little ducks and having a good laugh over what a fool Nick had made of himself, blowing out all his magic in a single spell. Knowing Smallbone, that was a whole lot easier to believe than that he actually didn't mind that Nick had learned magic on his own.

When Nick got back to the house, Smallbone had already eaten breakfast and was sitting in his rocker with Tom on his knees and his foul pipe stuck in his beard. The smell of sausage and onion and sage from the pan on the stove told Nick he was hungry. He got a plate and filled it with scrapple.

Smallbone emptied his pipe into the fire and set it back on the mantelpiece. "When you're done in here, Foxkin, you might as well come up to the tower. But clean up the kitchen first."

Nick choked on his scrapple. Was it possible the old man was actually going to teach him something?

Nick sped through the cleanup in record time and ran upstairs. The tower door was wide open, the stairs were lit, the curtain was drawn back, and the workshop was bright and almost neat. Smallbone had draped a sheet over the shelf of wooden carvings, stacked the maze of books, and swept the floor. Beside the worktable, Nick saw the corner of the box of magic he'd bumped into when he was a rat. It looked like an old sea chest, with a seal painted on the lid. He wondered what was in it.

A faint sour smell suggested that Smallbone had missed some of the rat poop. *I should teach him my gathering spell,* Nick thought, and grinned.

Across the room, Smallbone was hunched over

the worktable like a crow in a top hat. He flashed his glasses over his shoulder. "Come here, Foxkin, and tell me what you make of this."

"This" was a twisted framework of reddish iron with some bits of cloudy glass hanging from it like broken teeth. "It's a lantern," Nick said carefully. "It's rusty and the glass is all brown and bubbly. The corners are lumpy. No, wait." He looked more closely. "They're supposed to be lizards, aren't they? There's no fuel tank or wick, but I suppose you could put a candle in it, if there was a holder for it." He looked at Smallbone. "It's the Lantern, isn't it?"

Smallbone gave him a glittering look. "The Sentry of Fire," he said. "The glass is volcanic—Seaweed of Pele, it's called: very rare. And these critters"—the old wizard tapped one of the iron lizards—

"Are salamanders," Nick said. "They live in fire and speak with tongues of flame."

Smallbone poked at the Lantern irritably. "Ayuh. And right now, it doesn't do a jeezly thing. When it's up to speed, it lights up the Town Limits with magic fire. It's mostly for show—I ain't interested in starting a conflagration. That's why it went down, I guess. Not enough real fire behind it to keep it going."

"So Fidelou took it down?"

"Well, he certainly did what he could, howling around the Limits five nights out of seven, but the jeezly thing would've held up just fine if the Smallbone Covers had kept up their side of the Contract like they was supposed to."

Nick touched one of the salamanders. It was rough with rust, but Nick could feel a faint warmth in it, like old ashes waiting to be coaxed back to life. If he'd known how, he would have tried.

Smallbone jerked the Lantern out of reach. "You stop that! Land o' Goshen, Foxkin, didn't them jeezly books warn you about fummydiddling with enchanted doo-dads? With your Control, you'd most likely set a fire would burn a thousand years, and then where would we be? It takes a barn-load of figuring to create a ritual that'll keep it in its place."

"You did it once," Nick pointed out.

Between the glasses, the beard, and the hat, not much of Smallbone's face was visible, but that little looked distinctly uncomfortable. "Of course I did," he snapped. "Jeezly hard it was, too. You know"—another flash of the round glasses—"that Elemental Magic is the art of making things do what they'd do anyway, only in the direction you want. The Sentries are more complicated. First off, they're a trap, set to catch only certain kinds of fish. Second, they're tuned so the seals can reset them. That's why I made charts with everything laid out so I could build 'em again if I had to. Thing is," he went on casually, "two hundred and fifty years is a long time. Might be I'm having trouble laying my hand on one or two of the charts. Not that I need 'em, mind. I can just work faster if I don't have to start from scratch. I thought, with all your dusting and cleaning . . . ?"

He was wearing an expression that reminded Nick of Mutt when food was on the table—half hopeful, half resigned to disappointment. And he was going to be disappointed, because Nick had no intention of handing over his precious chart. Served the old man right for jerking Nick around with his threats and his tricks and his spell that kept him in the yard like a straying dog. The bookshop had given Nick that chart, and he was learning to understand it. He was sure it was based on earth, with other magics woven in. He recognized Protection, he thought, and that knot there was clearly meant to bind the stones in one place.

So the old coot could just put that in his pipe and smoke it. It'd probably smell a lot better than his tobacco.

Nick shook his head regretfully. "Nope. Nothing like that. Sorry."

⚜ ⚜ ⚜

That afternoon, a nor'easter blew up along the coast, with a howling wind that sent the rain driving sideways across the field. It would have been perfect reading weather, if the bookshop hadn't decided to go on strike.

It started with *Elements of Elemental Magic* going blank. Nick was startled, but he just figured the book was giving him an enforced vacation. Fine. He hadn't read anything but magic for ages. He could do with a little science fiction, he thought.

There wasn't any science fiction. There wasn't hardly any fiction at all, except in the ROMANCE section. There wasn't even any nonfiction Nick was interested in reading, only books on accounting and politics.

It took him a little while to figure out what had happened, and when he did, he couldn't believe it.

"It's not fair," he said, standing on the rug and facing the shelves. "It's not even the right chart!" His voice rose. "If it's so dad-blamed important to keep Fidelou out of Smallbone Cove, why didn't you give Smallbone the chart instead of me?"

He glared at the books, waiting for a response. No rustling or rattling, not the smallest prickle at the back of his neck. The bookshop was completely empty of any sign or scent or feeling of magic.

Nick got mad. "Fine," he said. "I don't give a fart in a high wind."

He stomped out to the barn. The goats were chewing their cud and flavoring the air with hay-scented burps, and Ollie was snuffling hopefully through the straw in his pen for something to eat or play with. The chickens strutted everywhere, heads bobbing as they searched for bugs. Nick climbed into Groucho's pen and picked up the curry comb and rubbed it in brisk circles along the donkey's bony shoulder, his anger draining slowly out of him.

After a few minutes, he rested his forehead against the dusty gray flank and closed his eyes. If he was honest with himself—and he couldn't be anything else, thank you, *Animal You*—he had to admit that he hadn't given Smallbone the chart because he wanted to fix the Sentries himself. If he did that, Smallbone would have to admit he was a real wizard and stop talking to him like he was just a dorky kid.

Groucho snorted and gave Nick's shoulder a reminding nudge. Nick wiped his face on his sleeve and went back to brushing.

Who was he kidding? Smallbone didn't make friends with his apprentices. He didn't even train them. If Nick pushed him too far, he might turn him into something that couldn't think—a brick or a chair or a plate. That would be the end of Nick, and nobody would ever know or care, except a handful of animals and possibly a magic bookshop.

When Nick finished brushing Groucho, he marched back through the rain. Curious, Mutt, Jeff, and Tom followed him into the bookshop.

"I'm sorry," he said into the waiting silence. "It's just I wanted to *do* something, you know? Something really wizardy. I know, it sounds dumb. If Fidelou's as powerful as Smallbone says, then I can't stop him. I'll give Smallbone the chart as soon as he comes down." He sent a pleading look into the shadows. "Can we go back to the way things were now?"

The silence grew thoughtful. Nick clenched his fists and fought the urge to keep talking, to shout and pull books off the shelves and throw them. The urge built and thickened, and just when Nick didn't think he'd be able to control it a second longer, a book sailed out of the darkness and landed in his hands.

It was called *The Dance of the Elements*.

⚜   ⚜   ⚜

Nick spent the rest of the day with his nose in a book.

His math teacher at Beaton Middle School would have been astonished to see him poring over charts of numbers and making calculations on sheets of stationery. It had rabbits on it, but paper was paper.

Smallbone had disappeared into his tower again. He'd even sent the dogs down at five thirty with a note tied to Jeff's collar saying he wouldn't be down for supper. Nick studied the chart as he ate chicken pot pie, trying to line its curves and numbers up with the charts in *The Dance of the Elements,* but all he'd achieved so far was a headache. He needed more time, was all.

Next morning, he was eating scrambled eggs when Smallbone came down at last, looking like a scarecrow who hadn't been to bed all night.

"Coffee," he said hoarsely. "Is there any bread left? I want an egg sandwich."

As Nick got up to fetch the bread, the shop bell clanged brassily.

Mutt and Jeff leaped up and tore out of the kitchen. Smallbone raised caterpillary eyebrows. "Well, what're you waiting for, apprentice? See who it is and tell 'em to go away."

Nick glared at him and went out to the shop. The

bell was still jangling as though it would never stop, and the dogs were under it, legs stiff and hackles up, loudly informing whoever was ringing it that they'd like to tear him to pieces. Nick had never heard them bark like that before.

He looked out the big bay window.

A huge, hairy white two-headed monster was on the porch, yanking at the bellpull as if he wanted to tear it out of the wall.

Nick drew back from the window, then took another, more careful, look. What he'd taken for a monstrous second head was really a white wolf pelt, complete with head and paws, draped around the shoulders of a man. They were massive shoulders, and the man was massive, too, with a mane of black hair and a proud, cruel face that might have been carved out of stone.

Though Nick had never seen him, he knew exactly who he had to be. The Evil Wizard Fidelou had broken into Smallbone Cove.

The bellpull popped out of the wall. Fidelou threw the chain behind him and battered at the door until the wood shook. "Smallbone! Open the door, Smallbone!"

Nick threw a hopeful glance at the kitchen door. Smallbone did not appear. And when he turned back, Fidelou was staring in at him through the window. His eyes were yellow, with pupils black as a starless night.

"Ah, a boy!" A voice like dark honey slid into Nick's ear. "Call off your dogs, boy, and open to me. I desire to speak to your master."

"We're closed!" Nick yelled. "Go away!"

The loup-garou grinned. His teeth were completely canine and horrible in his more or less human mouth. "But I am not in need of a book, me. I am a friend of your master—an *old* friend, you understand? We are brother wizards, he and I."

How dumb does he think I am? Nick wondered. "Smallbone doesn't have friends."

"I am not astonished, me, since his apprentice turns them away so rudely. Go to your master, boy, and tell him the Wizard Fidelou is here."

"Well, if it ain't my favorite loup-garou," Smallbone said.

He was standing by Nick, hat at a jaunty angle, his beard bristling.

Fidelou howled and launched himself at the window.

The air crackled and sparked like an electrical short, and Fidelou's hair stood up like a Halloween fright wig. Nick made a dive under the counter.

"You'll excuse me if I don't ask you in," Smallbone said gruffly. "We got too many wizards on the premises as it is."

Fidelou snarled. "You make the jokes, eh? You are foolish, old man. Foolish and weak."

"Not so weak as all that," Smallbone said. "I can still throw you into the middle of next week if I got a mind to."

"I think not." The wolf wizard sneered. "You have lived too long, old man. Your Lantern is dark, your Wind is stilled, your Stream is frozen between its banks. I have even breached your Wall. Soon Smallbone Cove will be mine, and my pack free to hunt as they will. It is a hungry pack, Zachariah Smallbone: hungry as death. And you will starve here in your magic house with this poor slave. Would you not rather face me upon the dueling field? You will lose, *bien sûr,* but at least you will die with honor."

Nick glanced up at Smallbone. Behind his bushy beard and round spectacles, the old man's face was stern. But the skirts of his coat shivered like water about to come to a boil. Smallbone was scared, and that scared Nick almost as much as Fidelou did.

With one last sharp-toothed grin, the wolf wizard disappeared. Nick scrambled up in time to see him swing himself into the saddle of a huge black motorcycle propped against the railing. It looked dangerous, a sleeping panther or a machine gun on wheels — a real evil wizard's ride.

Fidelou revved the engine and ripped out of the parking lot, his white fur cloak rippling behind him like a banner.

The dogs ran to Nick, very proud of themselves for scaring the intruder away and wanting to be petted. He fussed over them for a moment, then gently pushed them away.

"I got something to give you," he muttered, and

without waiting for an acknowledgment, raced to his room, where he grabbed the chart out of his bureau.

When he got back to the bookshop, Smallbone was still by the window, his shoulders bent. He took the chart Nick handed him, unfolded it, and peered at the lines and numbers. "This is for the Stone Wall. Thank you, Foxkin."

Smallbone mad and sarcastic Nick was used to. Smallbone sad and grateful scared him witless. "So what? You're the Evil Wizard Smallbone. Why not just fight him like he wants, blast him with a spell or something?"

Smallbone snorted. "Blast him with a spell? This ain't a jeezly movie, Foxkin. This is the real world — *my* real world, anyway. Magic has Rules. A wizards' duel ain't pretty, Foxkin. I could win and Smallbone Cove could still be stomped flat by a giant or burnt to a crisp by a dragon, and I would hardly know I was doing it." He tucked the chart into his pocket. "Best bet is to reset the Sentries and make sure them blubberhead seals keep 'em wound up proper. You attend to your studies. And keep your eyes peeled for the other charts. I wouldn't wonder if some jeezly apprentice didn't take and hide 'em somewhere for spite."

Since Nick had done just that, he knew Smallbone was right. Evil Wizard Books offered lots of places a frightened, angry boy could hide something he didn't want found. And Nick thought he knew where one was.

He said that, and Smallbone gave him a suspicious look. "You playing me, Foxkin? Because if you are, I swear I'll turn you into a cockroach and set Hell Cat on you."

Nick looked him in the eye. "No, you won't. But Fidelou would. That's why I'm telling you."

There was a startled silence. "So where's it at?"

"I don't know, exactly. I found it when I was a rat. It's stuck in a crack."

"An old newspaper, most likely," Smallbone said glumly.

"It felt like magic," Nick insisted. Smallbone lifted a bristly eyebrow. "No, really. Elemental Magic feels prickly, like static electricity."

"Well, you better get looking, then."

So Nick probed the baseboards in each of Evil

Wizard Books' empty rooms. He found two of the steel wool–stuffed rat holes, a yellowed copy of *Rocket Ship Galileo,* and some very old coins. In one of the small spare rooms, his probing fingers felt a tiny prick of electric energy. Unfortunately, the paper was stuffed in so tightly there was no way to extract it.

No natural way, that is. Smallbone got it out with a few sharp-edged words and a pair of needle-nose pliers, then sat down on the sagging bed and unfolded it. "I think . . ." He turned it around. "Ah! The wily old so-and-so. Ha!"

"What's it for?"

"The Lantern."

"Maybe I can help," Nick offered.

Smallbone's beard bobbed as he munched thoughtfully. "Maybe you can at that."

Chapter Nineteen

✦ ✦ ✦ ✦ ✦ ✦ ✦

A few days later found Nick standing on a flat granite stone in the Lantern Glade. There'd been a sudden return of winter. Snow dusted the ground, and the wind had a savage bite. Every few minutes, Nick swiped his dripping nose with the cuff of his jacket.

The jacket was red. So were his socks. Smallbone had insisted, since red was the color of fire. The old wizard was wearing a red muffler that shone with eye-aching brilliance against the dark background of pine and spruce and naked tree trunks around the clearing. The Lantern Glade itself was maybe half the size of a motel swimming pool, studded with rocks and carpeted with moss. An oak stood at one end. It was a giant of its kind, with a double trunk lumpy with galls, and twisted branches that would have blocked the sun if they'd been leafed out. Nick thought it was the most beautiful tree he'd ever seen. It was certainly the most alive.

To the south of Nick's stone, Smallbone was performing the ritual laid out in the chart Nick had found when he was a rat. The Lantern was looking a lot better than it had — more like a powerful magical artifact and less like something an elephant had stepped on. Nick had spent a whole day banging the dents out of the top and polishing the salamanders with stove blacking. He and Smallbone had mended the Seaweed of Pele, melting the volcanic glass in a crucible and cooling it in the pentagram without even scorching the floor.

The sun touched the top of the great oak, and Nick shivered nervously. When it was directly overhead, Smallbone would give the signal, and it would be up to Nick to light the Lantern.

"What do you mean, I'm going to light it?" he'd asked when Smallbone told him the plan. "You're the evil wizard."

"You want to help, don't you?"

"Well, yeah. But this is really big magic, right? What about all those complicated rituals and stuff?"

"I'll take care of those. All you have to do is light the jeezly thing. You do know how to light a candle, don't you?"

"Of course I do," Nick said, offended.

"It's like that, only bigger. There's no actual candle, you see. You'll have to give it all you got."

Smallbone was crossing and recrossing the Glade. Nick watched him stop at a rock, mutter, wave the Lantern, turn, check his heading against the chart, then march off in a new direction, leaving a bright little thread of magic behind him. He'd been doing it for some time, and the clearing was crisscrossed with a complex, brilliant web of red-gold light. Nick could feel the magic in it humming down his bones.

The sun stood directly overhead. It was noon, the hour of fire. Smallbone slid the Lantern onto a branch of the grandfather oak and nodded.

Nick closed his eyes and opened himself to fire.

It should have been easy. He'd lit hundreds of candles and lanterns—well, twenty or thirty, anyway.

But candles and lanterns had wicks, and fuel for the fire to feed on. The Lantern had only magic, which he must set alight. He and Smallbone had discussed it, and he knew he could draw it from the sun. But it was March, and it had snowed yesterday, and the sun, though bright, wasn't nearly hot enough to melt it. Nick's feet ached, his nose was numb, and he was horribly aware of Smallbone—and, oh, yes, the Lantern—watching him.

He couldn't mess this up.

Okay, he thought. *Big fire.*

Nick thought about how the sun felt at midsummer when the air was hot and close and the light on the water shone blindingly bright. He thought about sunspots and solar flares, about the magma that was melted rock.

His feet felt warmer.

Magma reminded him of volcanoes, which reminded him of seeing *The Return of the King* on TV and how scared he'd been when Gollum fell into the Cracks of Doom. Behind his closed lids, he saw the heaving mass of red and black and molten gold, with Gollum sinking into its depths. His body shook with the trembling of the earth beneath his feet. He smelled sulfur.

A familiar voice cut through the crackle of bubbling lava. "That's enough, Foxkin. You can open your eyes now. Land o' Goshen, Foxkin—STOP!"

Nick forced his lids open. It didn't help much, since all he could see was fire.

A freezing load of soft snow landed on his head, sliding icy fingers down his chest and neck. He gasped and shuddered and swiped it out of his eyes. "What was *that* for?"

Smallbone brushed the snow off his hands. His hat looked slightly singed and the hem of his coat was smoldering. "You needed cooling down."

Nick looked up. The Lantern was burning brightly, and the branch it hung on was charred black.

"I'm going to have to move it," Smallbone remarked. "That branch won't hold. When I told you to call fire, Foxkin, I didn't mean a thousand burning suns."

It was the nicest thing Nick had heard Smallbone say. He grinned. "I was thinking of a volcano. I sure lit the hell out of that Lantern, didn't I?"

"You durn near lit the whole tree on fire," Smallbone said drily. "And don't say 'hell'—it ain't manners."

Despite the chill wind, Nick was burning hot and his head felt light. He tumbled off the stone into the snow and lay still. "So, is Smallbone Cove safe now?"

A cool hand felt his forehead and withdrew. "Well, it should slow them down, anyway, which is all to the good. You didn't do bad at all, though you need to work on that Control. When you get your strength back, we'll make a start on the Wall."

Nick smiled weakly and passed out.

Chapter Twenty

✦ ✦ ✦ ✦ ✦ ✦ ✦

It took Nick three days to get his magic back, and that was without using any at all.

"Control, Foxkin," Smallbone told him. "Hardest thing to learn for a trickster like you. It's like spinning a good yarn: you need to know how to stop before you hang yourself."

Ever since Nick had relit the Lantern, Smallbone had been treating him like a real apprentice. Which seemed to mean wasting a great deal of time making sure Nick knew the Rules.

Nick hated the Rules. Nothing about them made any sense. They were confusing and ambiguous and annoyingly restrictive. Apparently every wizard worth his pipe knew them, even though they weren't written down.

"So how do I know if I've broken one?" Nick asked.

Smallbone chuckled. "Same way you know you've walked off the edge of a cliff."

"You *die?*"

"If you're lucky."

"So how do you know what they are?"

"You hark to your elders." The old man sighed. "Go away and take the dogs with you. I've had my belly full of company for one day."

Nick went down to the bookshop. "I want to know more about the Rules," he said.

A good-sized book sailed down the aisle. *Not written down, huh?* Nick thought smugly. *I guess the old coot just doesn't know how to ask.* And then he saw the title: *Glamourama: The Magic of Illusion and Disguise.*

Ever since *Animal You,* Nick had known that the bookshop had its own agenda. It gave him what it wanted him to have, not what he asked for. If it had been a person jerking him around like that, Nick would have been mad, but he couldn't be mad at the bookshop.

Unlike *Animal You,* this book got down to the good stuff right away. Right in the first chapter, he found a spell for making a spoon look like a flower.

Nick went to the kitchen, took a wooden spoon out of the dresser, and said the spell while imagining a flower, just like he was supposed to. The handle of the spoon turned green and the bowl turned pink.

Maybe if he imagined a particular kind of flower. A tulip, maybe. Tulips were easy.

An hour later, all he'd managed was a slightly pointy pink blotch sticking out of a pair of long green splinters.

Disgusted, he left the spoon on the table and started dinner.

When Smallbone came down, he was amused. "Strange color, that. Can't say I've ever met it before, outside a box of Crayola crayons. What was you aiming for, anyways? A sow's ear?"

Nick scowled. "A tulip."

Smallbone sat down. "You're going at this all barse-ackwards, Foxkin. Before you cast a glamour, you got to know how to recognize one." He picked up the spoon and frowned at it. A perfect scarlet tulip bloomed in his hand. He handed it to Nick. It felt like a wooden spoon. "Don't believe your eyes. Look with your magic. The tulip should start to shimmer like water just on the boil. Then you'll see the spoon and the tulip at the same time, only the tulip will be hazy and the spoon will be solid."

Nick stared at the tulip until his eyes stung. "It's not working."

"You're trying too hard," Smallbone said. "Cross your eyes a little and think of nothing." He gave a dry chuckle. "That should come easy."

Nick tried again. The image of the tulip shimmered, brightened, thinned into a scarlet mist around a solid wooden spoon. "I saw it!"

Smallbone shoveled chipped beef onto his plate. "Now remove the glamour so I can see it, too."

Nick concentrated on the scorches on the handle, the slightly lopsided shape of the bowl, the ding on one side. A moment later, a wooden spoon lay on the table.

"Good," said Smallbone. "Do it again."

Next morning Nick woke, as usual, to Tom's whiskers tickling his nose. He opened his eyes, and Tom yawned, displaying a curled pink tongue and all his teeth.

Nick sat up like he'd been spring-loaded.

Don't believe your eyes, Smallbone had said. And Nick didn't. He really didn't.

Nick scooped up the little cat, and Tom mewed indignantly, giving Nick an excellent view of one human tooth, flat as a Chiclet among sharp white thorns.

Still in his nightshirt, Nick ran down to the kitchen.

Mutt and Jeff greeted him with bouncing, slobbering, tail-swishing joy. "Sit!" Nick commanded. Two furry bottoms hit the wooden floor; two sleek black heads cocked sideways; two mouths opened in goofy doggy grins. Nick grabbed Mutt's muzzle, lifted the velvety upper lip, and unfocused his eyes. The tooth next to one long canine was square, crooked, and a little yellow — unmistakably human. Jeff, on the other hand, was all dog.

Nick hadn't thought about Smallbone's other

apprentices for weeks. He'd figured they'd been turned into animals and never restored, but he'd assumed that the old man had then let them go to live out their animal lives in the woods or between the walls — or even given them to Hell Cat to play with, as he was always threatening to do to Nick.

He'd never thought Smallbone would keep them as pets.

Or else, he thought glumly, he just hadn't wanted to think about it.

He didn't really want to now, but he couldn't help it. What about the farm animals? When he groomed Groucho, was he really combing a boy? When he gave Ollie his slops, was he feeding some poor kid potatoes, carrots, and bran mixed with sour milk?

And what about Hell Cat? Would Smallbone have a girl apprentice? Or the hens? It was bad enough that Nick had been shoveling transformed-apprentice dung all this time without worrying about maybe eating an egg laid by one.

He refused to think about milking the goats.

When he got to the barn, he examined every animal

in turn with unfocused eyes, looking for nonstandard body parts. As far as he could tell, the barn animals were all just animals, except for Ollie, whose human ear lay small and flat against his massive head.

Nick gave the nearest hay bale a good solid kick. Now that he knew the truth, he couldn't pretend he didn't. He had to turn the apprentices back. It's what he'd want them to do, if their positions were reversed. Tom and Mutt and Ollie were human beings, and nobody had asked them whether they wanted to be animals or not.

Besides, the bookshop seemed to want him to.

❧ ❧ ❧

Breakfast was a tense meal. Nick was so agitated he turned the fire up too high and burned the fried eggs black. Smallbone threatened to turn him into a cabbage and boil him for dinner, and Nick asked if he was a cannibal, and Smallbone said he might be if Nick didn't make him something fit to eat right soon. This time Nick broke the yolks, but Smallbone ate them anyway, then went upstairs, grumbling like a thunderstorm.

Nick left the dishes to the animals and went to the barn.

"I know about Smallbone's apprentices," he said, "and I'll turn them back. I just want to know if it's the same spell as the one in *Animal You.*"

It wasn't. The new book was called *Curses and How to Lift Them.* The spell it gave him wasn't particularly complicated and it didn't call for a lot of energy.

Good for practicing your Control.

There'd been a lot of rain the past few days, and the snow had been fretted down to dirty lumps and tattered patches of white scattered across the muddy barnyard. Nick put on a sou'wester and whistled to the dogs, who exploded out the door as soon as he'd opened it, ears flapping wildly. He scooped Tom off the rocker and was stowing him in one oversize pocket when Hell Cat jumped down from her perch over the stove and gave Nick her blue-eyed glare. She'd turned into a spitting ball of claws and teeth when he tried to examine her earlier, and he didn't think she was anything but a cat. But he didn't want to make any more mistakes.

"I'm going to turn these guys back," he said, feeling foolish. "You can come if you want to."

Hell Cat's tail shivered, and she trotted past Nick and toward the barn.

Nick closed the door and followed thoughtfully.

The barn was warm and shadowy and familiar. Nick brought out his chalk and string, drew a pentagram, and settled inside it.

According to *Curses and How to Lift Them,* animal-transformation spells were the easiest kind of curse to lift — for another wizard, anyway. *A living thing wants to return to its natural shape. All you have to do is create the conditions for that to happen.*

The spell was short and repetitive, easy to learn. Nick shut his eyes and started chanting, carefully feeding magic into the words bit by bit. Control didn't give him the rush of full-out spell casting, but it was oddly satisfying, like executing a perfect layup. As Nick chanted the last phrase, he felt his magical basketball swish right through the hoop.

There was a moment of silence, and then the barn erupted in panic-stricken squawking, baaing, and screaming.

Screaming?

Nick opened his eyes and saw a little kid in short pants and a frilly shirt sitting on a hay bale. Ginger-red hair the color of Tom's fur stuck out around his head, and he was howling like a strong wind.

While Nick was still taking this in, a hard body cannoned into him. "Grr!" the attacker said fiercely. "Bark! Bark!"

Nick squirmed, turned, and shoved him off. The boy who had been Mutt fell over sideways and floundered. Before Nick could get up, a second apprentice jumped on his back. This one knew how to fight. Teeth fastened themselves on Nick's ear and something sharp burned a line of fire across his cheek and lip.

At Beaton Middle School, kids got into fights all the time. They windmilled at one another with their fists and rolled on the ground. When one got a bloody nose or started to cry, most of them accepted that the fight was over, except for the inevitable trip to the principal's office.

Nick wasn't most kids. Nick never cried. Nick went berserk.

Twisting like an eel, he grabbed the apprentice who had scratched him by a fistful of cloth, and cocked back his arm for a good, hard, satisfying punch.

A pair of furious blue eyes glared up at him. They belonged to a skinny girl in a shapeless cotton dress and an even more shapeless gray sweater.

She showed her teeth and hissed. "Evil wizard!"

"Hell Cat?"

Nick dropped his hand and backed up a step. His mom had always told him he should never, never, not for any reason, hit girls or little kids—not even if they started it. He had promised he wouldn't, he never had, and he wasn't going to begin now, even though he really wanted to.

He could, however, set the record straight. "I am *not* an evil wizard!"

Hell Cat smoothed her sweater, turned up her nose,

and stalked off to sit by Tom. If she'd still had a tail, she would have wrapped it around her feet.

Mutt crawled up to Nick and bumped his head against Nick's leg. "Arf!"

It was then that Nick realized that he hadn't given any thought to what he would do with the apprentices once he'd freed them.

A rustle drew his attention to the pigpen, where a boy was leaning over the rails. He was older than Nick, maybe sixteen, with a body like a barrel and a face like a cheese thatched with yellow hair.

"You must be Ollie," Nick said.

The boy who had been the finest Yorkshire on the coast of Maine scratched his belly and blushed like a sunset. "Dunno. Sounds familiar, anyways. Who the Sam Hill are you?"

At least, Nick thought, *this one can talk like a human.* "Smallbone calls me Foxkin."

Hell Cat spat. "You must be evil. He's teaching you magic. He wouldn't teach you if you were good. I'm good, and he didn't teach me."

She was frowning at him as fiercely as Smallbone

ever did. Nick looked from Tom, who was smearing tears and snot everywhere, trying to wash his face like a cat, to Mutt, who was curled up on the floor, whimpering, while Jeff sniffed him over curiously.

"What's the *matter* with you guys?" Nick shouted. "I'm the good guy here. I *rescued* you. Why can't you just say thank you and go away?"

"Evil wizard!" Hell Cat snarled.

"Meow," Tom said.

"I'm hungry," Ollie grunted.

Nick stalked out of the barn.

⚜ ⚜ ⚜

Nick checked out the damage to his face in the bathroom mirror. He looked like he'd been in a cat fight.

Nothing like this had happened in "The Wizard Outwitted."

It was, as Smallbone would say, a jeezly mess.

Smallbone! He'd forgotten all about him! What was the old man going to say when he found out one of his dogs and both his cats were now people, not to mention his prize pig? Maybe if Nick just left them in the barn for a while, they'd all go away.

In the meantime, he had to start lunch.

Nick cast a glamour on his face to hide the scratches and went back out to the kitchen.

He was chopping onions for bean soup when Smallbone appeared, ferreted around in the fridge, and emerged with a cold drumstick in one hand and a glowing purple vial in the other.

"I'm eating upstairs today," he said.

Nick bent his head over the knife. "Okay."

The old man stomped to the door, stopped, and turned around. "By the way. That's a decent illusion you've cast on them scratches. For a beginner."

"Thanks," Nick said in a strangled voice.

"Your timing might have been better, what with Fidelou howling at the door and all," Smallbone went on with suspicious calm. "Now you turned them apprentices back, you got the same problem I had, which is what to do with a set of gormy nincompoops not worth the fire to cook their soup."

Nick looked up. "Then you're not mad?"

"The hell I ain't. I had 'em squared away all right and tight, with comfortable, easy, useful lives. If I wanted a passel of kids around the house, I wouldn't have transformed 'em in the first place. The problem with you is, you got power, but you ain't got sense. You made this jeezly foul-up, you fix it. Get 'em off the premises. I don't care how. You got three days, starting now."

Nick began to feel sick. "What happens if I can't?"

Smallbone's smile bared a tumbled graveyard of teeth. "I get rid of 'em for you."

Nick felt sicker. "Promise me you won't hurt them."

Smallbone gave him a sharp look, then shrugged. "You broke the spell. The Rule is, I can't touch 'em until and unless you fail to finish the rescue. So I guess you better get cracking."

⚜ ⚜ ⚜

Nick didn't have a plan or even the beginnings of one, but feeding the apprentices seemed like it would be a good place to start. So he heated up yesterday's oatmeal, dumped it in a bucket, and took it and some tin bowls and spoons out to the barn.

The apprentices were gone. Nick felt a sinking in his stomach, followed by something oddly like relief when he saw Mutt and Ollie and Tom huddled up with Jeff by the pigpen. Hell Cat was sitting by Groucho's manger, flexing and stretching her fingers with concentrated attention. When she saw Nick, she whisked her hands into the pockets of her baggy sweater.

"I brought you something to eat." Nick took the lid off the bucket. "Oatmeal."

Hell Cat scowled. "I want some milk."

"This is what there is," Nick said. "Take it or leave it."

Hell Cat shot him an offended look and turned her back.

Tom, Ollie, and Mutt weren't as picky. They came out of the pen and gathered around hopefully. Ollie and Mutt stuck their faces in the bowls and slurped. Tom tried to lap with his human tongue and got oatmeal all over his face.

Nick went to see if Thalia had a little milk left in her.

She did. Nick filled Hell Cat's bowl and held it out to her. "Here's your milk."

Hell Cat ignored him.

Nick gritted his teeth. "You probably won't believe this, but I know how you feel. I've woken up not knowing how many arms and legs I have or what I want for breakfast. I'd probably be a rat right now if I hadn't turned myself back."

Hell Cat growled. "That's because you're an evil wizard."

"And you're a snotty little brat!"

He had tried not to shout, but he'd failed. The boys lifted startled oatmeal-streaked faces. Tom started crying again.

Nick took a deep breath. "I'm sorry I yelled," he said, trying to sound like he meant it. "I'm sorry about the whole thing. I just wanted to help." That, at least, was true.

"You want to *help* us?" Ollie squealed.

"Smallbone was wrong to turn you into animals. I wanted to fix it." Nick sighed. "Guess I'm a numb-brain, huh?"

Nobody disagreed.

"Smallbone's going to kill us when he finds out," Hell Cat remarked. "You, too, probably."

"No, he won't," Nick said.

"How do you know?" Mutt asked.

"Because I'm still alive."

Everybody went very still. Nick looked up. Their faces were frozen, wide-eyed, white with fear. "What's up with you guys? I mean, it was totally evil of him to turn you into animals and keep you as pets—that's why I turned you back. But it's not like he beat you or starved you or fed you to the coyotes. You got to admit, the old man's not so bad, for an evil wizard."

Hell Cat spat. "Not so bad! Now I *know* you're evil!"

"Quit saying that!"

"Why? It's true."

Mutt was sitting with Jeff, cross-legged. He'd found a few words. "Devil!" he barked. "Evil wizard! Mean!"

"Mutt's right," Ollie said. "Last thing I remember, he told me he was going to make me into sausages come fall."

"That doesn't mean anything," Nick said. "He's always threatening to turn me into a slug and salt me, but he never does."

Ollie grunted skeptically. "How about this, then? He had this stick he kept by the fire, used to beat me all by itself. If I forgot to sweep under the stove or didn't scrub the pots just right, or took a piece of cheese more than I was allowed, it'd fly up and larrup me until I was black-and-blue."

Nick's mouth fell open. "But—"

"He set a spell on me once," Hell Cat said. "Made me scrub nonstop for nearly two days. When he took it off, I hit him with a frying pan. That's when he turned me into a cat."

Nick looked from face to frightened face. They were telling the truth. "Maybe he's changed," he said weakly. "I mean, he's crabby and all that, but he's never actually hurt me, if you don't count the spider thing. I've got warm clothes and enough to eat. He carves little wooden animals, for the love of Mike."

The apprentices exchanged looks. *He's lying,* the looks said. *He's crazy. He's an evil wizard.*

"Listen," Nick said earnestly. "He took real good care of you when you were animals. He liked you. Ollie, he played ball with you. Mutt, you were always following him around and wagging your tail and asking to be petted. You liked him. You all did."

"I didn't," Hell Cat said smugly. "I remember. I scratched him every chance I got."

Nick stood up and brushed straw from his jeans. "You can see for yourselves if you don't believe me. Come down to the house and have supper with us. It's fried mackerel and peas and mashed potatoes."

"And if we don't?" Hell Cat asked.

"I'll bring you sandwiches," Nick said. "If I remember."

"What about Smallbone?" Ollie said anxiously.

"He won't hurt you, I promise. Supper's at six — that's just after sunset. See you then."

☙ ☙ ☙

Nick was frying mackerel when Smallbone came down to the kitchen that evening. He took in the extra chairs, the steaming heap of golden-brown fish keeping warm at the back of the stove, the huge bowl of mashed potatoes, the economy-size package of frozen peas, and munched his jaws thoughtfully.

Tom scampered up to him, meowing in a little-boy

voice. The old man's beard twitched, and he reached down and stroked the ginger curls as if the boy were still a cat.

Nick let go his breath and started putting out the meal. It looked like Smallbone intended to keep his promise. There was some use to those Rules of his after all.

When the clock struck six, the back door opened. Hell Cat walked in.

"Evening, Hell Cat," Smallbone said. "You joining us?"

Her eyes narrowed. "You got a problem with that, Evil Wizard?"

"Only if you lick your plate. Foxkin, young Hell Cat needs a glass of milk. And a napkin."

It was a quiet meal. Hell Cat concentrated on drinking from a glass, eating with a knife and fork, and pretending Smallbone didn't exist. She managed pretty well until he moved to the rocking chair and Tom crawled up in his lap. She nearly choked on her potatoes when the old man put an arm around the little boy, lit his pipe, blew a smoke ring over his head, and rocked.

Hell Cat took a hasty gulp of milk, licked her hand, flushed beet red, and stalked into the bathroom, where she turned on the taps full blast.

Smallbone set the sleeping Tom gently on the rug.

"This place is like a jeezly nursery school," he grumbled. "I've half a mind to turn you into—"

The door opened and Jeff trotted in, tracking in lumps of sticky mud. Behind him was Mutt, a little unsteady on his pins, looking hangdog.

"Jeff's hungry," he muttered.

"I see you're looking yourself again," said Smallbone amiably. "Foxkin, you better heat up them taters. They're gone gluey cold."

Mutt wouldn't sit at the table, so Nick put his plate down on the floor next to Jeff's. He was a messy eater, but at least he was using his fingers now.

After a while, Hell Cat came out of the bathroom, pink faced and clean, her dark braid trailing water down the back of her baggy sweater. "I'm going to sleep," she announced to the room. "In a bed. Like a person."

"Take the first room to the left at the top of the

stairs," Smallbone said. "It's got a bed and a mattress. There's blankets in the bureau."

When Nick got back from doing the evening chores, Smallbone was gone and Mutt, Jeff, and Tom were asleep on the hearth rug in a pile. Nick went upstairs, put on his nightshirt, and climbed into bed.

He found himself missing Tom. No, not Tom, but the little orange cat who had slept on his pillow every night.

Apparently, Tom missed him, too, because it wasn't long before Nick heard insistent mewing outside the door. Nick put the pillow over his head and told himself Tom would go away if he just ignored him. Eventually, the mewing stopped, but Nick didn't fall asleep for a long time.

Chapter Twenty-One

✦ ✦ ✦ ✦ ✦ ✦ ✦

As the Spring Equinox approached, the seal folk of Smallbone Cove became exercised over the question of Walking the Bounds. Opinions varied wildly. On one side, there were those who agreed with Miss Lily and Miss Rachel that the Bounds should be Walked. On the other were those, like Saul and his friends, who were willing to see the Sentries come down if it meant they could fish farther out or even leave Smallbone Cove completely. Between them were the farmers and merchants who couldn't see the point of tromping fifteen or so miles through the mud and rain to perform a ritual nobody remembered for Sentries that weren't even working.

Miss Rachel didn't have any patience with this

kind of thinking. "It doesn't matter if we remember or not. We promised we'd do it, and we will. As for the ritual, perhaps the magic will take the intention for the deed. It's worth a try."

At dawn on the morning of the Equinox, all the Smallbones Lily and Miss Rachel could persuade or bully gathered in front of the white clapboard church. There weren't many—a few farmers, like Ruth and Naomi from the Smallbone Cove Goat and Dairy Farm; shopkeepers like Bildad and Zilpah Smallbone, who ran Three Bags Full Knitting; Joshua from Kites 'N Chimes; and Zery. Also Mr. Micah, who taught grades four through seven at the Smallbone Cove School, and Eb. Ruth and Naomi had brought their daughter Sarah, who was in kindergarten. And Dinah, of course. Nothing on earth would have kept Dinah away.

Miss Rachel was waiting for them in front of the church. To her sorrow, she wouldn't be coming with them, her chair not having been built for cross-country wheeling. There had been a path once, all the way around the borders, but most of it was as neglected as the ritual.

"Well," said Lily as they all stood looking up at the steeple, where the Weathervane pointed immovably east. "Here we are."

"What do we do now?" Ruth asked.

Everybody turned to Miss Rachel.

"We sing," she said. "There was always singing, I remember."

"What kind of singing?" Mr. Micah asked.

Miss Rachel sighed. "I don't know. I've thought and thought, and I've looked in every book I can think of, and I simply can't remember. I was only a little child when Mam stopped going."

There was an awkward pause. "Anybody know any songs about the wind?" Lily asked.

They tried "Oh, the Wind and the Rain"—or at least the two verses of it everybody knew—and "Blow the Man Down," because Zery said it sounded aggressive, and they wanted the wind to blow Fidelou down, didn't they?

The Weathervane didn't budge, even though there was a stiff wind blowing due north.

"It's completely broke," Eb pointed out. "The old

man never said we could fix 'em. He said we could make 'em stronger."

Which was true enough, but still, their total lack of success was discouraging.

They left Miss Rachel and headed west on the paved road that looped through Smallbone Cove, past Evil Wizard Books, looming tall and dark behind its empty parking lot, and followed a muddy, rutted path to the mouth of the Stream.

The ice had finally broken up, and the Stream was flowing again, though not with any real energy. The place where the fresh water flowed into the Reach was clogged with wood and clumps of leaves from upstream. Zery, Naomi, and Ruth waded in with their high waterproof boots to clean the debris away.

As they moved out into the current, Dinah watched with a mixture of dread and fascination. Her nerves were screaming, *Danger! Pain! Terror!* But her scientist's mind was watching to see what would happen as they got closer to the middle of the Stream. She was relieved, of course, when the bottom got too deep for wading well before the danger point. But she was still curious.

"I suppose we should sing a song here, too?" Bildad asked when the trio was back on shore.

They tried "Row, Row, Row Your Boat," and Mr. Micah recited a Robert Louis Stevenson poem that began "Smooth it glides upon its travel, / Here a wimple, there a gleam." Dinah thought the poem was very pretty but not remotely something that would make water want to rise up and swamp attacking enemies.

This wasn't going to work.

It was clear that everybody else in the little group was feeling the same way. Some of the farmers drifted back toward town, along with Joshua and most of the shopkeepers. Those who were left plodded along the path with their heads down, not talking.

It started to rain.

After a long, muddy walk, they reached the county road and turned east, still following the Stream. At the Stone Bridge, Bildad and Zilpah peeled off to rest and get dry at Zilpah's cousin's house. Ruth was carrying Sarah, and Dinah knew they'd lose her and Naomi, too, as soon as the procession got near their farm. She wondered if everybody else would go with them.

The Wall began where the Stream dove down under the county road and ran in a shallow curve all the way down to the shore, where it disappeared into the waters of the Reach. There was no obvious place to stop and sing. They stood by the road and argued for a bit, then decided they'd walk to the end of the Wall and sing there, stopping by the Lantern on the way.

As they squelched along the muddy path, Lily fell back by Dinah. "Your dad and I were thinking we could have some hot chocolate at Ruth and Naomi's before we finish the circuit. It's a long walk and everybody's cold and—"

"We can't do that," Dinah burst out. "If you're going to conduct an experiment, you have to complete it. It's bad enough we don't know what songs to sing. We can't stop and come back when we feel like it."

Lily sighed. "I hear what you're saying, sweetie, but we might have to. My feet hurt. And Sarah's too young to be out in the cold so long."

They were nearly to the turnoff to the goat farm when Mr. Micah, who was walking in front with Eb, gave a yell.

There was a gap in the Wall.

Dinah's stomach fell into her boots. The Wall was down! It was inconceivable—like the library burning or the Weathervane falling off the church steeple. Mr. Micah was wringing his hands, Sarah was crying, and Joshua and Zery and Naomi were trying to fill the gap with the stones tumbled below the breach. But the stones slipped from their hands or rolled out of place.

"It's no use," Lily said. "We need the song. Do you think if one of us ran to Evil Wizard Books and begged, Smallbone would tell us what it is?"

Mr. Micah, looking desperate, said he could try, but Eb's opinion was that it would be a waste of time.

Mr. Micah looked relieved.

"Maybe," Dinah said, "it doesn't matter what we sing. Maybe we just have to really mean it."

Lily looked around at the group. "Anybody know a song about rocks?"

There was a long silence broken only by the sound of rain plopping into mud, and then Sarah started to sing. She couldn't carry a tune and she was singing more to herself than anyone else, as little kids do, but Dinah recognized the song. She'd sung it herself, playing with the other kids in the schoolyard when she was small.

"Build the stones, build the stones,
High, high, high.
Pile them and stack them
Up to the sky."

There was a game that went with it, involving making piles of rocks and kicking them over. One team was the wolves and one was the builders, and it all involved a lot of squealing and rolling around on the ground and getting your clothes dirty.

"Pack them with earth
And wedge them with moss.
Kick the wolf in the ribs
And show him who's boss."

The little girl sang the song through once and started again. Dinah joined her at "High, high, high."

At "Pile them and stack them," the stones began

to move, slowly and awkwardly because stones in a good stone wall aren't really shaped for rolling. Dinah could see them trying to pile and stack themselves, but something was preventing them. She moved closer. Something dark and curved and tapered—a feather, lying on the bare earth where the Wall should be.

By now, the adults had seen it, too. Dinah could hear them behind her, arguing about what to do, all but Mr. Micah, who was singing along.

The thought of stepping in among all those grinding, creeping stones was terrifying. But the thought of coyotes taking over Smallbone Cove was more terrifying still. Dinah squared her shoulders and, singing, danced as close as she could, leaned over, and blew the feather into the woods. Then somebody grabbed her by the waist and lifted her out of the way as the stones rushed in to fill the gap with a thundering crash.

"And show him who's boss!" Sarah shrilled, and it was done.

There was a certain amount of crying and scolding and hugging as the adults reacted to what had just happened, and then they all headed off toward the Lantern.

"But it's all so *silly*," Ruth said. "Can you imagine the Evil Wizard Smallbone expecting grown men and women to dance around singing nursery rhymes four times a year? I can't."

Dinah had been thinking about this. "But they weren't grown men and women," she said. "They were seals, or at least they had been not too long ago. I don't know how turning animals into people works, but I bet there was a learning curve."

"Besides," Mr. Micah said, "can you think of a better way to make sure everybody knows the words to something, whether they know how to read or not?"

"Fine," said Lily. "Sarah, do you know a song about fire?"

Sarah buried her face in her mother's shoulder.

"Sarah," Dinah said, "can you play Roaring Fire with me?"

The little girl nodded.

When they got to the Lantern Oak, the adults made a circle around the two girls, who sat cross-legged on the very rock where Nick had stood to light the

Lantern a week earlier. Properly speaking, Roaring Fire was a jump-rope rhyme, but there was a clapping game that went with it, too.

> *"Roaring fire, pretty light,*
> *How many wolves have you burnt tonight?*
> *One, two, three, four . . ."*

The first time, they only got to six before Sarah messed up, but by the third time, twenty wolves got incinerated, or at least singed. The flame in the Lantern leaped and flared before settling down to its usual steady glow.

Zery cheered and hugged Lily. Eb hugged Mr. Micah.

By the time the little procession got back to the center of town, everybody was wet and muddy and almost too tired to put one foot in front of the other. They'd had plenty of time, however, to figure out the songs for the Wind and the Stream.

Adults and children stood in a group in front of the church, looked up at the Weathervane, and sang:

"The wind blows south and north;
It blows both west and east.
Come, wind, and keep harm far from us,
Safe from man and beast."

Saul, who was hanging out on the wharf, nearly bust something laughing at them.

The Weathervane didn't move. Sarah burst into tears again.

"We should take her home," Ruth said over her daughter's head.

"You go," Naomi said. "I'm going back to the Stream."

Everybody groaned. "We were already there!" Zery exclaimed. "We cleared out all those leaves! We even sang to it!"

Lily sighed. "We didn't sing the right song. Micah, you game?"

Mr. Micah nodded.

"I'm coming, too," Dinah announced, and then Sarah said she wanted to go with Dinah, and of course Ruth had to carry her, and Zery wasn't about to be the only one to flake out. So they all traipsed out to the Stream, moving a lot more slowly than they had earlier, lined up along the banks, and sang:

"The Stream runs free
Down to the sea
And runs out into the bay.
It rises up high,
It ripples down low,
And it sweeps the pirates away."

The Stream gave no indication that it had heard, but Dinah didn't care. It was the Spring Equinox, and for the first time in years, Smallbone Covers had walked the Bounds, just as they were supposed to do. The Stream ran clear, the Lantern burned steady, and — most important of all — the Wall ran from the road to the sea without a gap. And the Smallbone Covers had mended it all by themselves.

As far as Dinah was concerned, the experiment had been a success.

Chapter Twenty-Two

+ + + + + + +

The sun was up when Nick woke. He was tired and weighed down with the feeling of vague dread he used to get on exam days. For a moment he didn't know why, and then he remembered the apprentices and groaned.

It didn't improve his mood when he opened his door and found Tom curled up on the threshold, fast asleep. When he stepped over him, the little boy woke, stretched, yawned lavishly, and meowed.

Two more days, Nick thought. *I wish I was dead.*

Downstairs, the sink was full of dirty dishes. A note lay on the kitchen table, held down with a wooden spoon. Nick unfolded it and read:

It's the first day of spring. I'm going into town to see if them blubberheads are keeping their part of the bargain. I'd bring you along, but you'll have your hands full. Clock's ticking, Foxkin. Don't forget.

Nick got the bacon and was beating up a bowl of eggs when Hell Cat trotted in, looking perfectly at home in a pair of overalls and a shirt she'd found somewhere. Her dark hair was tied back with a red bandanna. No longing for the good old days of kitty-hood for Hell Cat, no siree.

Leaving her to oversee breakfast, Nick put on his sou'wester and squelched out to the barn to see if he could lure Ollie into the house.

The usual early-morning chorus of bleats and brays was replaced by munching and the occasional contented cluck. Judging by the rustling and the gentle rain of high-quality straw from above, Ollie was taking care of the chores.

"Breakfast's ready," Nick called out. "Better go get some before the others scoff it all."

Ollie's head peered down from the loft. "So they're

okay? Smallbone didn't turn 'em into mice or any-thing?"

"They're fine. Hell Cat's making bacon." Ollie frowned, and Nick felt a pang of guilt. "Sorry, Ollie."

The former pig clambered down the ladder. "You bet you are! Cats can't cook. She'll burn it or forget to pour the grease off, sure as apples." And he thundered out of the barn.

Nick milked the goats, cleaned the pens, and cast the egg-gathering spell. When he got back to the kitchen, Ollie was kneeling by the fire, toasting bread on a long fork with Mutt, Tom, and Jeff gathered around him, watching eagerly. Hell Cat sat at the table, eating bacon with her bare ankles primly crossed.

Ollie pulled the toast off the fork, pushing Jeff's muzzle out of the way. "Eggs!" he exclaimed when he saw Nick's basket. "Toss 'em here and I'll scramble 'em up. Mutt and Jeff ate the old ones. They was tough anyways."

All his life, Nick had considered any eggs that weren't rotten or burned good eggs. Ollie's scrambled eggs were more than not burned. They were tender and buttery, like fluffy yellow clouds. He took another helping and wondered why Smallbone had turned anybody who could cook like that into a pig.

While he was eating, Mutt, who had consented to sit at the table, yelped suddenly.

Nick stared at him. He'd gone as pale as a fish's belly and was gazing at the kitchen calendar as if he'd seen a ghost. "What?" Nick said. "It's the first day of spring."

"The year," Mutt quavered. "Is that the right year?"

Ollie was staring, too, his mouth opening and shutting noiselessly, his wooden spoon dripping egg on the floor.

"Golly," said Hell Cat. "It's the twenty-first century!"

Nick looked from one strained face to the next. "What do you mean, it's the twenty-first century? When else should it be?"

There was an uncomfortable silence, and then Mutt said, "I ain't got much schooling, but my ma learned me how to cipher. If that there calendar is right, I reckon it's about two hundred and forty years since the old man turned me into a dog."

Nick stared at him. He looked scared but not crazy. "You don't look it."

Sensing that something was wrong, Jeff came and put his chin on his former packmate's leg. "I still feel like I'm fourteen," Mutt said, rubbing Jeff's ears. "But what if them two hundred and forty years creep up and jump on me all at once? Dogs don't think about things like that."

Nick didn't want to think about it, either. "You'll get used to it," he said uncomfortably.

"Not sure I want to." Mutt sighed heavily. "I wish you hadn't turned me back."

"I don't," Hell Cat announced.

"I don't, either," Ollie said. "Being a pig isn't all that interesting. Slop is slop."

"Meow," Tom said, and tried to jump up into Nick's lap. He bumped his head on the chair. As he started to wail, Nick knew what he had to do. He didn't know how. But if he could pull it off, it would solve half his apprentice problem. All it would take was lots of Will and Confidence. Plus the right book.

He stood. "You guys clean up. I got something I need to do."

"What's that?" Hell Cat asked suspiciously.

"You'll find out," Nick said, and left.

The bookshop looked bleak and gloomy. Nick took up his favorite position and folded his arms. "I did what you wanted," he said. "Okay, I wanted to do it, too, and I admit I didn't think it all the way through. Now they're in the way and everything's kind of a mess. Smallbone needs me to get rid of them, and Mutt wants to be a dog again, and Tom doesn't even know he's not a cat. So maybe you could help me turn them back?"

There was a long silence. Nick folded his arms tighter and bit his lip. If the books were testing his patience, he'd be patient. If they were testing his Control, he'd be controlled. If they were testing his persistence, then he'd go back in the shelves and examine every title until he found what he needed. He was a wizard, and that, apparently, was what wizards did.

A palm-size shadow flew down the aisle and slid onto the table. Nick picked it up and took it over to the counter so he could see it in the light. It wasn't really a book at all — just pages folded between thin wooden covers tied shut with black tape. It was handwritten, not printed, and the first page read:

THE ARTE OF TRANSFORMATIOUN REVEAL'D
by Zachariah Smallbone, Wizard
Boston, 1755

Nick stared. Using Smallbone's own spells from Smallbone's own book felt like reading his diary or using his toothbrush or — well, he didn't know exactly what it felt like, except wrong. Still, the book had come to him and the spells would certainly work. Besides, he was curious.

He sat at the counter and started to read.

Some time later, he heard a noise and looked up to find a tray on the counter beside him. It held a plate with a sandwich and a cup of strong tea. Nick ate and drank and went back to reading. When the light began to fade, he lit a lamp, almost without thinking about it, and read until Hell Cat appeared and told him that if he wanted supper, he was going to have to come and get it.

To his surprise, Smallbone was there, eating spaghetti with homemade sauce and looking as harmless as an evil wizard in an ancient black coat and a bashed-in top hat could look. Mutt had retreated to the fire with Jeff and Tom, but Hell Cat and Ollie sat across from their former master, looking wary but determined.

Nick sat down. Ollie's sauce was delicious.

The grandfather clock struck midnight as Nick finally finished reading Smallbone's book. His head was spinning with words and ideas and magic he didn't really understand. But he knew enough to do and say what he must to give Tom and Mutt what they wanted.

Now he just had to do it.

⚜ ⚜ ⚜

Only Hell Cat and Ollie were in the kitchen when Nick came down next morning, a lot later than usual.

"Mutt said he'd do the chores," Hell Cat informed him. "He took Jeff and Tom with him."

Nick stared at her blankly. Between nerves and strange dreams, he wasn't at his best.

"You need breakfast," Ollie said. It was flapjacks with wild-blueberry syrup, and when Nick had eaten and drunk a cup of coffee, he pulled on his Christmas sweater and a pair of duck boots. Smallbone's book was back on its shelf. He knew the spell now. He could either cast it or he couldn't. At this point, the book wouldn't help.

Ollie wished him good luck.

It had rained overnight, and the barn was veiled in a damp gray mist. Mud sucked at Nick's boots as he walked across the meadow. He knew how to clear the mist and dry the path, but he didn't. He needed all the magic he had in him for what he was about to do.

Out in the barn, Nick found Mutt and Jeff and Tom curled against the goat pen in a heap. Tom and Jeff were asleep, and Mutt was pretending.

Nick swept the floor, took out his pentagram-drawing kit, and carefully inscribed a pentagram. Then he sat down inside.

"Okay, Mutt," he said. "I'm ready."

Mutt got up, lifted Tom in his arms, and put him in the pentagram, careful not to step on the lines. The little boy woke and crawled into Nick's lap, making a soft growling noise like he was trying to purr.

Nick lifted his hand and concentrated.

He'd never done a spell this complicated before. Elemental Magic was basically suggesting to fire that it burn, to water that it flow, to earth that it support, to air that it move in exactly the way the elemental wizard wanted it to. Every transformation spell he'd cast had been meant to return something to its natural state. This spell went against nature, bending bone and dispersing mass, going against the natural course of biology and evolution to turn an actual human boy into an actual cat.

I'm Nick Reynaud, he thought. *I'm an evil wizard. I can do anything I want to do. And I want to do this.*

The words of the transformation spell hurt his

mouth as if he'd been eating rocks and thorns. They tried to stifle him, leaving Tom a boy with a cat's head or maybe a shapeless bag of fur and guts. But Nick spoke on, determined. And when he finished, sweating and dizzy, a little orange cat was draped across his leg, purring like a motorboat.

Nick picked Tom up and set him outside the pentagram, careful not to smudge the lines. The little cat sneezed, bounded over to Groucho's stall, and jumped through the rails.

Nick took a deep breath. "Your turn, Mutt."

The former dog was backed up against the goat pen with his arms around Jeff's neck, white as a sheet. "I changed my mind."

Relief swept through Nick even as he said, "It's a one-time offer, Mutt. What about those two hundred and forty years?"

"Don't matter. That was the scariest thing I ever did see. I'd sooner get used to thinking than go through that. Besides, Jeff don't care, do you, boy?"

Jeff lifted his muzzle and licked Mutt's neck and ear.

With the energy of a boy who suddenly discovers he's not going to have to walk over hot coals a second time, Nick rubbed out the pentagram, extracted Tom from Groucho's manger, and went back to the house with Mutt and Jeff.

Mutt still looked spooked, but he perked right up when Ollie handed him a bowl that smelled richly of butter and the sea. "There was salt fish," Ollie said to Nick. "So I made chowder. I hope you don't mind."

The chowder was the best Nick had ever eaten—even better than Eb's. By the time Nick had finished it, he knew what to do with Ollie, and maybe Mutt and Hell Cat as well.

The apprentices, when he told them, were not enthusiastic.

"Take us to Smallbone Cove?" Hell Cat sneered. "Are you crazy? Those fellers hate us."

"No, they don't," Nick argued, hoping this was true. "Why should they?"

"I dunno," Mutt said. "Smallbone never had much good to say about the Cove Smallbones. Said they're a bunch of lazy cusses."

"He said the same about you," Nick said, disgusted.

He went upstairs, went to bed, and slept the rest of the day and all night. When he woke up, a little orange cat was curled on his chest and the delicious smell of sausages was perfuming the air.

Downstairs, Mutt was sucking his fingers and Hell Cat was licking her plate. She stopped when she saw Nick. Mutt didn't.

"We've decided," she announced. "We'll go to Smallbone Cove. If we hate it, we can always run away."

※ ※ ※

They couldn't leave immediately, though Nick wanted them to. Hell Cat said, rather snottily, that nobody was going to hire anybody who looked and smelled as bad as Ollie and Mutt, so there was a fight over that, and then Ollie and Mutt had to wash.

While they were getting ready, Smallbone took Jeff up to the tower with him.

"He should be with me," Mutt said almost tearfully when he came out of the bathroom and found Jeff gone. "We belong together. Mutt and Jeff."

"I'll bring him to visit," Nick promised. "Tom, too."

The apprentices exchanged a look. Mutt knelt down and scratched Tom behind the ears, then marched out the back door and toward the path to Smallbone Cove without looking back. The rest of them had to run to catch up.

Nick was surprised that the apprentices knew the way as well as he did, and said so.

"It ain't changed all that much," Mutt said.

"Where're we going?" Ollie wanted to know. "Nate's?"

"Nate's?"

"Clam shack down by the wharf. Best fried clams I ever ate."

"Well, it's Eb's now," Nick said. "The chowder's good, but not as good as yours. I'm taking you to Smallbone Cove Mercantile, so you can meet Lily."

"Who's Lily?" Hell Cat asked.

"You'll see."

When they reached the porch of the Mercantile, Hell Cat made a small unhappy noise, almost like a mew. To Nick's astonishment, Mutt and Ollie took her hands. She let them.

Nick opened the door and they all went in.

It was warm inside and smelled of sugar and chocolate. Lily looked up from laying out a batch of chocolate-chip cookies in the bakery case. "Well, hello, Foxkin. Who are your friends?"

This was it. Nick put on his brightest smile. "They're old apprentices of Smallbone's. They were under a spell, but I released them. I thought you—not you personally, but Smallbone Cove generally—could take them in."

Lily turned a deep, angry red. "You've got a nerve, Foxkin, waltzing in here with things in the state they're in! If Smallbone wants his spare apprentices housed and fed, he'll have to come and ask himself."

Nick thought quickly. "It's not a favor for Smallbone. He just wants to get rid of them. Come on, Lily. They hate him even more than you do. That's got to count for something. Besides, they don't have anywhere else to go."

Mutt took a shy step forward. "Pleased to meet you, ma'am. I'm Mutt. I used to be a dog."

Lily's lips twitched. "Lily Smallbone," she said.

Ollie stuck out a large pale hand. "My name's Ollie. I was a pig."

Lily shook the hand. "Hello, Ollie." She turned to Hell Cat, who was hanging back, scowling. "And what were you, honey?"

Hell Cat folded her arms across her skinny chest. "My name's not Honey. It's Hell Cat."

"Hell Cat. I see." Lily examined them with a business-like air. "So, what can you fellers do?"

"I can cook," Ollie offered.

"Ollie's real good," Nick put in helpfully. "Best fish chowder I ever ate. Magical, really. And Mutt here can get along with anybody."

Mutt gave Lily a brilliant and slightly goofy smile. She blinked. "That's nice. What's your work experience?"

In the next ten minutes, Nick learned a great deal about the apprentices. Ollie and Mutt were orphans and had run away and ended up somehow at Smallbone's, just like Nick. Mutt had worked for a greengrocer and Ollie had worked in his uncle's tavern. Mutt was the oldest, having worked for Smallbone in 1781. Ollie had worked for him in 1916. Hell Cat had been separated from her family when they hit the road after the bank took her father's Massachusetts farm in 1931.

"And what do you do?" Lily asked her. "Besides raising hell?"

Hell Cat glowered. "Pa taught me to shoot a rifle. I used to get rabbits and woodchucks for the pot. And I can take care of myself, if that counts."

"It does. Well," Lily said, looking around at the three anxious faces, "there's quite a collection of talents here. Ollie, Eb can always use a good cook at the Klam Shak, especially when tourist season starts. Hell Cat, there's not much call around here for a sharpshooter, but Miss Rachel at the library could use some help."

Hell Cat looked panicky. "I ain't a big reader."

"Miss Rachel doesn't need you to read. She's not as young as she used to be and she's in a wheelchair. Truth is, she could use some help around the house, and she might even accept it if she knew she was doing you a favor."

"Let Mutt do it," Hell Cat said. "He's good at taking care of folks."

"You'll learn," Lily said firmly. "Mutt, you can work here. Room and board to start with, salary to be determined when I see what you can do. Everybody happy?"

Her tone suggested that they better be. The three apprentices nodded. "Good. Nick, take them to Eb's and wait for me."

Outside, apprentices past and present exchanged dazed looks. "What just happened?" Mutt asked.

"You got Lilied," Nick said.

"I don't like her," Hell Cat announced, glowering. "She's bossy."

Nick shrugged. "Good thing you won't be working for her, then. Come on. I want to get back to Evil Wizard Books before Smallbone comes looking for me."

Chapter Twenty-Three

✦ ✦ ✦ ✦ ✦ ✦ ✦

In the days following the Equinox, half the town went to look at the mended Wall and the glowing Lantern and agreed that there might be something in this ritual thing after all, and wasn't it just like Smallbone to leave all the hard work to them while he hid in his tower. And what about those kids who'd showed up in town? Old apprentices of Smallbone's, Lily said, but they seemed ordinary enough, even if they had been animals for all those years.

Dinah wasn't so sure about that. She'd been a coyote for only a few weeks, and she sometimes still dreamed about it. As soon as she had the chance, she headed right over to the library to see how Miss Rachel was getting on with the girl from Evil Wizard Books.

What did a cat know about the Dewey decimal system, anyway?

Hell Cat had turned out to be strange but fascinating. She didn't seem to think that having spent the last eighty-some years as a cat made her peculiar or weird. She had a mind of her own and she didn't care who knew it. She hissed when she was mad and told stories about Smallbone that almost curled Dinah's hair. And she was a demon for work. In the week she'd been with Miss Rachel, she'd done more to clean up the library than Dinah had managed in a year.

She couldn't read a word, but Miss Rachel had taught her how to alphabetize.

When Dinah got to the library the next Saturday morning, Miss Rachel was by her window as usual, a steaming mug of tea on her desk, looking somewhat exercised. The floor had been cleared and its boards still glistened with water from the first scrubbing they'd had since Dinah could remember.

"As you can see," Miss Rachel said in the tone of a woman who has been tried to the limit, "we're in the middle of spring cleaning here. I only hope I can find my books again when it's done."

Hell Cat popped out of the kitchen like a jack-in-the-box. Her hair was tied up in a bandanna and her middle in a big flowered apron. "Miss Rachel's mad because I want to move the sofa."

They all looked at the sofa. Once, it had been the pride of some nineteenth-century Smallbone's front room, carved with cavorting seals and upholstered in ocean-blue plush. The seals were cracked and the plush was faded and worn bald in patches, and the sofa itself was very much in the way, but Miss Rachel considered it a part of the library's quaint charm. Tourists sometimes had their pictures taken sitting on it.

"That sofa can stay right where it is," Miss Rachel said. "It's been there since my grandma was a girl, and likely long before."

Hell Cat looked sly. "Can't we at least get that box out from under it so I can clean? There could be something really historical in it." Her sapphire eyes gleamed. "Treasure, even."

"She's right," Dinah said. "We might find something you could use for your book on Smallbone Cove."

Miss Rachel looked thoughtful. "Go ahead, then. But be careful!"

The box was made of metal, welded by age and damp to the floor below. Hell Cat fetched a hammer and a screwdriver, and finally, with Dinah pulling and Hell Cat pushing, they worked the box free of the sofa, which promptly cracked and collapsed in the middle.

"My sofa!" Miss Rachel bleated.

Dinah pulled cautiously at the box's old-fashioned iron latch. "Drat. It's rusted shut."

"I think there's some WD-40 in the kitchen drawer," Hell Cat said, and ran to get it, coming back a moment later with the oil.

It took some doing, but they got the latch open at last and lifted the lid, releasing a sour smell and a puff of what looked like soot.

Miss Rachel put her hand over her nose. "Mold! Get that thing out of here, right away, before it infects everything."

Dinah helped Hell Cat wrestle the box into the

kitchen. They were debating whether to leave it there or take it out back when Miss Rachel gave an amazingly seal-like bark of alarm.

The two girls raced into the reading room. The library door was open, and two Howling Coyotes were surveying the room with the air of tourists at a county fair. They both had brown Howling Coyote jackets zipped to their throats like armor. One of them, not much more than a kid, wore a red baseball cap over his sandy hair. They smelled of rot, gasoline, and wet dog.

Dinah knew that smell. It was the smell of the pelt she'd found in the Stream. It made her nose sting and filled her with terror and confusion. She shrank back against the bookshelves.

Red Baseball Cap Guy narrowed his eyes at Hell Cat, who was bristling like a porcupine. "You got a problem, little girl?"

"I sure do," Hell Cat hissed. "I—"

"Wanted to tell you how easy it is to get a temporary library card," Miss Rachel boomed. "We usually only issue them in the summer, but we're willing to make an exception for dedicated readers."

Red Baseball Cap sneered. "That right, little girl?"

Dinah glanced at Hell Cat, who looked like she was ready to explode.

Miss Rachel cleared her throat warningly.

"Yeah," Hell Cat said finally. "I wanted to give you a library card." Dinah allowed herself a small sigh of relief. "You know how to read?"

Red Baseball Cap's face twisted.

Dinah looked around for something she could use for a weapon. The hammer was too far away, but Hell Cat's broom was right over . . .

"Aw, leave it alone, Jerry," Red Baseball Cap's companion said. 'There's no fun in beating up old women and babies."

"Baby?" Hell Cat yowled. "I'll show you baby!"

The next few minutes were crowded. Hell Cat jumped on the biker called Jerry, scratching and kicking. His friend plucked her off and threw her against the shelves. Miss Rachel roared, Dinah caught up the broom, and Jerry laughed and jerked it out of her hands. He used it to sweep out shelf after shelf of books, which thumped down on Hell Cat like papery bricks.

A chorus of yammering and yipping and roaring broke out in the street, accompanied by the sound of breaking glass.

"Let's *go,* Jerry!" his companion said, and ran out the door. Jerry threw one last book at Dinah and followed, taking a moment to knock over Miss Rachel's desk, tea and all, before dashing out the door and plunging into the hullabaloo in the street.

Dinah ran over to Hell Cat, who was sitting in a pile of books, rubbing her head and using the kind of language that would have earned Dinah a good old-fashioned talking-to if she'd ever been dumb enough to use it.

"You all right?" Dinah asked breathlessly.

Hell Cat glared. "Shut the door, you idiot!"

Dinah looked out at the running, struggling crowd of fishermen in yellow oilcloth and Howling Coyotes in brown leather and ran to close and lock the door. Then she turned to Miss Rachel, who was staring out the window, her eyes like polished black pebbles and her mouth in a straight, grim line.

"Coyotes," she remarked, "are perfectly nice animals. And there are many respectable motorcyclists. These creatures are neither the one nor the other." She paused, then added, "Poor things."

"Poor things nothing," Dinah said. "They're horrible."

"*Fidelou* is horrible," Miss Rachel corrected her. "He gave them those wicked pelts. They can't call their souls their own. Still, I hope Saul and his crew give them a larruping they won't forget."

Dinah looked out the window.

After Smallbone had freed her from the magic coyote pelt, Dinah read every book the library held on coyotes and seals. She'd learned that coyotes ate anything, including fish, and that they didn't usually run in packs. She'd also read that seals, while usually peaceable animals that would rather flee than fight, had been known to attack killer whales — and beat them, too — by ganging up and tearing at them with their strong, sharp teeth.

The fishermen of Smallbone Cove had only ordinary human teeth, but their arms were strong from hauling nets and they outnumbered the bikers almost two to one. The Howling Coyotes, on the other hand, had knives and tire irons and chains, and they'd been in a lot more fights than the fishermen had.

Hell Cat got up and went to the other window. "Ham's down!" she shrieked, dancing with excitement and fury. "No, he's up again, but he's bleeding! Doesn't look too bad, though. Go, HAM!"

Dinah looked out over the crowd of bodies surging and tumbling along the street. Here Cain the animal doctor and a hulking biker pummeled each other on the porch of Three Bags Full Knitting. There a leather-covered arm brandished a crowbar. At the edge of the parking lot, a fisherman in yellow oilcloth was beating a biker's head against a wooden bar. Even through the storm windows, she could hear cracks and shouts and groans.

"This is horrible!" she cried. "What're we going to do?"

"There is nothing we can do," Miss Rachel said.

"The coyotes are Smallbone's concern. This library is mine."

"Well, Smallbone should know about it, then!"

Dinah turned and fled though the kitchen and out the back door. Then she took off behind the church toward the path that led to Evil Wizard Books, running as though all the coyotes in Fidelou's pack were howling on her heels.

Chapter Twenty-Four

+ + ✦ ✦ ✦ + +

Nick was sweeping the kitchen floor after lunch, thinking about how to make the Stream rise up in monster shapes if a coyote tried to cross it.

The shop bell jangled sharply. His bones turned to ice.

The bell rang a second time. Jeff raced out of the kitchen, barking. Nick dropped the broom, hurried to the shop, and peered through the window. It was Dinah, the girl who had been a coyote. She looked furious.

Nick grabbed Jeff by the scruff of his neck and opened the door.

Dinah was red faced from running, and her mottled hair stuck up around her head. "I want to talk to the evil wizard," she said. "It's real important."

"He's working on the Sentries," Nick said. "Anything I can do?"

Dinah clenched her fists. "I have to talk to Smallbone. The coyotes are back and everybody's fighting." Her voice trembled a little. "They tore up the library."

"The library?"

Dinah made a frustrated noise. "Are you going to get Smallbone or not?"

"I'll get him," Nick said. "You want to come in?"

The seal-dark eyes moved to Jeff, who was growling gently. "What about the dog?"

"Oh, Jeff doesn't bite." He couldn't resist adding, "Not hard, anyway."

Leaving her to work things out with Jeff, Nick took off up the stairs two at a time.

Over the past weeks, Nick had noticed that the tower door moved, depending on Smallbone's mood — or maybe its mood — Nick wasn't sure. Today it was at the end of the hall his bedroom was on, with the door wide open. He stood at the bottom of the steps and shouted, "Smallbone? The bikers are back, and they're tearing up the Cove!"

Nick heard Smallbone roar "Land o' Goshen!" then the clatter of rings as he swept back the curtain. "You interrupt me again, Foxkin, I'll turn you into a mackerel and fry you. What if I'd been in the middle of a spell?"

"But the bikers—"

"Confusticate the bikers!" Smallbone said. "What's your source for this choice piece of scuttlebutt?"

"Dinah Smallbone. She's downstairs, and she wants to talk to you."

"Land o' Goshen!"

Nick stepped out of the way just in time to avoid being knocked over by the evil wizard, who marched down the hall, muttering.

In the bookshop, Dinah was pacing back and forth in front of the shelves, while Jeff sat watchfully by the door. Smallbone thundered down the steps and confronted her, his hair crackling under the bent pipe of his black top hat, the skirts of his black coat flapping and flaring like vulture wings. "Well?"

His voice was low and hoarse and menacing. Nick had to admire Dinah's moxie. She paled, but her voice was firm as she announced, all in one breath, "The Howling Coyotes are tearing things up and the fishermen are fighting them and they've got knives, and you have to help!"

Smallbone's glasses flashed irritably. "What makes you think that?"

Dinah's fists clenched. "We Walked the Bounds and did the ritual—we even figured it out all by ourselves. We fixed the Wall, too. We did our part. Now you have to do yours."

"I'm *doing* my part," he snapped. "Or I would be, if I wasn't talking to you. Foxkin, take this seal back to town, look around, see what's going on."

Nick came down from the landing and stood by Dinah. "Okay," he said. "But what should I do if they're still fighting?"

"Blast 'em with a fireball," Smallbone said, clutching his hat with both hands as if it were about to fly off. "Call up a wind and blow the whole boiling of 'em to Halifax. You got the strength for it. And when you've sent Fidelou's coyotes packing, you can go to the library and see how Miss Rachel's doing. Maybe you can look around, see if there's anything good to read. You know what I mean."

He scowled at Nick through his glasses with awful intensity. Nick grinned at him, suddenly filled with certainty. "Don't worry," he said. "I got this."

Dinah grabbed Nick's arm. "Come *on!*" she said. "We have to run!"

He opened the door and they ran.

⚜ ⚜ ⚜

If Smallbone Cove had a fault, it was that it looked just a little too much like the perfect Maine Seaside Town. The houses were charmingly old, with tiny-paned windows, weathered gray shingles, and white picket fences in front of three of the shops. Commercial Street was paved with cobblestones. The windows were always shiny, the shingles in good repair, the trim picket fences nicely painted, and the cobbles smooth and tightly fitted.

It didn't look like that now.

When Nick and Dinah arrived at the edge of town, red faced and out of breath, they could see right away that the fight was over. Commercial Street was empty — if you didn't count a couple of cars with slashed tires and broken windshields — but it was the emptiness of a field after a battle. Even from the end of the street, Nick could see that the wooden shutters that covered the shop windows in the off-season had been splintered, and broken glass sparkled among the cobblestones. Half the tiny panes in the Klam Shak's front window were smashed, and the door was open and hanging off its hinges. As they got nearer, Nick saw a familiar figure sweeping what looked like the shattered remains of several chairs out into the street.

"Ollie!" he called. "What's been going on?"

Ollie leaned on his broom. "Big fight," he said. "Howling Coyotes and the fishermen. Worse than Saturday night at my uncle's tavern, and that's saying something."

"Who won?" Dinah asked.

"We did. The fishermen started it, though pretty much everybody took a hand in the end. I hit a biker with a cast-iron pan." Ollie grinned. "A hot one. Anyway, they ran off 'bout fifteen minutes ago with their tails between their legs." He nodded toward the parking lot. "Some of them left their motorcycles behind."

"Anybody hurt?"

"Saul's got a slash on his arm. Pete and Goliath got goose eggs on their heads. Other folks got cut up and bruised. I didn't hear about everybody."

"And my mom and dad?" Dinah asked.

Ollie shrugged.

Dinah turned her frightened eyes to Nick. "I gotta go home," she said. "Tell Miss Rachel. And good luck finding whatever it was Smallbone was being so cagey about."

"Thanks," Nick said, surprised, and, as she went racing away down to the Mercantile, added, "I hope your folks are okay!"

Nick crossed the street, climbed the steps to the Smallbone Cove Public Library, and went in.

Miss Rachel was in her chair by the window. "You're Smallbone's apprentice, aren't you? I saw you at the Town Meeting. What did he call you again?"

Hell Cat's head popped up from behind the circulation desk. "Foxkin!" She glowered at Nick. "What are you doing here?"

Nick took in the scattered books, the broken sofa, the pale scar on the circulation desk where something had smashed into it, the mess of broken wood, crockery, and paper beside the wheelchair, and he started to get mad. "I want to help," he said.

"Are you going to help us clean?" Hell Cat asked.

"That's not his job, dear." Miss Rachel held up a clump of boards and rumpled paper that had once been a book. "Can you fix this?"

As a boy whose best friend was currently a bookshop, Nick was horrified. "Maybe," he said. "I don't know. If you trust me with it, I'll take it home and see what I can do. What I meant was, I want to help get the Sentries fixed, so this won't happen again. I'm looking for charts. Old, thick, kind of stiff. They'd have lines all over them, and numbers. Some words. It's hard to describe," he finished lamely.

"Sounds it." Miss Rachel waved a plump hand at the stacks of cardboard boxes piled against the stairs.

"As you can see, we're a little behind on the cataloging. You're welcome to look, though."

Nick's heart sank to his toes. Going through all those boxes would take days, months, maybe years. By the time he found the missing charts — or, more likely, didn't find them — Fidelou would be the Evil Wizard of Smallbone Cove and he himself would probably be eating flies in the pond, if a coyote hadn't eaten him first.

Hell Cat tipped her head. Nick could almost see her ears prick up. "What do you need charts for?"

Nick hesitated. Smallbone wouldn't tell them — he was sure of that. He'd just threaten Miss Rachel into finding them herself, with a one-day deadline, probably. Nick couldn't do that. He could lie, but it would be easier just to tell the truth.

Besides, he found he didn't want to lie to Miss Rachel.

"They're charts for the Sentries," he said. "Fixing them is real complicated, and it would be a lot faster if he had the charts to help him. I was hoping you might know something about them."

Miss Rachel shook her head. "I don't think—" she began.

Hell Cat was looking thoughtful. "There's that box we found under the sofa," she said. "That's old."

"But it's full of mold!" Miss Rachel exclaimed.

"He's a wizard," Hell Cat argued. "Maybe he knows a spell to make mold disappear."

Nick followed Hell Cat into the kitchen, where the metal box sat where the girls had left it, looking the worse for wear. "We WD-40'd the hinges," Hell Cat said. "It'll open easy. But it smells pretty bad."

Nick opened the lid, releasing a stink of rotten mushrooms and stagnant water that reminded him of Uncle Gabe's cellar. He put his hand in and felt a familiar tingle as his fingers closed around something soft and slimy. "Yuck!"

"I told you," Hell Cat said.

There was something magic in there. He just hoped it wasn't completely rotted. He thought for a moment, then closed his eyes and felt the water diffused throughout the box. If he just gathered it up, like that, and made it into a bubble, like that, and floated it out of the box and over to the kitchen sink . . .

"Golly!" Hell Cat said. "I didn't know you could do that!"

This broke Nick's concentration, as well as the bubble, which splashed all over the floor. But it didn't matter. The box was dry inside, and so was whatever he'd felt. He sneezed as the dry mold flew into his face and he pulled out a package wrapped in oilcloth.

It was a chart, all right. For the Stream, appropriately enough. Whatever else was in the box, however, had crumbled and mixed with the mold. He hoped it hadn't been another chart.

Hell Cat leaned over his shoulder. "It looks like spaghetti," she said. "Are you sure this is magic?"

Nick refolded the chart and put it in his pocket. "Yep."

"Can you read it?" Hell Cat wanted to know.

"Like print," Nick said, which was only a stretcher, not a downright lie. "We'll have the Stream back online in no time."

The fog was rolling in when Nick left the library. It hid the Cove and the point and lay on the wharf like thin gray wool, muffling all sound except the hollow, mournful honk of the foghorn.

He stood on the steps and looked across Main Street at the parking lot where four motorcycles lay on their sides, surrounded by glass from their shattered headlights. Four Howling Coyotes had been hurt too bad to ride by themselves, then. Good.

As he watched, a skinny figure slid out of the shadowy porch of Joshua's Kites 'N Chimes and scuttled toward one of the bikes.

It was wearing a red Portland Sea Dogs baseball cap.

Nick's heart stopped and started up again, pounding fit to bust out of his chest. His cousin Jerry had a Portland Sea Dogs cap. Uncle Gabe had gotten it for him for his fourteenth birthday, and the only times Nick had seen him without it since then were when Uncle Gabe snatched it off his head so he could whack him with it.

There wasn't anything special about Sea Dogs

baseball caps, Nick told himself. Plenty of guys had them. And Jerry was with Uncle Gabe in Beaton, way off inland. He couldn't be riding with Fidelou.

The boy in the baseball cap looked up.

It was Jerry. Even in a Howling Coyote jacket, with his hair in his face and a shiner coming on, Nick knew him.

The mean pale eyes—or at least the one that wasn't swollen shut—looked straight into Nick's and widened.

Nick dashed down the steps and ran.

Chapter Twenty-Five

✦ ✦ ✦ ✦ ✦ ✦

Seeing Nick on the library steps hit Jerry like a bucket of ice water.

When his cousin ran away in December, Jerry thought he was rid of the little pest for good. Never in a million years had he thought that Nick would turn up again, much less in Smallbone Cove.

The shock lasted only for a moment before it turned into pure hatred.

Jerry pretty much hated everybody in the world, but Nick was special. Ever since he and Aunt Brigitte had come to live with his dad when Jerry was ten, Jerry had resented him. Jerry had wanted Aunt Brigitte to himself, baking pies and reading bedtime stories and chasing nightmares away. Her noisy, snot-nosed, clingy little brat just got in the way and spoiled things.

Then she died, and the things about home that had already been bad got ten times worse. Jerry had given it a lot of thought, and ended up concluding that it was all Nick's fault. He decided to make Nick's life as hard as Nick had made his. When the little snot-nosed brat ran away, Jerry had gone out and celebrated. And now there he was, or somebody who looked mighty like him, well fed, rosy cheeked, and cheerful until the moment his eyes met Jerry's, when he took off down the street like the wimp he was.

Jerry righted a motorcycle and got on, hoping it was fit to drive. He didn't want to walk all the way to Fidelou, but he would if he had to. He had something to tell the Boss he just thought might help him win his pelt at last.

Chapter Twenty-Six

Nick didn't see any point in telling Smallbone about seeing Jerry in Smallbone Cove.

It wasn't like Jerry was going to come for him — Nick knew how much Jerry hated having him around. And Jerry wouldn't tell Uncle Gabe, either, because if he was riding with the Howling Coyotes, chances were he'd run away from Uncle Gabe just like Nick had.

No, it was going to be fine. All he had to do was help Smallbone get the Sentries working again, and everybody would be safe.

Smallbone was delighted with the chart Hell Cat and Dinah had found in the library. He even smiled a reasonably non-evil smile when he unfolded it. "Looks like you're worth your keep after all," he said. "Two, three days to make sure we got this nailed down, and them coyotes'll be shaking water out of their ears. Fetch me *Mysteria Acquam,* Foxkin. We got us some figuring to do."

Nick researched tides and currents and underwater springs until Smallbone sent him down to make sand-wiches, then made charts of numbers until Smallbone sent him to bed. He should have been too tired to dream, but even Bow-Wowzer Meowzer couldn't keep him from waking up in a lather, sure he was back in the cellar in Beaton, sure he'd heard Jerry's—or worse, Uncle Gabe's—step on the stairs. After a particularly vivid dream that featured Uncle Gabe sniffing around Evil Wizard Books like a hunting dog, Nick went out to the barn with *The Hobbit.* He hung his lantern on a hook, made himself comfortable on a bale of hay, and read, wondering if Gandalf's pipe smelled as bad as Smallbone's.

It was still dark when Nick woke with a start to a chorus of yelling goats. Startled, he tumbled off his hay bale.

"Glad to see you're up bright and early, Foxkin," Smallbone said. "We got a big day ahead of us. There's a visitor coming."

Nick went over to the cranky old hand pump and started priming. "Visitor?" he said, as if he didn't care.

Smallbone opened a bin, scooped out a bucket of goat feed, and dumped it into the trough. "Did a little scrying this morning, looking for Fidelou, found this feller instead. Big fat cuss, face like a walrus. He ain't magic, and he sure ain't with the State, so he's got to be a relation. A father, I think you said. Or maybe an uncle?"

Nick pumped furiously. Water gushed out of the pump, flooding the buckets, slopping on the floor, and soaking his jeans to the knee. He jumped back, swearing, and fell onto a hay bale, where he lay, blank with terror.

"You better tell me," Smallbone said.

"I saw my cousin Jerry in town yesterday," Nick told the beams above him. "He's with the Howling Coyotes. He must have called Uncle Gabe and told him where I was."

"Would that be the famous Jerry Reynaud whose name you stole when we first met?"

"I thought if you started throwing curses around, maybe they'd land on him instead of me."

"I see." Smallbone picked up the hay fork. "This Uncle Gabe, he with Fidelou, too?"

His tone was mild, but Nick could hear the edge under it. "He lives way out in Beaton and works in a garage and watches races and wrestling on TV. And drinks. He doesn't get out much."

"Well, he's out now." Smallbone pulled his pipe from his pocket and stuck it in his mouth, unlit. "And he's coming here."

Nick's mind raced. He could hide in the woods, or he could swim out to one of those little islands in the Reach. What he really wanted to do, though, was turn his uncle into an ant and step on him, or even stop the spell halfway and see if any of the horrible things *Animal You* had threatened would happen.

He must have said some of this out loud, because Smallbone cackled. "Bloodthirsty, ain't you? Not that I blame you, mind—far as I can tell, it wouldn't be more than he deserves. But that ain't how this story goes. The Rule is your nearest kin gets three free shots at rescuing you."

Nick sat up so suddenly his head spun. "I don't want to be rescued. I want to learn magic."

Smallbone gave him a thoughtful look. "So you can be an evil wizard?"

"Maybe I can be a good wizard, like Gandalf."

The bristly beard twitched briefly. "Maybe pigs can fly."

Silence fell, punctuated by goaty munching and slurping and the occasional impatient cluck from the chickens. Nick got up to feed them. He even cast his egg-gathering spell.

"There's a way out of this," Smallbone remarked as eggs floated from their hidey-holes to the straw-lined basket.

Nick shot him a suspicious look. "Really? What?"

"There's more than one way to spin a story. Think, Foxkin."

Thinking wasn't easy with one part of Nick's brain shouting *RUN* and another shouting *FIGHT,* but he came up with the answer at last. "It's like 'The Wizard

Outwitted,'" he said. "Except what I have to do is *not* give Uncle Gabe a hint so he won't know which animal is me."

"Light dawns over Marblehead," Smallbone said.

"Then will he go away and leave me alone?"

"He'll have to. One chance to a customer." The old wizard smiled toothily. "After that, you belong to me."

Nick thought about this. "That's too easy."

"Maybe it is and maybe it ain't," Smallbone said. "Animal bodies got minds of their own, you know."

Nick did know. Remembering some of the things he'd done as a rat still made him squirm. "I guess that means it's on me now, huh?"

"It always is, Foxkin. It always is."

❧ ❧ ❧

Some time later, Nick was on the hearth rug in the kitchen, waiting for Uncle Gabe to show up. Jeff, who'd been out in the woods all morning, slept beside him, whuffing and jerking in a doggy dream. Tom was investigating something under the stove. The clock was ticking loudly and, Nick thought, much more slowly than usual.

He didn't know where Smallbone was.

The shop bell jangled hoarsely. Jeff jumped up, ears pricked, growling; Tom galloped across the floor and tried to hide under Nick's leg. Nick put his arms around Jeff's neck and told himself there was nothing to worry about. Smallbone was doing all the magic. All Nick had to do was keep his head.

Out in the front room, the door opened with a long nerve-wrenching screech. Nick jumped nervously.

"I'm here for my nephew, old man," a familiar voice shouted. "You going to hand him over, or do I stuff your scraggly whiskers down your throat?"

"Neither one," Smallbone said calmly. "There's Rules that govern these things, Rules even a cross-grained cuss like you has to follow."

"You think?" Uncle Gabe snarled. There was a grunt, followed by a flood of very bad words. Apparently the Rules didn't prevent Smallbone from showing Uncle Gabe who was boss.

"Here are the terms," Smallbone went on as though nothing had happened. "You recognize your nephew three times in a row, you can have him. You get it wrong once, he stays with me."

"Yeah, yeah," Uncle Gabe said. "You think you can't lose, don't you? Seeing as you're holding all the cards?"

"Anybody can lose," Smallbone said. "That's why it's a test. And it's starting *right now!*"

It was like movie magic—*Alakazam!* You're a frog! Poof! You're a fish! As Smallbone spoke, Nick, Jeff, and Tom turned into three black Lab puppies, identical in every detail except for one being a boy in a body he didn't really know how to use.

A puppy knocked him over and bit his ear playfully. Nick growled and snapped at it.

Somewhere in the air above him, Smallbone's voice said, "Your nephew is one of these dogs."

"I know the drill," Uncle Gabe sneered. "And I know you got to let me get a good look at 'em. So move your skinny butt before I move it for you."

A shadow fell across Nick, and the stink of beer and stale sweat filled his nose. The other puppies bounced up and started to bark, their tails windmilling wildly. Nick bounced up, too, only his tail had tucked itself between his hind legs and he couldn't figure out how to wag it. He whined in frustration.

A giant hand reached out of nowhere and grabbed him by the scruff.

The world spun around. Nick found himself kneeling in front of the fireplace, half choked, with Uncle Gabe's grip tightening on his neck.

"Once," Smallbone said.

⚶   ⚶   ⚶

Nick was squatting in the middle of a web. He was spitting mad—at himself, mostly, though Uncle Gabe was mixed up in there, too—and determined not to give himself away again. It should be easy. He'd been a spider before. He knew how it felt.

Two shadows fell over his web. *Flies,* Nick thought. *Yum.*

"One of these spiders—" Smallbone began.

"I got it," Uncle Gabe growled.

Silence fell, thick as flannel. Nick thought he could feel his heart beating along his back. If spiders had sweat glands, he would have been sweating.

"Give up?" Smallbone said.

"Nope. I already know which one he is. I'm just

thinking how I'm going to make him pay for putting me through this malarkey."

Nick flinched. It wasn't much of a flinch, but it shook the delicate threads of the web, which moved as if in an invisible breeze.

Uncle Gabe crowed. "That one!"

Nick found himself squatting on the barn floor with Uncle Gabe and Smallbone standing over him. Uncle Gabe was grinning like a jack-o'-lantern. Smallbone's face was still as stone.

"Twice," he said.

❧   ❧   ❧

Nick was among a herd of goats he knew very well, staring at the two men standing outside the pen. Beside him, the billy goat Harpo stamped his foot and baaed uneasily. The herd separated into a line.

"Can't see 'em clear, way back there," Uncle Gabe said. "It ain't a fair trial if I can't see 'em clear."

Smallbone climbed into the pen and tried to shoo them all forward. Nick kept an eye on Harpo and Thalia and bounced to one side. There were three billy goats, besides him — Tom and Jeff, probably, making things harder for Uncle Gabe. Maybe this would work after all.

"You give up?" Smallbone asked.

"I ain't even got started."

Uncle Gabe grabbed a hayfork and hit the rails of the pen with it. Thalia reared up on her hind legs and yelled like an angry toddler. Nick found himself rushing to the front of the pen with the intention of giving Uncle Gabe the head-butting of his life. When he hit the rails, he stretched his neck between the slats and spat straight into Uncle Gabe's face.

"That one," Uncle Gabe said triumphantly.

Then Nick was standing in the goat pen with Jeff trying to hide behind his legs and Tom crouched by his feet, mewing.

"Hey, there, Nick," Uncle Gabe said. "How's tricks?"

Smallbone's gaze moved from Nick to Gabe and back again. His mouth was a thin line in his beard.

"Thrice," he said, dry as a rainless month. "Seems like he's yours after all."

"You heard the old-timer," Uncle Gabe said. "Come on. We're going home."

Chapter Twenty-Seven

✦ ✦ ✦ ✦ ✦ ✦ ✦

Uncle Gabe dragged Nick to the pickup, shoved him inside, and slammed the door. Nick sat up and moved his butt off the spring sticking out of the seat. He didn't fasten his seat belt, because there wasn't one. Like everything his uncle owned, his truck was beat up and worn out and sad.

Like Nick.

He'd always been proud of being the kind of kid who never knew when he was beat. When a kid hit him, he hit back with interest. Every time Uncle Gabe had belted him, every time Jerry had gone at him or ripped up one of his books or thrown his shirt in the toilet, he'd spat and struggled and fought. Well, he was beat now.

Through the smeared windshield, he saw Smallbone on the porch of Evil Wizard Books with Tom
in his arms and Jeff beside him, stiff legged and alert.
With his black dog and his ginger cat and his coat and
beard and hat he didn't take off even when he ate, the
old man looked more than ever like something out of
a horror movie.

The Evil Wizard Smallbone. He used to be a nasty
customer, but now he carves souvenir wooden figures
and he's nice to animals. He even lets his apprentice
help him with his spells.

I hope Fidelou gets him, Nick thought. *I hope Fidelou
gets them all.* Well, not the animals. It wasn't their fault
Uncle Gabe could pick him out three times out of
three. It wasn't even Smallbone's fault, though Nick
would have liked it to be. Thanks to *Animal You,* Nick
knew himself well enough to know that he'd given
himself away.

Uncle Gabe got into the truck, slammed it into
gear, and peeled out of the parking lot. His eyes were
slits under his cap, his mouth set like iron. Nick knew

that expression. It promised pain, maybe a trip to the hospital. It promised that Nick was going to be sorry he'd ever been born.

They drove through Smallbone Cove, going far too fast. A few startled Covers looked up as the pickup rattled by, then looked away again. No help there, Nick thought, even if they knew he needed helping. He was Smallbone's apprentice and Smallbone's problem. The only person Nick had left to count on now was himself. He slumped hopelessly in the seat.

"Well, aren't you a useless lump of misery," Uncle Gabe said. "Almost makes me glad your ma's dead and gone."

The habit of poking somebody until they cracked was obviously a family trick. Well, Nick wasn't going to fall for it this time. Uncle Gabe might be bigger than Nick, and a whole lot meaner, but he wasn't very smart.

"If it wasn't that I promised your ma I'd keep you in the family," Uncle Gabe went on, "I'd have put you in care soon as she was in the ground. Still, what goes around comes around. Just because I got no use for you don't mean nobody does. The Boss wants you, devil knows why."

Nick sat up. "The boss? Do you mean Fidelou?"

Uncle Gabe shifted gears. "Mean son of a so-and-so, ain't he? He'll make mincemeat of that old coot, when he catches him."

Nick set his teeth. He wasn't useless and he wasn't helpless and he wasn't going to let a clueless old bully use him as bait. Uncle Gabe might be big and mean as a snake, but he didn't know magic.

Nick did.

The truck climbed a long hill and the trees thinned. At the crest of the hill, the road ran through a blueberry barren. Low bushes and gray boulders tumbled down the hillside like a thick, lumpy carpet to a stand of pines. Beyond it, the Reach shifted and sparkled under the bright spring sun.

Nick scanned the roadside for something he could use to stop the truck. A tree branch across the road would do it, but he'd never called wood before. The water was too far away. There were plenty of rocks, however. This was Maine; there were always plenty of rocks.

Nick closed his eyes and thought of stone. He liked stone. He'd been one, after all. You could make a knife out of stone, if you chipped it right. He'd cut his foot once, walking barefoot in a field just like the one they were driving through now. When he concentrated, he could sense them, slices of quartz, clusters of feldspar, shards of granite sharp enough to slice through the pickup's balding tires. He called and felt them answer, drawn by his magic like iron filings to a magnet rolling out over the road in an avalanche.

The truck bounced and rocked over the tumbling stones, then there was a loud rubber *POP* as a tire blew. Uncle Gabe clung to the wheel, cursing all the devils out of hell as he tried to keep the pickup on the road. With a crunch and a tooth-jarring lurch, the pickup came to rest with its rear wheels off the ground and its front wheels in a ditch.

Nick had wedged himself under the dashboard as soon as they'd started to skid and pretended to be knocked out. He didn't move when Uncle Gabe kicked the door open, got out, still cursing, and crunched around to the front to check out the damage.

It was now or never.

Nick knew that to turn himself into an animal, he had to have perfect Will and Concentration. Oh, and he had to be Confident, too.

He certainly had the Will. He'd find the Concentration. As for Confidence, there was only one way to find out.

The world turned inside out and around.

When it stopped, he was hit by a stench of stale beer, old cigarettes, and garbage festering behind the seats, overlaid with a sharp, peppery, sour stink that had to have been Uncle Gabe. He sneezed and shook himself.

The world was strangely colored—all blues and greens and shades of gray—and painfully bright and sharp. His nose was telling him more things than his brain could take in. He wasn't sure he knew how to run with four feet.

Uncle Gabe shouted hoarsely, and instinct took over. Nick leaped out the open door and fled the asphalt stink of the road. The rocks didn't offer much cover, and the low, thick bushes dragged at his fur. What he wanted was trees to hide in and rotten logs to hide under.

A sharp crack sounded behind him. Something zipped past and slammed into a nearby boulder, knocking off a shower of stone chips. Nick dodged behind the rock and burrowed into a thicket, where he lay among the twigs, panting.

His fox-self told him to try for the trees, but his boy-self knew he couldn't outrun a bullet. And Uncle Gabe was getting closer, his big boots shaking the ground, his sour, beery, furious stink floating on the air. Nick heard a loud, concentrated buzzing. Wiggling forward, he saw a handful of yellowjackets hovering like tiny helicopters around a hole at the base of the rock.

Uncle Gabe hated yellowjackets.

Nick's jaw dropped in a foxy grin. He crawled out of the thicket, gathered himself, and leaped up onto the rock, to find himself a stone's throw from Uncle Gabe.

Nick put back his ears and hissed. Uncle Gabe

grinned, reversed his rifle, and raised it like a club. Nick wheeled and jumped behind the boulder, landing bare inches from the entrance to the yellowjackets' nest. He kicked some dirt into the hole, then dove into the bushes.

Behind him, the yellowjackets boiled up out of their nest in a swarm, looking for something to sting.

What they found was Uncle Gabe. He stomped and yelled and swung his rifle at the swarm like a baseball bat, but that just riled them up. He dropped the rifle and lit out downhill with the yellowjackets after him in a furious, buzzing cloud.

Nick crawled out of the bush, sniffed at the rifle, lifted his leg, and peed on the trigger. With any luck, the yellowjackets would sting Uncle Gabe until he swelled up like a balloon. In any case, he wasn't likely to come back. In the meantime, Nick's nose told him there was another fox nearby.

A moment later, he appeared on the boulder. His fur was a rusty red and his paws and muzzle were soft black. He twitched his black-rimmed ears. Nick ran over and touched his muzzle with his nose.

It was Smallbone.

"If you concentrate," the fox said, "you'll find you don't need a human throat to talk like a human. It ain't nature, but it is magic."

Nick concentrated. "It's a trap," he said. "Fidelou sent Uncle Gabe to get me so you'll leave Smallbone Cove."

The red fox sat and swept his tail around his front paws. "That ain't exactly the surprise of the year, Foxkin."

"Aren't you worried?"

"My story is what it is," Smallbone said, "and it's moving on to the climactic scene. You, on the other hand, got choices. You've passed all the tests, young Foxkin, outwitted the evil wizard, and slain the ogre—or at least made him mighty sick. You belong to yourself now, fair and square. You can go out into the world and seek your fortune, like them other young fellers who escape evil wizards. But," he went on stiffly, "I'd take it kindly if you stayed with me. Only if you want to, though."

"I want to," Nick said.

"Then we better head on home," Smallbone said. "No need to make this any easier for Fidelou than we have to."

֍ ֍ ֍

A little while later, they were trotting through the woods, heading north. Smallbone was moving fast, stopping from time to time to sniff for the next tree he'd peed on to mark the way home, and talking about foxes.

"Gray foxes," he said, "ain't like red foxes. Red foxes get the publicity, but you can do things we can't. Climb trees, for instance." He stopped, nose lifted. "Dang. Coyotes."

Nick smelled them, too — rank, meaty, rotten, wrong. His lips drew back and he chattered angrily.

"Whole pack of 'em," Smallbone said. "The old wolf, too. Dang."

Now was the time, Nick thought, for the old man to turn into something big and dangerous, something that could fight coyotes. But Smallbone just pricked his ears and dove into the undergrowth.

The coyote stink was getting stronger. Instinct sent Nick skinning up the nearest tree, his paws turning in to pull him up the trunk. Once safely out of reach, he balanced on a sturdy branch and looked around. Through the trees, he saw a bush-tailed red fox perched on a giant boulder. His ears were glued against his skull, his teeth were bared, and he was surrounded by coyotes.

Nick danced on his branch with frustration. Why didn't Smallbone blast the coyotes with a spell? He was the Evil Wizard Smallbone, for Pete's sake. Why didn't he turn into a dragon and eat them?

A huge wolf appeared, glimmering unnaturally white against the dark pines. As Nick watched, whimpering, the air crackled, and there stood the Evil Wizard Fidelou, shaking back his long black hair and howling with laughter.

If the coyotes smelled wrong, Fidelou smelled worse. He smelled like rotten eggs and raw sewage and dead rats in a muddy basement and spoiled milk. He smelled of pure evil. Nick crouched down on his branch and stayed very still. A land wind tossed the pine and ruffled his fur, blowing Fidelou's scent into his nose and his own scent out to sea.

Fidelou kicked the coyotes aside like so many

puppies, grabbed the snarling Smallbone by the scruff of his neck, and held him high.

"Well, if it is not my old friend Smallbrain!" The harsh voice crept along Nick's bones like a chill wind. "How I have longed to meet you again! But you grow cautious: you keep to your den. So I find your weakness, eh? Your new apprentice, the apple of your eye. I remove him, and voilà! You follow, like a dog after her pup. Where is he, then, this precious apprentice of yours? Not here? Perhaps your rescue has failed, and he waits in my dungeon for you to join him. Perhaps I will kill him, eh? Or perhaps I will give him a pelt, make him my own obedient little dog, and teach him to hunt seals."

Smallbone, who had been hanging limply in Fidelou's grasp, snapped.

The wolf wizard tightened his grip. "You have no honor, you. I bring you a formal challenge, and you sulk, you hide, you decline to answer. By the Rules of Story, I have the right to fight you here and now, but I will not. Fidelou is honorable, even to a mortal hedge wizard. Before we duel, you will eat, drink, rest. And then it will be my great pleasure to kill you."

With a flick of his hand, Fidelou produced a sack, stuffed Smallbone into it headfirst, and slung it over his white-cloaked shoulder. Then he gathered up the coyotes with a huntsman's whistle and strode off among the trees.

Nick intended to follow him; he really did. The thought of Smallbone in the power of that stinky, horrible wolf wizard made him want to yip like a kit. He had to rescue him. If only he could figure out how to climb down the tree. If only he weren't so hungry. If only he weren't so very, very sleepy.

⚜ ⚜ ⚜

The sky was navy blue when Nick stretched, licked his paws, backed down the tree without thinking about it, and sniffed around for something to eat. When he came to his human senses, he was crunching on a bone, and the fur of his muzzle was sticky and matted. Licking it, he tasted fresh blood.

Concentrate. He had to concentrate.

Slowly, he remembered. Fidelou had captured Smallbone—or maybe Smallbone had let himself be captured. Anyway, Fidelou hadn't killed Smallbone. He wanted to duel him. He was even going to give him time to rest.

There had been a wizards' duel in "The Wizard Outwitted." It had been exciting to read about, with lots of shape-shifting into wind and clouds and dragons. Since it was a fairy tale, the good guy had naturally won. Which brought up the question of what would happen when the dueling wizards were both, officially, evil.

Nick's sensitive ears picked up a tiny rustle under a bush nearby. A mouse, or a shrew. His mouth filled with saliva. Sweet eating on a mouse. No—he shook his head sharply. Smallbone. Smallbone was in danger. He had to rescue him.

Alone? his boy-self sneered. *When you can't even keep your mind on him for two seconds? You need to get rid of this fox while you still can and get some help.*

Man, those mice—they were definitely mice—smelled good.

Nick dug out the mice and scarfed them up like extra-crunchy chicken nuggets with fur. After he'd licked his paws clean, he brought his mind back to the problem at hand, which was what?

Oh, yes. Rescuing Smallbone. Which he couldn't do the way he was now, with his fox senses screaming to him to hide or go home, anywhere but after those coyotes.

Home, he thought. He'd go home. Turn himself back, get the bookshop to help him, make a plan.

Raising his nose, Nick searched the air until he sensed Smallbone's mark. He trotted off through the undergrowth.

The first mark was on a tree stump, the second beside a rock. The third was a pile of scat, followed by a spruce tree and a cushiony patch of lichen growing on an old stone wall. As Nick clambered over, it was as if he woke up out of a long dream. He knew he was at the western boundary of Smallbone's territory, and that this Wall was the Sentry that guarded it. Evil Wizard Books was not far now. He sniffed the air. *That way.*

Night fell as Nick trotted briskly past a pond full

of fat frogs and through the woods toward the smell of magic. His paws hurt from the long run and he was hungry again, but he was home.

With the last of his strength he changed himself back into a boy and collapsed on the porch of Evil Wizard Books. As the world began to fade, the door opened and a cloud of books flew out around him. Nick closed his eyes and passed out.

Chapter Twenty-Eight

✦ ✦ ✦ ✦ ✦ ✦

Nick woke up on the bookshop floor with Jeff licking his face. The sky out the window was a pale gray, and the birds were tuning up their morning chorus. He felt gritty and sore and guilty.

"It's because of me," Nick told Jeff. "He'd be safe if he hadn't come after me. I've got to go save him."

Jeff whined hopefully, and Nick realized that none of the animals had eaten since the day before. The goats hadn't been milked. He himself was so hungry that his stomach hurt. And he needed a plan. He couldn't go up against Fidelou without a plan.

He'd ask the bookshop to help him — as soon as he'd seen to the animals. Smallbone would skin him if he let the animals go hungry and dry.

Nick pumped water and handed out hay and feed and milked, then turned Groucho and the goats out into the meadow to graze just in case he wasn't back by nightfall. Then he went to the bookshop.

It was quiet and cool and darker than it should have been, given the sunshine outside. Nick lit the lamp and turned to the shelves. There was no reason to beat around the bush, so he came right to the point. "Fidelou's got Smallbone," he announced. "I'm going to rescue him."

His words were met by silence. No rustles. No book soaring or fluttering or floating out of the shadowy aisles. His heart began to pound.

"Is this one of your stupid tests? Because I don't have time for that. Fidelou's dead set on a wizards' duel, and I don't know if Smallbone will win!"

There was an uncomfortable pause, and then a book fluttered down the stairs and landed neatly in Nick's hands. It was *E-Z Spelz for Little Wizardz*. It wasn't a joke—as far as Nick could tell, the bookshop didn't make jokes, although sometimes the books did.

And *E-Z Spelz* had always been his friend. He opened it and read.

We've done what we can. Now it's up to you.

⚜   ⚜   ⚜

It was coming up on noon when Nick went to rescue the Evil Wizard Smallbone. He had Smallbone's pipe in one pocket, a map of Maine in the other, and a basket on his arm containing a very indignant Tom. He closed the door behind him, whistled to Jeff, and headed toward the path to Smallbone Cove. He did not lock up.

It was a beautiful day. The weather had softened, and the path through the woods was almost dry. Leaf buds were swelling on the trees, and pink and white flowers were blooming among their roots. The air was alive with the faint, high creaking of peepers and the shrill voices of birds arguing over nesting spots. Nick unbuttoned his jacket and walked faster. He'd drop by the Mercantile, leave Tom and Jeff with Lily and tell her what was up, then walk to Fidelou town.

What he really needed was a car, but he didn't think Lily would lend him hers. Maybe he could thumb a ride.

Smallbone Cove was quiet. The fishing boats were still out on the Reach, the kids were in school, and Nick didn't care where the rest of the Covers were. They couldn't help him anyway.

The Mercantile's window was boarded over, and the sign said CLOSED. Nick opened the door and went in.

Four pairs of startled eyes — two blue, two dark — turned to him from different parts of the store. They belonged to Ollie, Hell Cat, Mutt, and Dinah, who were putting the Mercantile back in order after the Howling Coyotes' last visit.

"Hi, Foxkin," Dinah said.

Nick had no time to waste on manners. "I got to go somewhere," he said, "and I don't want to leave Tom and Jeff at the house in case I don't come back right away. Will you take care of them?"

Dinah looked alarmed. "I don't know if Mom —"

"C'mon, Dinah. She could handle a coyote, she can handle a couple of pets. Or maybe you can get one of the farmers to take them." He thrust the basket containing Tom into her arms. "Where is she?"

Dinah clutched the mewing basket. "Town Meeting. She'll be a while."

"Why do you need somebody to look after them, anyway?" Mutt broke in. "Where's Smallbone?"

"Gone," Nick said flatly. "Fidelou got him. They're going to fight a wizards' duel, and I have to try and stop it." He felt better saying it, even if it didn't make any difference. "I was going to tell Lily, but you can do that."

"Wizards' duel?" Ollie asked uncertainly.

Nick jittered impatiently. "It's like a giant game of rock, paper, scissors, only the wizards turn themselves into dragons and winds and try to kill each other."

"What happens if Smallbone loses?" Dinah wanted to know.

"Smallbone won't lose," Hell Cat said. "His speciality is turning people into things. What're you worried about?"

"You don't get it, do you?" Nick said. "Fidelou's not human. He's really old and really powerful and really horrible. As bad as you think Smallbone is, Fidelou's a thousand times worse. He stinks. And if he kills Smallbone, you're next."

He looked around the circle of frightened faces. He saw excitement, fear, and suspicion. "You'll tell your mom, right?" he asked Dinah. "'Cause I gotta go."

Mutt had been down on the floor, wrestling with Jeff, but when Nick started for the door, he stood up. "Hold on. I'm coming, too."

Nothing else would have stopped Nick, but that did. "What?"

"You heard me. I'm not mad at Smallbone anymore. You're right. He's different from who he was. He even smells different." His thin upper lip lifted slightly. "Besides, I hate coyotes."

Ollie cleared his throat. "I'll come, too, if you think there's anything I can do."

It was a brave offer. Nick considered it. "I don't know. Can you drive?"

"Do you have a cart and a horse?" Ollie asked.

Nick shook his head. Ollie looked relieved.

Dinah bounced impatiently. "We've got a car. And I know how to drive it, too."

Everyone's attention shifted to her. There was a thoughtful silence.

"But you can't leave Smallbone Cove," Mutt pointed out.

"We don't *know* that, not for sure. Nobody's tried, not in living memory. Besides, the Weathervane and the Stream are still weak, right?" Nick nodded. "Then it's worth a try." She turned faintly pink. "I'm a scientist. I experiment. And I've always wanted to see outside Smallbone Cove."

Nick wanted to tell her no, but he didn't. It was her decision, not his. The fact that he'd feel better if she came was beside the point. "That's it, then," he said. "Mutt, Dinah, and me will go to Fidelou."

Hell Cat looked affronted. "I'm coming, too."

Everybody stared at her. Mutt snorted. "That's a hoot and a holler. What about 'Smallbone's evil and I hate his guts forever'?"

"I've changed my mind," Hell Cat said loftily. "You need somebody with brains along on this picnic."

Chapter Twenty-Nine

Dinah stole her mother's car.

"She'd only say no if I asked," she said. "Besides, if we rescue Smallbone, he'll square it with her, and if we don't, I'd rather she killed me than be a coyote."

Mutt and Hell Cat got in the backseat, Mutt looking like he'd rather be in Smallbone's kitchen, Hell Cat bouncing with excitement. Nick got in the front seat next to Dinah, and they drove off toward the Stone Bridge. Nobody talked about what might happen to Dinah when they crossed it, but Nick, at least, could think of nothing else. He was pretty sure what happened to Covers who ventured outside the Town Limits, and he thought Dinah knew, too.

Dinah slowed down as the car approached the Stone Bridge, then gave it the gun. The car lunged over the Stream, then stopped with a lurch, its front wheels resting on the county road.

Nick looked at Dinah. She was staring at her arms in horror as they sprouted a coat of thick, glossy fur—silver gray with black spots like her hair. Her fingers spread into flippers, her head lengthened into a snout, and then Nick was sitting next to a harbor seal wedged between the seat and the steering wheel, groaning.

There was a shocked pause, then Hell Cat said, "Golly. Who's going to drive now?"

Nick reminded himself he couldn't hit a girl. "Shut up, Hell Cat. Mutt, help me get Dinah out of the car."

It wasn't easy. Dinah flapped her flippers when they tried to move her and threatened them with a mouthful of small sharp teeth. In the end, she fell out of the car on her own and galumphed awkwardly across the bridge. On the far side, she collapsed against a tree.

She was still a seal.

"What'll we do now?" Mutt asked.

What Nick wanted to do was jump in the car and see how fast he could drive to Fidelou. But he couldn't stand seeing Dinah so sad and helpless when he knew she was so brave. She'd stolen the car for him, after all, and done her best to get him where he needed to be.

"We take her back," he said.

Hell Cat's eyes went wide. "All the way to town?"

"There was a sign for the Smallbone Cove Goat and Dairy Farm back down the road. We'll take her there. I'll get the car, and you bring her some water from the Stream. It can't hurt her, and it might help."

Like Jerry, Nick had learned to drive on Uncle Gabe's pickup. Lily's old Ford was a lot easier. Nick turned it around and pulled up near the tree where Mutt was trickling water into Dinah's mouth from his hands. The three of them shoved her into the backseat and drove back the way they had come.

Whether it was the water or being on the right side of the Stream, Dinah was definitely regaining her natural shape. She still looked like nothing you'd want to find on your front porch on a bright April morning, but she'd lost her muzzle and her whiskers and reabsorbed some of the fur. Mutt and Nick helped her to the porch, rang the bell, and ran for the car, getting in just as a woman in a red shirt opened the door and saw Dinah slumped on her porch swing.

Nick stamped on the accelerator and laid rubber out of there.

When they got to the Stone Bridge, Nick took a piece of string and Smallbone's pipe out of his pocket and hung it on the rearview mirror.

"What's that for?" Hell Cat asked.

"Finding spell," Nick said shortly. The stem swung left and right, then stopped, quivering. "Inland," Nick said. He took out the map and handed it to Mutt. "Here. You navigate. We got us a wizard to rescue."

It was a horrible drive. No state trooper alive was going to believe that Nick was old enough for a license, so they kept to the back roads, some of them dirt, none of them straight, all of them treacherous with potholes and frost heaves. Nick was ready to jump out of his skin.

Suddenly, the pipe stem swiveled to the right. Nick spun the wheel and screeched to a halt.

"Why are we stopping?" Hell Cat asked.

Nick rolled down the window. The rotten stench of Fidelou's magic hung in the air like smoke. He unhooked the pipe from the rearview mirror and spun it gently. The stem whipped around once, then pointed straight at what looked like an impenetrable tangle of bushes and briars. Nick unfocused his eyes.

The road to Fidelou was a track barely wider than the car, unpaved and rutted, with branches dangling low enough to brush the top of a coyote-biker's unhelmeted head. "There it is," he said.

"I don't see nothing," Hell Cat complained.

"Good thing you're not driving, then."

Nick rehung the pipe on the rearview mirror and, keeping an eye on the stem, drove forward. They crawled along, the axles complaining as they bumped over the deep ruts. *If Fidelou didn't kill them,* Nick thought, *Lily would.*

"So, Foxkin," Mutt said, "what's the plan?"

Nick hadn't made one. But he wasn't going to tell Mutt that. "We check out the lay of the land."

Hell Cat made a rude noise. "By driving up to Fidelou's lair in Lily's old Ford?"

Nick kept his eyes on the pipe. "You didn't have to come, Hell Cat."

"I suppose you got a better idea?" Mutt asked her nastily.

Hell Cat grinned. "Glad you asked. First off, we ditch the car before we get to town."

"That makes sense," Mutt admitted.

"Thank you," Hell Cat said. "Second, we split up. Puppy-boy here and I sneak in one way and Foxkin sneaks in another."

"That's it?" Mutt barked. "That's your plan? Those are *coyotes,* Hell Cat. They have noses. They'll smell us before we even get close."

"Not if we find some really smelly mud and roll in it," Hell Cat said. "Besides, Dinah said coyotes mostly sleep during the day. Also wolves. So there."

After some discussion, Nick pulled the Ford into a gap in the trees and cast a glamour to disguise it as a lichen-covered boulder. Hell Cat saw through it right away, but Mutt didn't, even when Nick explained the trick. Hell Cat said it was because cats were naturally more magic than dogs, and Mutt said if Hell Cat was so magic, she could go rescue Smallbone by herself. They were still arguing as they went off down the road.

❖   ❖   ❖

Spring had not yet come to Fidelou's woods. The trees were silent, dark, and barren, the undergrowth dry and dead. The only sound Nick heard as he walked was his own feet crunching through last year's dried leaves. Nick pulled out Smallbone's pipe and let it swing. The stem wavered, then quivered to a standstill, pointing straight ahead. He moved on until finally he reached a tumbledown shack with dirty yellow paint flaking off its warped clapboards like sunburned skin. Behind it, two motorcycles were parked under a spidery drying rack hung with coyote pelts, their empty heads dangling between their empty paws. Beyond it, he saw another drying rack in another muddy yard, and on down a row of racks and pelts and garbage-studded mud.

The smell of the pelts made his eyes sting.

Keeping to the edge of the woods, Nick crept along behind the shacks until he came to a gray-shingled general store, where he stopped and got out the pipe. This time, the stem pointed toward the store. Nick scuttled across the muddy clearing and squatted behind a friendly barrel, then peered around the corner and saw Fidelou's castle.

It looked just like the sort of place an ancient French wolf wizard who liked motorcycles would live. Nobody was around except a burly Howling Coyote standing guard by the door.

Nick drew back behind the barrel and considered his options. If that was where Smallbone was, then he had to get in, hopefully without getting caught. Castles in movies always had side doors. Maybe this one did, too.

A hand grabbed his wrist and twisted his arm up between his shoulder blades. A wiry arm clamped around his throat, and an unpleasantly familiar voice said, "Where's Dad at?"

Nick stiffened, his heart pounding. His body wanted to struggle and kick like he always did when Jerry jumped him, but his brain told him that the only thing struggling would get him was a dislocated shoulder. Fighting wouldn't help him. He would have to use his wits.

Fox by name, fox by nature, he thought grimly, and said, "I don't know where he's at, and I don't care."

Jerry gave him a shake. "Liar. You wouldn't be here if he hadn't brung you."

"He run off," Nick muttered.

"Good." Jerry jerked Nick to his feet, sending an agonizing pain through his shoulder. "Time to see the Boss."

As his cousin frog-marched him toward the castle, Nick concentrated on keeping his legs moving. He didn't want to see the Boss. The very thought of being that close to the wolf wizard, of meeting those mad yellow eyes and listening to that hoarse, insinuating voice made his belly clench.

That's right, his inner voice said. *Scared is good. Bullies like people to be scared of them. He's less likely to hurt me if I'm scared. He'll think I'm weak. And I'm not.*

This thought carried Nick past the trailers and to the door, where the burly guard hefted a long tire iron and growled, "Whaddya want, punk?"

"Hey, Audrey," Jerry said cheerfully. "I got a present for the Boss."

The guard leaned toward Nick and sniffed. "He smells funny."

"The Boss won't care," Jerry said. "Trust me."

"Your funeral," Audrey said, and waved them through to a cramped and dusty courtyard with a door on the other side, pointy and ancient and banded with iron. In front of it stood another guard, who also thought Nick smelled funny. He opened the door, though.

A powerful stink of decaying meat, rust, wet dog, mold, and rotten eggs hit Nick square in the nose as Jerry propelled him forward into Fidelou's den.

Between the stink and the ache in his shoulder, Nick didn't have much attention left for his surroundings. They were big, he knew that much, and lit only by two sullen torches on the columns nearest the wide platform at the far end, where Fidelou lounged on a throne covered with fur.

Jerry marched Nick to the foot of the platform and shoved him sprawling onto a red carpet that felt like it might have been stolen from a cheap motel. Nick was breathing in the scent of mildewy acrylic when a dark voice said, "The estimable Jerry, is it not? What is it that you bring me, Jerry?"

"This loser"—here Jerry planted a kick in Nick's

ribs that made him grunt and curl up like a shrimp—"is my cousin Nick, the kid you sent Dad to rescue from Smallbone?"

"Ah." Fidelou's voice was smooth as chocolate syrup. "And your excellent papa? Where is he?"

Nick heard Jerry swallow nervously. "I dunno, Boss. Maybe Nick gave him the slip."

"Or killed him," Fidelou said. "*Dommage*. He understood my Vincent as no other. Still, we have Smallbone's apprentice. Well done, *mon brave*."

"Does that mean I get my pelt now?" Jerry asked eagerly.

Fidelou laughed. "Why not? Hiram, a pelt, if you please."

From his position on the carpet, all Nick could see of Fidelou were his boots and the top of his throne. The boots were large and scuffed across the instep and propped on a stool draped in black cloth. The back of the throne was decorated with an old top hat, considerably worn and beaten in on one side.

It was Smallbone's hat. And the cloth under Fidelou's boots was Smallbone's coat.

Nick went cold with dread.

Hiram's leather-clad legs stood beside the throne. "Here you go, Boss. One coyote pelt, slightly used."

Fidelou stood and moved forward. "On your knees, *mon brave*," he said gently.

Jerry whipped off his red baseball cap and knelt on the red carpet.

Fidelou unfolded the pelt, holding it by snout and tail. It was black, with white markings on the muzzle and forepaws. "With this pelt," he said, "I welcome you as a member of the pack. It gives you the power to run on two legs or four, to speak as men do or howl with your packmates under the moon. As long as the coyote remembers the man, the choice is yours. Do you understand?"

Jerry's eyes were fixed on the pelt. "'Course I do," he said.

Nick almost felt sorry for him.

"Bon."

Fidelou dropped the pelt over Jerry's head. It heaved and rippled as it took hold. Jerry gave one startled yell that slid into a howl, and then a black-and-white coyote stood and shook himself like a dog coming out of the water.

Fidelou leaned forward and growled at Jerry, who whined and crouched and lowered his head submissively.

"Bah! A coward, this one, fit only to eat offal." The burning yellow gaze fixed on Nick, who did his best to pretend he was unconscious. "Get up, boy. I know you are awake."

Nick stood, a little unsteady on his feet.

Fidelou looked him up and down, a sneer on his thin lips. "You are Smallbone's apprentice? But you are nothing but a child!"

"I'm fourteen," Nick lied.

Fidelou showed fangs the color of old ivory. "Had you forty years behind you, you would be a child to Fidelou, whose years number more than five hundred. Still, I am generous, me. I offer you a place in my pack."

Nick looked at his cousin, currently engrossed with chasing an itch across his black-furred flank with frantic nibbles. "No, thanks."

Fidelou was amused. "Your cousin has the soul of a

mouse. But you, you have *esprit;* you have *courage.* Join me of your free will and you will stand at my right hand." His eyes bored into Nick's. "What do you say to that, eh?"

Nick wondered just how dumb Fidelou thought he was. "That you're a liar."

"You do not trust me?" The torchlight reflected redly off his long, wet teeth. "I will give you proof of my goodwill. You hate this cousin of yours—I can smell the hatred upon you. *Bon.* I will kill him. Better, I will let you kill him with your own teeth. In return, you will be my lieutenant and run by my side. It is a good bargain, no?"

It was beginning to dawn on Nick that Fidelou, though powerful, wasn't very smart. "You're a psycho," he said flatly.

"You refuse, then? *Dommage.* Yet see how kind a master I can be. I give you time to reflect! Think well, Smallbone's apprentice. For if you do not take the skin I offer you, you will certainly lose your own. Hiram, take him to the dungeon."

Chapter Thirty

✦ ✦ ✦ ✦ ✦ ✦ ✦

It said a lot about Fidelou that the entrance to his dungeon was right behind his throne. Hiram manhandled Nick through a narrow arch and down a long twisting stair that gleamed like snail slime in the flickering torchlight. Nick fought to keep his footing and tried not to think about what might happen next.

At least Smallbone would be there.

The stairs ended. Hiram shoved Nick down a short dark hall and into a long low room smelling of damp and tar and smoke. In the sullen light of a few torches, Nick saw a rack, an iron maiden, a brazier ringed with pokers, and a heavy table holding a selection of tools and devices of unknown but certainly painful uses. Against one wall hung four narrow iron cages, three of them empty except for a scattering of bones that might or might not have once belonged to animals. The nearest one was occupied by a pale, chunky man in a plaid shirt and dorky red suspenders—some stupid upcountry hick who must have gotten in Fidelou's way somehow.

There were no other prisoners.

The bottom fell out of Nick's world.

Hiram shoved him into the middle cage and turned the key in the lock with a hollow *clunk.* "Better think fast. The Boss ain't what you might call patient," he said, then put the key in his pocket and left.

Nick collapsed onto the bottom of the cage. Iron bars—or possibly bones—dug into his legs and butt, but he hardly noticed. He was too busy trying not to think about what might have happened to Smallbone. He rested his head against the bars and fought the urge to cry.

"If this ain't a jeezly mess, I don't know what is," said a voice. "What're you doing here, Foxkin?"

The words were Smallbone's, but the voice was not. Nick jerked upright. "What did you call me?"

"Your proper name." The prisoner snorted. "Jerry, indeed. I've seen Jerry. You ain't a thing like him."

Nick squinted through the forest of bars between them. This guy wasn't any older than Dinah's dad, and though he wasn't exactly fat, he was a lot more solid than the skinny old man Nick knew. It wasn't a glamour, either. Nick had seeing through glamours down cold.

"And you're not a thing like Smallbone."

An impatient sigh. "What did I tell you about believing your eyes? Use your noggin, Foxkin. Who else knows you said your name was Jerry? Who else knows you figured out a way to gather eggs by magic? Who else knows you lied about knowing how to read? Who else would you expect to find locked up in Fidelou's jeezly magic-proof dungeon?"

"I don't know!" Nick groaned. "Maybe Smallbone told Fidelou all that under torture or something and you're just messing with my head."

"Ain't you the suspicious cuss!" the prisoner exclaimed. "All right. You got me dead to rights. I confess. I ain't Smallbone. Nobody is Smallbone, not at the moment, anyway. There ain't no Evil Wizard Smallbone."

Nick swore.

"You watch your mouth," the man who said he wasn't Smallbone snapped. "Properly speaking, the Evil Wizard Smallbone is a coat, a top hat, a house that runs itself, and a bookshop with a mind of its own."

Nick shook his head like Groucho getting rid of a fly. "If you're telling me it was the bookshop that turned me into a spider, I don't believe you."

"Land o' Goshen!" the man said. "Maybe it'll help if you think of Smallbone as a job, like being president. There always is one, but it ain't always the same feller. Evil Wizard Books and the clothes come with the job, like the White House and the red phone."

Nick thought about this. It made sense, in a Smallbonish way. And it did explain a lot. Why Smallbone never took off his hat and coat. Why the Smallbone Mutt and Hell Cat and Ollie described was so different from the Smallbone he knew.

"So what you're saying is that it's just the coat and the house doing all the magic for you?"

"All that stuff don't *do* magic. They *are* magic. There's a difference. I learned magic from the books, same as you. I got a thousand spells at my fingertips and I know how to use 'em. The coat just makes 'em stronger, like a magical battery. Makes me stronger, too."

"And the hat?"

"It covers my bald spot." Not-Smallbone held up a plump forefinger. "What was that?"

"What was what?"

"Shut up and listen."

In the darkness overhead, Nick heard a faint thumping and scraping, like somebody letting a bucket down a well. A closer, louder thump was followed by a bitten-off yowl. The yowl was familiar. So were the muddy legs clutching what looked like a clothesline descending in jerks from the ceiling. A few feet above the floor, Hell Cat released the line, landing on her feet. She smelled like rotting leaves.

"Hell Cat," Smallbone said wearily. "What a surprise. How many apprentices you bring along on this expedition, Foxkin?"

"Just her and Mutt. Hell Cat"—Nick gestured

through the bars—"meet Smallbone, without his coat and hat."

Hell Cat trotted to Smallbone's cage and looked him up and down. "You sure? I wouldn't have thought Smallbone'd be a red-suspenders kind of feller, myself."

"Then you'd be wrong, wouldn't you?" Smallbone said drily.

"So," said Nick. "Are you going to get us out of here?"

Hell Cat shrugged. "Probably not, unless you know where the keys to the cages are." She went over to the rack and the iron maiden. "Golly." She poked a rusty spike with a curious finger. "What's this for?"

Smallbone growled. "Torturing little girls who were a whole lot more useful when they were cats."

"Very funny." Hell Cat turned to the rack, gave the wheel an experimental twirl. When it squealed rustily, she levitated backward, rattling the tools on the table like castanets.

Smallbone made an exasperated noise. "Go away, Hell Cat. In fact, go as far away as you can. Mutt, too. Fidelou wants a fight, and I'm going to give it to him.

If I win, you can come back to Smallbone Cove if you want to. If I lose —"

"What do you mean, if you lose?" Nick exclaimed. "You can't lose."

"You sure of that?" Smallbone asked grimly. "I ain't. Fidelou may be crazy as a coot, but he's old and he's strong. He's fought more wizards' duels than you've had hot dinners."

A panicked buzzing ran along Nick's bones. "But you beat him before, didn't you?"

There was a long, uncomfortable pause. "That wasn't me. That was my master Smallbone. Mean old cuss, with a temper like dry powder. Knew pretty nearly everything there was to know about transformations, but even he needed the coat to stand up against Fidelou." Another pause. "And Fidelou wasn't even out to kill him. Fidelou just liked a good fight."

Like Jerry, Nick thought. "But he's out to kill you?"

The cage rattled gently as the latest Smallbone shifted his position. "Ayuh. He's bored, Fidelou town is falling apart, he wants a new town to spoil. Without the coat, I'm pretty strong, but I'm still human. He's not."

Hell Cat looked determined. "We'll just have to rescue you, then." She picked up a mallet and a pair of rusty pincers. "I bet I can get the locks open with these."

Smallbone shook his head. "You're forgetting the Rules. Evil wizards work alone. They don't have help and they don't get rescued. Ain't nobody never read you a fairy tale, Hell Cat?"

"My mama couldn't read," Hell Cat said. "Besides, that ain't even true. Fidelou has lots of help. What about the Howling Coyotes?"

"Minions don't duel. This is between him and me, and may the best villain win."

Smallbone's voice said the topic was closed, but Nick wasn't so sure. Maybe the Rules couldn't be broken, but they could be gotten around. The beginnings of a plan came into his head.

"Hell Cat," he said slowly, "can you come over here a second?"

"What're you up to, Foxkin?" Smallbone asked sharply.

"Nothing," Nick said.

"Uh-huh."

Nick beckoned to Hell Cat and whispered to her through the bars.

Hell Cat gave him a slit-eyed glare. "You're nuts."

"I know," Nick said. "Will you do it?"

Suddenly, Hell Cat grinned. "Sure."

Nick couldn't quite manage to grin back, so he pulled Smallbone's pipe out of his pocket. "Use this to find us. Just hold it up and let it swing. The stem will—"

"I know, I know," Hell Cat said. "Good luck!" She ran back to the clothesline, tugged it twice, and hung on as it jerked up into the ceiling. When she was gone, the dungeon seemed darker and danker than ever.

"Foxkin," Smallbone said, "you going to tell me about this plan of yours?"

"What plan?" Nick said.

"The one you was telling Hell Cat just now. Unless all that whispering was about how you've been sweet on her all this time and was afraid to say."

This struck Nick as funny. "That's right," he said.

"I asked her for a date. Now can I get some sleep? It's been a long day."

Nick had no intention of actually sleeping, but when he woke up with a jerk, the dungeon was pitch black. The torches had gone out. Time had passed; he didn't know how much. At least it was still night—at least he hoped it was. In any case, if he was going to go through with his plan, he'd have to do it now.

He pulled himself stiffly to his feet.

Smallbone's voice came out of the blackness. "Whatcha doing?"

"You'll see."

"Is it a fool piece of nonsense?"

"Probably." Nick felt sick. "Well. Here goes. Hey!" he shouted, banging his cage against the wall. "What's-your-face! Hiram! Come down here! I want to talk to the Boss!"

꒐   ꒐   ꒐

A few minutes later, Nick was back on the dirty red carpet in front of Fidelou's throne. The stink of evil was making his stomach churn, and Hiram's grip on his arm was like a steel band, but he was on his feet and he had a plan. It depended on a whole bunch of things going right that were more likely to go wrong, but still, it was a plan.

Fidelou was lounging against his wolf pelt with his feet on Smallbone's coat. "You wished to speak to me?" he asked. "Speak, then."

Nick took a deep breath of carrion-scented air. "I want to be a coyote," he said.

Fidelou appeared to find this amusing. "You will excuse me if I decline to believe you."

"Why? You told me to think it over, and I did." Nick looked the wolf wizard straight in the fierce yellow eyes. "I want to join your pack."

"Do you deny that you hate me, apprentice of Smallbone?"

"No. But I hate Smallbone worse."

"My enemy's enemy is my friend, eh?" Fidelou yawned, giving Nick an excellent view of a jawful of pointed teeth. "Well, I too have thought, and I think it would be foolish to trust my enemy's enemy when he is himself a wizard."

Nick's face tingled with fear. "Who me? I can't do magic!"

His voice was shrill with panic.

Fidelou frowned. "You are Smallbone's apprentice, are you not?"

"He *said* I was. But so far, all I've done is cook and wash dishes and milk goats. He never said nothing about teaching me magic."

He was babbling. A good liar never babbles.

But Fidelou only shook his head. "He is a fool. Magic rises from you like heat from a fire. A mortal fire, *bien sûr,* and not to be compared to my own, but great. Perhaps that is why he has not taught you. He is afraid you would destroy him. But me, I am afraid of nothing. Five hundred years I have lived, in the Old World and the New, and never once have I been afraid." He leaned forward on his throne.

"Fear is a mortal failing. You, for example, fear me to the point of madness."

I'm dead, Nick thought. He'd thought that before, when Uncle Gabe was on a tear, but now he knew he'd never believed it. His uncle wouldn't kill him — not on purpose, anyway. Fidelou would, without thinking twice. He'd enjoy it.

Nick sagged in Hiram's grip. Concentration. It was all about Concentration and Will. Let Fidelou think he was a wimp and an idiot. What Fidelou thought couldn't change who Nick really was.

Neither could his stinking magic pelt, not if Nick could help it.

"Yeah," he muttered. "I'm scared. That's why I want to join you—so I don't have to be scared anymore."

Fidelou sat back against his pelt, the picture of satisfaction.

"I accept your offer. It will amuse me to take Smallbone's pup for my own. Release him," he told Hiram. "He is too smart to run. And bring to me a pelt—the white pelt, I think." He grinned at Nick. "It is very special, that pelt. I give it only to those whose natures are truly wild."

Hiram released Nick, and he collapsed onto the red rug. He was shaking and felt sick to his stomach. *Okay, I'm scared,* he thought. *But I have a plan.*

"It is time," Fidelou announced dramatically.

Nick raised his head. The wolf wizard was standing on the platform, a pelt stretched between his hands. It was silvery white from head to tail, and its legs dangled in a spooky, almost lifelike dance.

"It is nearly dawn," Fidelou went on. "Kneel before me, apprentice of Smallbone. Soon you shall see your enemy defeated."

This was it. There was nowhere to run, no way to fight, no clever trick or lie to tell, just Nick the stubborn kid with the bad attitude against Fidelou's special magic pelt. At least he'd stopped shaking. He looked up at the pelt dangling over his head. The lolling head stared at him with empty eyes. Nick stared back.

It's just a transformation, he told himself. *You've gone through this before. You know how to turn yourself back. You're Nick Reynaud of Beaton, Maine, and no full-of-himself, big-mouth wolf is going to get the best of you.*

Fidelou released the pelt and it settled over Nick like a furry blanket, stinking of bad magic and mothballs.

Suddenly, Nick felt fine. In fact, he felt wonderful. He was a good dog, and good dogs don't have to be afraid. Good dogs obey their master and their master keeps them safe.

Except you're not a good dog, said the voice of his human self. *You're a magic coyote. And coyotes are tricksters, just like foxes. You have this, Nick.*

The coyote part of him whined. It knew coyotes couldn't kill wolves.

Who said anything about fighting? Fidelou's not all that smart. Think of it this way: if he's all that big and bad, why's he holed up in a drafty castle in the poorest, rockiest hardscrabble stretch of woodland in the entire state of Maine?

The coyote became aware that the mad yellow eyes were staring at him. *He wants to know if you're in his power,* the back of his mind informed him. *And you're not, are you? So you'll need to pretend.*

The coyote crouched submissively.

A shadow fell over him and sharp nails sank painfully through the thick fur of his ruff. "Apprentice of Smallbone"—the harsh voice was affectionate—"you make me a fine dog, eh?"

The coyote whined and waved his tail, but inside

his head, Nick was saying, *I'm not a dog! And you're not the boss of me!*

The loup-garou straightened. "Bring up the hedge wizard," he said.

Hiram disappeared.

Fidelou grabbed his pelt from the back of his throne and swirled it around him. Nick lay down and rested his muzzle on his crossed paws. He didn't know what was going to happen next, and he was scared again, but he was in control of himself, and that was the important thing.

That, and Hell Cat's sneaking abilities.

Clanking and scuffling sounded from the dungeon stairs. Nick sat up and pricked his ears. Hiram led Smallbone forward by a chain bound around his hands. With his shirt and his red suspenders and his plump face all stubbly and streaked with dirt from the dungeon, he looked more like a farmer than an evil wizard.

He still didn't have his glasses.

"My old friend Smallbone!" Fidelou said. "Have

you slept well? Victory is not so sweet when it is too easily won."

Smallbone munched his jaws. Without the bushy beard, it looked like he was grinding his teeth. "If it's a fair fight you're after, you'll have to give me back my coat."

Fidelou shook back his mane of black hair and laughed. "Fair is for heroes and little children. Evil wizards take what advantage they may." He gestured at Nick. "See, here is your apprentice. Does he not make a pretty pet?"

Smallbone squinted at Nick.

Deliberately, Nick put back his ears and growled.

"I see," Smallbone said. "You're welcome to him. Useless as shoes on a cat."

One of the squinting eyes closed briefly. It could have been a twitch or it could have been a signal. Nick decided to believe it was a signal.

The tiny windows at the top of the Great Hall had begun to grow pale with the approach of day.

Fidelou sniffed the air and scowled. "The sun rises. It is time!" He snapped his fingers, Nick came to his heel, and the two wizards and their attendants marched out of the hall and into the pearly mist.

⚡ ⚡ ⚡

The ground Fidelou chose for his long-desired wizards' duel was a scraggly meadow dotted with rocks and weeds and a few scruffy pines. The sun cast spears of light through the trees as Fidelou's pack trotted out of the woods. Some went on two legs and some on four, but all were coyotes and all were his, from the gnarliest veteran to the young white male trotting at his heel.

The pack followed Fidelou to the tallest of the pines and stood in a semicircle behind it like an audience at a play. Fidelou pulled Smallbone up onto a boulder and unchained his hands.

Smallbone rubbed his wrists and pulled up his suspenders. Without his horror-movie coat and hat, he looked half dressed and exposed, a snail without a shell.

Fidelou, on the other hand, looked just like an evil wizard ought to look: tall and wild and strong and sinister, and completely in control of the situation.

"I challenge you, Zachariah Smallbone," he howled.

"By sky and stone, by sea and flame, I challenge you. By your name and your nature, by your magic and your skill, I challenge you. By the Rules and Rituals of Battle and Story, I challenge you." His voice dropped to a gentle growl. "Do you accept?"

"I expect I got to, seeing as how you won't give me a moment's peace until I do."

Fidelou growled. "I ask you again. Do you accept of your own will and desire?"

Smallbone sighed. "I, the Wizard Smallbone of Smallbone Cove, accept the challenge of Fidelou the Loup-Garou. You happy now?"

Fidelou began to lift his hands.

"Hold your horses," Smallbone said. "I got the right to set the terms. I call a Standard Western European Wizards' Duel. Shape-shifting only, no taking the same shape twice, no returning to your original form until the other one is dead."

"Done." Fidelou stretched his mouth in a wide inhuman grin. "I hope you are prepared to die."

"I ain't worried," Smallbone said. "Unless maybe you aim to jaw me to death."

At that, Fidelou snarled and lunged, beginning as a man and ending as a wolf, jaws wide, aiming for Smallbone's throat.

Nick went rigid with fear, then breathed again when he saw a gray fox streak up the pine like a scalded cat. The duel had begun.

The wolf turned into a giant eagle and rose from the ground in a thunder of wings. It circled the pine, gaining height, then folded its wings and stooped.

The fox disappeared.

The eagle turned into a red-crowned woodpecker and drilled his powerful beak into the pine.

A big striped tomcat erupted from the tree trunk and swiped at the woodpecker with extended claws. The woodpecker became a tawny bobcat with tufted ears and wicked teeth. It sprang at the tom, then screamed in pain as a yellowjacket buzzed up between its paws and stung it on the nose.

Nick whined uneasily. Smallbone was holding his own so far without the help of the coat, but sooner or later he'd run out of magic and Fidelou would get him. Where were Hell Cat and Mutt?

A giant snake attacked a knight with a gleaming sword. The sword became a roaring flame and the snake a black cloud streaming rain and thunder.

Nick looked around him. Every one of the two- and four-legged coyotes had its eyes riveted on the field. He slipped away into the shelter of the trees, lifted his nose, and sniffed. Coyote, of course—lots of magic coyote—and the burned-metal smell of magic. But he could also make out, if he concentrated, rotting leaves and pine and mud and—very faintly—scents that he recognized: Mutt and Hell Cat, nervous as the first day of school . . . and a familiar mixture of tobacco and old man.

Moving like a pale mist through the brush, Nick followed his nose to where the former dog and cat crouched behind a bayberry bush with an untidy bundle between them, arguing in whispers.

"*Smallbone's* the pond, Mutt. I was keeping track."

"That would mean Fidelou's the basketball now, and I don't see him turning himself into a basketball, do you?"

Nick nudged Mutt's shoulder with his nose. Mutt

yelped and Hell Cat punched his arm. "That's Nick, stupid." Her eyes gleamed—she was enjoying herself. "What do you want us to do?"

Nick whined.

"Stop kidding around," Hell Cat said.

He concentrated, opened his mouth, and barked. It was no use. The pelt wouldn't let him speak.

Hell Cat unfolded the bundle. It was Smallbone's coat, all right, looking strangely sad and ragged without Smallbone in it. For the first time, Nick saw the lining, which was completely covered with tiny black writing. The collar was frayed.

"His hat's in the pocket," Hell Cat said helpfully. "We had to collapse it."

"What do we do now?" Mutt asked.

Hell Cat punched his arm again. "He can't talk, dummy. We'll have to use my plan."

"You mean the one that's practically guaranteed to get us both killed?"

Their squabbling was interrupted by a tremendous roar from the meadow.

Three heads turned to the field.

A dragon and a giant confronted each other across a wasteland of uneven furrows and ridges punctuated with muddy puddles, uprooted bushes, and displaced boulders. The dragon was enormous, green, and scaly, with claws like steel scythes. The giant had four arms and two heads, each sporting a single pale-blue eye in its forehead, and looked extremely fearsome, although the pine tree he held like a club was probably not the best choice of weapon against a fire-breathing opponent.

Nick tried to unfocus his eyes. It was no good. He couldn't tell which monster was Smallbone and which was Fidelou. They both looked real to him.

Up to now, the duel had been more like a game than a fight. The wizards had been testing each other's abilities, seeing which shapes the other chose, thinking how to counter them. Now they were really getting serious.

The dragon opened its whiskered jaws and spouted an arc of bright flame at the giant, who vanished.

Nick stuck his muzzle under Smallbone's coat and wiggled his way into it.

Power roared into him. His brain reeled. "Whoa!" he said. "Awesome!" and scrambled to his own two feet.

The dragon was stomping around, bellowing as it looked for its prey. Now that he was wearing the coat, Nick could see the white wolf inside the dragon, like the nucleus of a frog's egg. Smallbone, cloudy and indistinct, surrounded a small brightly colored snake coiled up behind a rock.

It was time to do something. The question was, what? Even with the coat, Nick couldn't fight Fidelou: it was against the Rules.

Nick's cheek itched. He scratched it, or tried to, but his fingers met a springy, wiry barrier. A beard? How did a twelve-year-old grow a beard? He looked at his hands. They were liver spotted, bony, gnarled — Smallbone's hands.

He stared at them a moment, then smiled. It felt like an evil smile.

Nick lifted both arms and waved. "Hey! Dingy dragon!" he yelled, putting magical force behind it. "You lose something?"

It wasn't the cleverest taunt in the world, but it did

the trick. Everybody was staring at him — were-coyotes (four- and two-footed), Hiram, the dragon that was suddenly not a dragon anymore but a big man wearing a white fur cloak, his eyes shooting yellow fire and his outstretched finger shaking with rage, screaming, "Cheat! Cheat! I win! You *cheated*!"

"Did not!" Nick yelled.

"But yes! A duel to the death, you said, and no person to take his true shape until the other lies dead!"

"Ha!" Nick gave his best Smallbone sneer. "But this ain't my true shape!"

Fidelou raised his face to the cloudy sky and howled. It was a truly impressive howl, somewhere between a wolf pack serenading a full moon and a jet plane taking off. It was the howl of a wizard who had well and truly lost his temper. Which, as *E-Z Spelz for Little Wizardz* could have told him, was really bad for a wizard's Concentration and Control.

Nick slapped his hands over his throbbing ears and counted.

One.

Two.

On three, a huge black grizzly flowed up from behind a rock and took the wolf wizard into its massive arms. The howl cut off, muffled in fur and muscle. In the sudden silence, Nick heard a growl and a sickening crunch.

The grizzly turned into a plump bald man in red suspenders. He looked down at the heap of torn flesh and fur at his feet, wiped blood from his mouth, and squinted shortsightedly in the direction of Fidelou's pack.

"Get out of here right now and we'll call it square," he said. "Attack me, and I'll turn you into rabbits. Up to you."

A handful of four-legged coyotes bolted to the woods, their ears back and their tails between their legs. One of them, Nick noted, was black with white feet. It looked like Jerry was going to be a coyote for a very long time. But then, Nick thought, maybe the coyote was Jerry's totem animal anyway.

Then a handful of two-legged pack members made a break for it — women with kids, plus some guys who looked more relieved than shocked. This left the real hard cases, coyote and currently human, the scarred and the one eared, with narrow eyes and mean, tight smiles. They produced knives and chains and tire irons and bared their teeth and moved toward the flannel-shirted man who had killed their leader.

The biggest coyote, a big tan brute with a scar Nick could see across the field, sprang. The wizard threw his arm out in a gesture that should have sent the animal flying into the woods but, to Nick's dismay, only knocked him onto his back. The coyote lay there for a moment, picked himself up, shook his head angrily, and prepared to charge again.

Smallbone was running out of magic.

With a steam-engine scream, Nick took off across the field, stepped in a ditch, and pitched headfirst into a tangle of brambles.

If it hadn't been for the coat, he might have gotten tangled and pricked like one of the unluckier princes who went to find Sleeping Beauty. As it was, his face and hands stung like he'd been cuddling a porcupine, and his leg felt like it had been hit by a red-hot poker.

Smallbone was still a long way off, and the ring of coyotes was tighter than it had been.

Healing spell. Why didn't he know a healing spell? Because he'd never thought to ask for one. He swore, then heaved himself out of the brambles and shucked off the coat. Holding it over his head, he closed his eyes and thought about wind. He imagined drafts and breezes and sudden, gusty blows strong enough to rip a sheet off a clothesline, pegs and all. Behind him, he heard the soft rustling sigh of pines bending in the wind. And then his hair was whipping at his cheeks and the coat was flapping and straining like a living thing. Nick released his grip and the coat glided away like a huge bat toward Smallbone and the furious coyotes.

The wizard — and he was a wizard, coat or not — had his hands full, holding a protection around himself that shrank moment by moment as his power drained. Teeth clenched with concentration, Nick directed his wind to float the coat above Smallbone and lay it gently on his shoulders.

The coat dropped on his head, then heaved and flapped as Smallbone struggled to find the sleeves. The coyotes fell on him in a yammering, shouting mass.

Nick closed his eyes and put his hands over his ears, his mind blank with shock. He couldn't have failed. He was the hero of this tale. He'd done all the right things. He'd paid his debts and been kind to animals and learned his lessons. He'd put himself in danger, fooled the evil wizard, and called up a magic wind. It should have worked.

The pack fell silent. *It's over,* Nick thought. He suspected he'd be next. He didn't much care. He opened his eyes, feeling oddly calm.

A pack of little brown rabbits was scattering across the meadow. Some of them hopped past him, their long soft ears laid back, their round black eyes staring, stinking of fear and musk. And then they were gone, white scuts twinkling as they headed toward the safety of the woods.

"Well, that's that."

Nick looked up to see Smallbone standing beside him. The old wizard's beard was bristling, his hat was waggling, his coat was flapping, and his graveyard teeth were prominently displayed.

"You're not dead," Nick said weakly.

"Takes more than a bunch of mangy coyotes to kill the Evil Wizard Smallbone." The old man reached into a pocket, pulled out his glasses, and perched them on his beaky nose. "That's a nasty mess you made of your leg, there, boy."

Nick grinned helplessly. "I'm fine."

"Ha!" Smallbone's glasses glittered in the sun. "Better learn some healing magic, Foxkin. Boy like you'll find plenty of use for it."

Hell Cat and Mutt came puffing up, looking pale. "That was some wind you called," Hell Cat said. "Nearly blew the hair off my head."

"You all right?" asked Mutt.

Smallbone reached down and poked at Nick's leg. Nick yelled.

"I ain't no doctor, but I guess it ain't broken. Some ripped up, though." Smallbone directed a glare at Mutt. "I hope you got a car. It's going to be a long haul home if you don't."

✦ ✦ ✦ Epilogue ✦ ✦ ✦

Smallbone Cove in June was very different from Smallbone Cove in January. Shops were open all up and down Commercial Street, from Three Bags Full Knitting to Joshua's Kites 'N Chimes. Artists set up their easels in the municipal parking lot and painted views of the harbor. Lovers of seafood from all over New England flocked to Eb's Klam Shak, where Ollie's fish chowder and corn bread special was getting a real reputation. The weather was hot and clear and bright. Smallbone Cove Mercantile did a brisk business in sunscreen, as well as postcards, coyote and seal plushies, and black T-shirts with EVIL WIZARD BOOKSHOP in Gothic letters below a white-line drawing of Smallbone at his horror-movie best.

It was Midsummer Day.

Just before dawn that morning, Lily, Zery, Dinah, and the ancient proprietor of Evil Wizard Books had led a festive procession through the woods. A convenient path, newly cleared and graded, ran just inside the inland boundary, but it was still a long walk—fifteen miles, just about, mostly through the woods along the banks of a bright, chattering stream. The procession made four stops along the way, and everybody—even the grown-ups—sang something that sounded like a children's jump-rope rhyme. When they got back to the pretty white clapboard church, with its unusual weathervane shaped like a harbor seal, everybody danced.

When it was all over, the procession broke up to buy Moxie and iced tea and chowder from the stands in the parking lot in front of Eb's, and jump ropes, reproduction Weathervanes and Lanterns, and other Midsummer Magic merchandise from the shops on Commercial Street.

Smallbone himself headed for the Smallbone Cove Public Library with Lily, Dinah, Mutt, and Miss

Rachel. She had Walked the Bounds, too—or rolled them—in her new electric wheelchair.

The library had gone through a lot of changes since April. The boxes of books and papers had all been sorted and arranged in drawers and shelves, newly installed on the second floor. The downstairs had been scrubbed and freshly painted, its shelves lined with mysteries and biographies and guides to Maine wildlife. The circulation desk now boasted a computer. A little carved wooden cat perched on the monitor.

The seal sofa had been repaired and re-covered and placed in the new reading alcove.

Dinah had made herself responsible for the online catalog and the computerized checkout system. Hell Cat shelved returns, processed late fees, and ran a reading group for little kids on rainy weekend afternoons. Owing to all the sorting and alphabetizing, she was getting pretty good at reading, though her favorite book was *Millions of Cats,* which hardly had any words in it at all. Miss Rachel supervised, answered questions, and made progress on her history of Smallbone Cove.

Dinah ran up the wheelchair access ramp (also new) and opened the door. Hell Cat was peering intently at the computer screen. Judging from her expression, she was playing Angry Birds.

"Getting some work done?" Dinah asked innocently.

Hell Cat clicked the mouse and spun her chair around. "How'd it go? See any coyotes out there?"

"Ha, ha," Mutt said. "Very funny."

Miss Rachel backed into her workstation by the window. "The ritual worked fine and dandy. I'm just sorry young Foxkin couldn't come. He's worked so hard repairing the Weathervane and all."

"Somebody had to mind the store," Smallbone said. "Lily, them jeezly black undershirts you ordered're selling like hotcakes."

"Of course they are." Lily's voice was smug. "And after your performance this morning, you'll have to reorder. I didn't know you could dance like that."

Smallbone tugged on his beard. "Magic makes you do strange things," he said gruffly. "Ain't it time we got on with what we come for? Hell Cat, did Foxkin remember to bring that chest over from Evil Wizard Books?"

"Last night," Hell Cat said. "It's in the back."

"Well, haul it out, then. I ain't got all day."

After some discussion about the respective strength of boys and girls, Mutt and Hell Cat went to the kitchen table and came back lugging a wooden sea chest between them. It was very old, with rope handles and a big iron padlock. A painted harbor seal gazed mournfully from the lid.

Lily gave it a doubtful look.

"You sure this is right?" she asked. "It doesn't look big enough."

"They fold up smaller than you think," Smallbone said, handing her an ornate key.

Dinah was surprised to see her mother's eyes well with tears as she knelt by the chest, turned the key, removed the lock, and lifted the hasp.

Everyone leaned forward eagerly.

A smell rose from the chest—bitter and wild, like a salt marsh at high tide. Lily brushed aside a tangle of dry seaweed and lifted out a seal skin, dappled silver and black.

"Golly," said Hell Cat reverently.

"Are they all there?" Miss Rachel asked.

Lily laid the pelt on the old librarian's lap. "We'll count them together, Miss Rachel. But they seem all right. In fact, they're wonderful."

Dinah hunkered down by the open chest, breathing in the sea smell and looking at the pelts Smallbone had taken from her ancestors, but not quite daring to touch them. They were beautiful and magical, but they were dangerous, too. If she put one on and went out to sea, would she have to be a seal forever? Would she forget about Smallbone Cove, her mother, the library, everything she loved? Would she forget she wanted to go to college or be a scientist?

Hell Cat had no such qualms. She picked up a skin and rubbed her face over it. "Oh, it's *soft*!" She looked at Smallbone. "Can I try it on?"

"No!" Smallbone and Dinah shouted in unison. Smallbone's cheeks bunched. "You want to tell her why not?"

Dinah shot him a nervous look. "I can't— I mean, I don't know how magic works. Except it's only logical that putting on a skin that isn't yours is not right. It leads to bad things like, well, like Fidelou and the Howling Coyotes."

"Oh, pooh," Hell Cat said. "I ain't like them loser bikers. I'm just curious, is all."

"You might recall," Smallbone said mildly, "what curiosity does to cats. And we got business to do. Lily, you got them papers?"

Lily got up. "It's in the library computer. Dinah, will you print it out for me?"

Everybody watched, mesmerized, as Dinah called up the file and sent it to the printer. As the printer was thinking things over, Miss Rachel said, in a making-conversation tone, "Anybody heard anything from Fidelou town?"

"It's still there, far as I know," Smallbone said. "Though there ain't much left of it."

Lily frowned. "Now I'll worry every time I hear a motorcycle."

"Don't," Smallbone said. "I promised to protect

Smallbone Cove from all evil and I done that." As he spoke, a hot metallic tang tinged the air. "If a single coyote tries to pass the Sentries, on two legs or four, the Wall will bar his way, the Stream will rise to drown him, the Wind will blow him into the middle of the next county, and the Lantern will set such a fire under his skin that he'll be sorry he was born."

He stopped and coughed. "Well," he said in a more ordinary tone, "if that paper's ready, Dinah, let's see what else I promised."

The new contract between Zachariah Smallbone and the residents of the town of Smallbone Cove was a long document. It had clauses and subclauses and what Dinah's dad, who had helped to draw it up, called contingencies and Hell Cat called boring parts. What it all boiled down to was that, for the first time since Smallbone had dragged their ancestors out of the sea and given them human form, speech, and the ability to think, the inhabitants of Smallbone Cove could come and go as they wished. The Sentries that kept were-coyotes, stray evil wizards, shoplifters, guns, and drunk drivers out of Smallbone Cove no longer kept the townsfolk in. Dinah could study at the University of Maine or Caltech, if she wanted to. Lily could go to trade shows in Augusta or even Boston. Fishermen who were tired of the Reach could fish off of Portland or even Cape Cod, if they wanted.

The seals of Smallbone Cove were free.

"Town Meeting'll be different," Dinah said.

Smallbone sighed. "A lot of things'll be different. But that's for another day. Let's get this jeezly thing signed so I can have my breakfast."

Lily and Miss Rachel signed, then the old wizard took the library ballpoint and wrote *Zachariah Smallbone* on the proper line with a flourish. Dinah signed as a witness for the next generation. Smallbone turned down an invitation to join Lily and Dinah for breakfast at Eb's, a cup of tea, and Mutt's offer of a ride home in Lily's car, and left the library.

Nobody, not even the most sunburned of the tourists, said hello as he walked down Commercial Street. He was the Evil Wizard Smallbone, and you never knew when he might do something to prove it.

He marched down the woodland path, whistling

under his breath. When he reached the pond, he took off his top hat, banged it shut against his leg, and stuffed it into a pocket. He scratched his head energetically, unbuttoned his coat, and walked on, the skirts of his coat brushing the ferns and moss and small white trilliums growing along the edge of the path.

When he emerged from the woods, Jeff bounded up to him, his legs muddy and his coat rough with burrs. The black Lab licked his hands and tore off toward the house, ears flapping.

The parking lot was empty. Smallbone ran up the porch steps and entered, flipping the little wooden CLOSED sign as he shut the door behind him. Evil Wizard Books looked downright cheerful. The piles of books in the windows and on the tables were decorated with carved wooden figures of animals and fishermen and pirates and mermaids. Evil Wizard T-shirts in assorted sizes were piled on the counter between the old brass cash register and a wire rack of scenic postcards.

In the kitchen, a plump man in an Evil Wizard Books T-shirt was sitting in the rocker, reading a book propped against the furry orange ball that was Tom, asleep on his lap. He had a bald spot and a new and scruffy-looking brown beard. Judging from the state of his clothes, he'd been digging in the garden.

"How'd it go?" the man asked, not looking up from his book. "Anybody get turned into anything untoward?"

Nick slipped off the Smallbone coat and draped it over the back of a kitchen chair. "Nope. It went off real well." He sniffed the air. "Is that sausages I smell?"

"Ayuh."

"Any left? I'm hungry enough to eat a boiled owl."

"Look in the oven."

Nick had only taken a couple of bites when the shop bell clanged.

Smallbone turned the page. "Don't look at me," he said. "You're the Evil Wizard today."

Acknowledgments

This book is based on a short story I wrote for *Troll's-Eye View*, an anthology of stories told from the point of view of classic fairy-tale villains. I chose to retell "The Wizard Outwitted," which I read as a child in *Fairy Tales from Many Lands*, edited by H. Herda and published by Franklin Watts in 1956. It's a Russian fairy tale, and I've never seen it collected anywhere else. So I'd like to begin with a big thank-you to H. Herda (whoever they may have been), and to Ellen Datlow and Terri Windling for inspiring me to think of Nick in the first place. And to my BFF Eleanor Hoagland and her husband, Leigh, for lending me their beautiful house on the Reach to write in, thus giving me the setting for Nick's story.

Once inspired, however, a book needs to be written and rewritten—a process that should not be undertaken without the guidance of good and magical friends. I count myself lucky to have had Iris Wilde, Doselle Young, Karen Meisner, Will Alexander,

Terri Windling, Theodora Goss, Kat Howard, Lev Grossman, Edith Hope Bishop, Claire Cooney, Carlos Hernandez, Holly Black, Hillary Homezie, Elizabeth Dulemba, Chip Sullivan, and Ruth Sanderson as readers, advisers, and cheerleaders, with special callouts to Stu Segal and Stan Dulemba, who gave me valuable tips on the care of motorcycles; Kay Crabb, who checked out Nick's psychology; and the Maine trapper, the pig farmer, and the goat farmer at the Blue Hill Fair who patiently answered my rather strange questions about gray foxes, Maine coyotes, pig games, and how goats behave when upset.

I am also grateful beyond words to Jill Grinberg, who handled the whole mysterious process of submission and negotiation with verve and grace, and to Deb Noyes and Miriam Newman of Candlewick, who gave me and Nick the kind of rigorous and useful editorial attention I've always dreamed of.

Most of all, I thank Ellen Kushner for keeping me supplied with industrial-strength chai and support while I took this book apart and put it back together again multiple times, complaining all the while. I owe you one, dear.

Porter County Public Library